WHERE THE DEVIL WON'T GO

E.J. FINDORFF

Copyright © 2016 by E.J. Findorff.

All rights reserved. This book or any portion thereof may not be reproduced or used in any manner whatsoever without the express written permission of the publisher, except for the use of brief quotations in a book review.

Printed in the United States of America

First Printing, 2015

www.ejfindorff.com

To my good friends Walter, Danny, and Brian

ONE

The murder suspect had yet to arrive at his home in New Orleans East, an area which could be considered one huge crime statistic. I reclined in my Accord, parked a safe distance away, under the shadow of a streetlight's absence. My windshield revealed a bleak painting of neglected houses and residential apathy as a rogue tabby shot from curb to curb.

My wife and daughter had dinner waiting for me at home, but I wanted to give this at least an hour. I'd had a run of bad luck and I could smell the collar. The gangbanger, suspected in a recent murder, had to feel safe to come back at some point.

A beat up, non-descript van with one headlight pulled under the carport of a house across the street from the banger's address, well-hidden from the glow of the moon. The red shine from the brakes resembled the devil's eyes before they shut off. I secured my mini-binoculars for a better view, merely due to boredom as my target had yet to show. The driver stepped from the van and slid the side door open. From his size and manner, I could tell it was a man. He leaned forward, throwing a hard punch at something inside.

His frame bent at the waist, coming out of the van with a small body, like a teenager. The long hair could mean it was a female and she appeared young. While waiting for a murderer, I stumbled onto a kidnapping, and certainly something more sinister.

I called into dispatch, identifying myself. "I got a sixty-seven with a possible seventy-seven at eight-two-nine Marquette Street in the East. Suspect is a possible white male, stocky build."

The scratchy voice came back. "Affirmative, Detective Peyroux. Dispatching units to your location."

"I don't have time to wait for them. Make sure they know that."

"Affirmative, Detective."

The moment the man entered the house with the person on his shoulder; I jumped from my car with my Glock tight at my side. No lights came on as I crossed the street onto his cracked driveway. That's when I saw the boarded windows. A scan of the neighboring houses told me that people minded their business on this block. That cat brushed against my leg as I stopped and considered my entry. I crouched to scratch its ears, feeling that he was in this with me. The Tabby purred in appreciation.

I extended my arm to push open the side door, which he hadn't closed in his efforts to get his prey inside. The aroma of stale air from a lack of ventilation brushed my face. A single bulb illuminated the next room where tense noises emanated. It seemed the place had been cleared of its furniture, but plywood covered all the windows. I inched out of the cramped kitchen, trying to get a visual of the living room. On the floor in the distance, long shadows struggled. A fist rose for a sure blow.

I charged into the room and shouted, "Police. Don't do it."

"What the shit?" He straightened with the girl in a chokehold. With the lamp directly behind them, his face remained black under his hood. A gun swung up to her head. "Stay where you are, or she's dead."

Braced together, the man's sweaty arm had merged with her throat. Long hair escaped from his hood. His thick frame stood just under six feet. The teenager's backside pressed against him, both facing me. The barrel of his gun disappeared in the tangles of her hair while my Glock pointed at his forehead. His hidden face revealed the whites of his eyes. The three of us were locked in a deadly game of chicken.

"Let her go before this goes too far. You haven't done anything bad yet."

He dragged the girl to the dark solidity of a long wall, gauging my actions. We both realized the only exit was behind me, unless he tried the bay window, which was the only one not boarded.

His voice shook. "I'll kill her. Stay right there. I swear I'll kill her."

"You're not leaving. I'm not moving. Let's talk this out."

"No, you're going to let me leave, and then I'll let her go. I promise."

I prayed the reinforcements would appear silently, because this guy seemed spooked. I had to trust my instincts for the girl to leave this house alive. If I let him escape with her, it would just be a matter of time before we found her body.

Despite his agitated rocking, my aim remained steady. He shuffled to his left, thinking I would mirror his movement and give him a clear line to the door. My feet remained planted, my aim never in doubt.

The girl panicked, getting her senses back. She was no longer just dead weight in his arms. She erupted in a wave of crying; her hair was knotted and pasted onto her face. He tightened his grip, cutting off her air. Small coughs emanated from her mouth, forcing me to quicken my decision.

If I let them leave, I wouldn't be able to pick him out of a lineup. But taking the shot could mean her death, too. Even if my bullet found its destiny, his weapon could still discharge while pressed against her head. His muscles would soon tire, which might quicken his own decision.

Bits of saliva popped off his lips as he spoke in desperation, "Throw me your gun and cuff yourself to the refrigerator and I'll let the girl go. A head start, that's all I want."

"No." With both hands on my gun, my breathing deepened.

"You want her to die, man?" he hissed. "I'll let her go if you let me go."

He rocked back and forth several more times before taking a full step to his right, jerking the girl along. He swayed again and then stepped left. He didn't realize it was a repetitive motion, a pattern, his own specific dance. My aim changed angles along with his head, praying he wouldn't turn his gun on me. If he did, I was screwed.

"All you've done is a kidnapping. Slap on the wrist."

"Don't talk to me like I'm stupid. I let her go and you shoot me."

"Not if you put your hands in the air and you lie face down for me. I already called in for back up."

The girl's struggling ceased for the moment, hanging like a rag doll.

"Her only hope rests on you." He pressed his nose against her head. "I'm walking out of here and you're going to let me. Throw down your gun right now."

"Can't do that." *I have the shot.*

"Throw it down and cuff yourself to the fridge."

"Not going to happen." *I have the shot.*

"Do it." The gun left her temple and tilted towards me.

It sounded like a firecracker when the gun lit up in my hand. A retaliatory crack exploded from the other side of the room and it felt as if a wasp had stung my chest. My legs gave out and gravity took over. He had kicked over the lamp and I could barely make out the figure pointing the gun, but the girl was gone from his grasp. I let several rounds fly from where I lay, but the guy ducked out of sight. Sirens wailed; the window smashed. Bright red and blue lights splashed through the room as squad cars pulled up to the front of the house.

The girl. What happened to the girl?

That cat I had befriended licked my face – *some partner.*

TWO

Two months later...

A floater in the Mississippi River rarely presents a neat corpse. Humans bloat, and skin becomes delicate like tissue paper. I progressed from the Moon Walk parking lot to the riverbank with my badge clipped to my belt and my holster heavy on my shoulder. The Crescent City Connection loomed in the skyline over the Mississippi River, looking like a tether keeping New Orleans from floating away. This eighty-degree day turned out to be hottest yet in an otherwise cool start to spring.

At the end of the brick walkway, police tape had been strung around several lamp posts and some uniformed cops kept citizens at bay, but it didn't stop curious tourists from recording a true-life New Orleans crime scene. The body lay draped under a white sheet, atop the large rocks, which sloped to the river's current.

Part of a policeman's job entailed informing tourists of the sketchy areas to avoid, which when heeded, would equate to less crime and less paperwork. If this lady had wandered into the wrong neighborhood, then traveling all the way back here and dumping her in the river wouldn't make sense.

The Crime Scene Unit had yet to arrive, but my Captain told me they were on the way. Ever since I returned to the job, everyone continued to ask how I was doing, not understanding the *salt-wound* relationship. I wanted to send out a blanket email to the entire NOPD in hopes of avoiding the questions about Cozy Robicheaux, the girl I'd shot two months ago, and letting a kidnapping rapist escape.

I shook Cozy's bullet wound from my mind and zeroed in on the lumpy shape under the sheet. The medical examiner had better rule this a suicide because I wanted my first case back to be quick, and the Quarter didn't need more bad press.

My nostrils flared while taking in the smell of decomposition, in stark contrast to the usual smells of fried seafood and Creole cuisine one enjoyed in the French Quarter. CSU had to know this body needed refrigeration soon, but clocks in New Orleans ran slower than most places. I ducked under the tape, hoping the breeze stayed constant off the river.

A muscular patrolman stepped up, his chest reaching me before the rest of his body. "I'm Officer Tatum, first on the scene."

"Detective Peyroux. Any identification?"

"None."

"Where was the body found?"

The young policeman pointed a few feet away from the body at the water's edge. "The body was face-down. Me and three other guys pulled her out to where she is now."

"Hopefully, you didn't do any damage."

"You wanted us to leave her in the water?"

"No. I just hate that CSU isn't here yet." I looked around. "So, nothing else out of the ordinary?"

"Sorry, Detective." He gave me that familiar, lingering stare. I sensed what he was thinking. He'd heard my name before.

I stepped forward almost bumping into his chest. "You got something to say to me, officer?"

"No, Detective. Not a thing."

"Then go mind the on-lookers."

My ankles swiveled on the rocky terrain as I made my way to lift the sheet to inspect her face. This woman could have been my mother and I wouldn't have known it. She looked like bratwurst ready to explode on the grill, but there wasn't a tattoo in sight that might help with identification. She could have been thrown in right where we stood, or the river's current could have brought her down from the north.

I pulled out my sunglasses and returned to the amber bricks that paved the Moon Walk, hoping Dr. Jerry with CSU had pulled up behind the succession of squad cars. No such luck. I sat on a bench and jotted notes that I'd easily remember anyway, letting my Ray Bans hide my worry. Forensics needed to do their thing before I could do mine. Once they collected her properly, all I could do was check missing persons and wait for lab and autopsy results. My colleagues back at the station would probably start a pool on whether it was a tourist, local, or prostitute. And behind my back they might place bets on whether I'd finish the case.

Detective Tara Gray stepped onto my crime scene wearing big reflective shades and a thin, white jogging suit. Her hair was cropped short, but styled like an advertisement for a beauty salon. Her lean frame seemed to glide forward while a badge swung around her neck like Mardi Gras beads. The cluster of freckles on her nose reminded me that her family tree had a white branch. She stopped by my feet, but never faced me.

"Dobson didn't send . . ." I fingered the corners of my eyes under my sunglasses.

"Yep. I told her I don't like you, but she insisted." She put her hands on her hips.

"Is that your badge around your neck, or did you join a rap group?" I crinkled my eyes at her.

She lifted her glasses. "You drunk again, mother fucker?"

I broke into a laugh and she finally smiled. If we had been meeting for lunch, a warm embrace would have been in order. Tara and I had gone through the academy together, each making detective the same year and assigned to work Homicide out of Headquarters on Broad Street. We worked well together, and the Captain knew it.

Her smile faded. "How are you, really? Chest still hurt?"

"Nope. Healed up nicely. Good as new. Pass it on."

She nestled in by my side. "I'm going to tell you again, because it can't be repeated enough. You had to take the shot. He would have killed her otherwise."

"I shot an innocent young girl in the throat in an abandoned house, Tara."

"The shot *deflected* into her throat," she countered.

"A half-inch from killing her."

"And she's alive because of you."

"She's alive only because the bullet slowed as it passed through the killer's forearm first. And he got away. The van was stolen, the house wasn't his."

"Yeah, but now his DNA is on file. You faced an impossible choice; and yet you made the right choice." Tara slapped her hand onto my thigh. "You let him escape, but if he'd held onto her, it was a hundred percent he'd kill her. The odds just didn't fall in your favor, honey. Every cop out here knows you made the right call."

"It's been hell: the hospital stay, the investigation, the administrative leave, my therapy sessions. I had Heather in my ear telling me it was okay to quit."

"No favors from your buddy, the Mayor?"

"You know me better than that. I've never used my friendship with Chance."

"I know. Bad joke."

"I'm used to them." I pushed her shoulder with a smile.

"Since you've been on a leave of absence, Dobson wants me to take lead on this one. Let you get your groove back." She waited with a furrowed brow.

"That's why she sent *you*. I'd tell anyone else to shove it."

She rested her face on my shoulder with a short hug, and then stood, ready for business. "Identification?"

"None." I showed her the sparse notes on my notebook to prove it.

"Sucks."

"Been waiting on CSU forever. Thinking about getting a beignet."

She walked forward. "I'm going to examine the vic."

"Under the sheet." I pointed and kept my grin for a moment. "See? Joking . . . I'm fine."

Tara was a stellar detective, and I could have been paired with much worse. She almost mimicked my exact movements when I had first arrived, lifting the sheet and checking the surrounding area. The river's currents framed her body while her head tilted toward me as if hearing my thoughts. I waved at her with my fingers.

The boats and barges floated effortlessly under the bridge. The Riverboat Natchez spun its giant rear wheel a hundred yards out, slowly making a getaway. It wasn't hard to be reminded of Mark Twain, or even Louis and Clark when they first floated past this crescent of land full of Native Americans.

For the thousandth time, I imagined the bullet finding the kidnapper's forehead.

If only.

THREE

Missing persons files from across the country monopolized the rest of the day. I'd searched for the ones with the matching criteria of race, weight, height, and hair color. CSU couldn't offer anything useful just yet, and DNA results wouldn't come back for a week. Tara unofficially let me take lead as she typed up paperwork on three other cases, which were denied my involvement. Our River Doe would appear on the evening news, so we expected to be flooded with tips and leads to follow in the morning.

Before heading home, I stopped at the Crescent City Firing Range near Headquarters to test if I still had my nerve. The outside of the building looked like it could be an adult video store you see from the highway. It needed a new paint job, new façade, and a new sign. The empty lot insured I would have fifteen minutes of alone time before closing. The owner would give me thirty minutes if I needed it.

My muscles tensed while checking the Glock, a piece that rested comfortably at my side since the Academy. The poster of the generic black-silhouetted target loomed twenty yards down the line as I put my headphones on and slapped in the magazine. My knuckles cracked in a finger stretch. I had just taken a piss, but needed to go again. If there was anything else to do before shooting, I couldn't think of it.

As I raised the gun with both hands, the target blurred into Cozy Robicheaux being held by that madman. I had never believed that a memory or a hallucination could actually take the place of true vision, but here she was, standing before me, innocent and scared. After blinking her away, the target came into focus and I exhaled, firing six rounds in succession with no hesitation—easy, when no lives are on the line. My lungs took air again and I lowered the gun, hoping the cluster on the target was wrong.

The sheet of paper raced towards me, stopping with a ripple and a nice grouping of six bullets to the left of the target's head. My head swiveled around as if there would be gawkers laughing at me. The harder I focused, the worse I did as two more targets offered a similar result. Being alone, I allowed myself to curse and slap my face to wake up my aim. The closer the distance, the better I did, but that hardly put me at ease. How the hell do you compensate for that kind of drifting on the job? I had to fix this fast.

Lush shrub bushes and oak tree leaves surrounded my house right off Magazine Street. Huge tree roots caused sections of broken sidewalk to dip and rise, creating an obstacle course common to the Uptown area. My living room window glowed with permanent light from the corner lamp, a menial constant that gave comfort after a long day.

As soon as I shut the front door my wife accosted me with an embrace. "How was it?"

"Good. It was good." My hands traced her slender torso, stopping at her hips. I pecked her lips with a smile and she let go. "Alicia here?"

She gave a quirky half-smile and shrugged. "In her room talking with Jane on the phone."

"Of course."

"I saw you and Tara at the Moon Walk on the news. That's your case?"

"Yeah. Nothing much to it right now. Doe dumped in the river."

"Don't want to talk about it?" Her curious face frowned.

"Not right now. I'm hungry. Let's eat."

Spaghetti and meatballs with my wife and daughter started subdued. Forks tapped plates until Heather broke the silence. "Alicia's soccer games are going to start soon. You should see her cute uniform."

Alicia cocked her head in a challenging manner. "Jane says perverts get their rocks off on girls wearing soccer uniforms."

That caught my attention. "You're only twelve. Do you even know what that means?"

She thought for moment. "Jane says it's an *orgasm*, which we learned about in *sex ed*." My daughter emphasized the proper words. "They taught us a man's *orgasm* releases *sperm,* which is used to make a *baby*, but Jane says a woman's *orgasm* feels really good."

"Jane's just a wealth of information."

"Is that right, Mom?"

Heather sighed, slightly red. "Yes, but in terms of making a baby, a woman's orgasm isn't just to feel good. The muscle contractions help a man have his orgasm. As it turns out, most men don't need that help."

I smirked. "Men don't become perverts because of outfits. But you still need to be vigilant of strangers approaching you at the games."

"I know, Dad. Whatever." Alicia rolled her eyes as only a tween can.

"I do want to see your uniform, though."

"Is Mr. Chance going to come to my games?"

"Being mayor doesn't give him a lot of time for that, dahlin'. But, I'll ask."

The rest of dinner conversation stayed light. Television time passed in a blink. Before I realized it, we had brushed our teeth for bed, where the term *sleep* would be used loosely. I didn't know if more therapy would solve my restless nights, but something had to be done before I turned to alcohol as a sleep remedy.

Heather sashayed from the bathroom wearing a sexy red lace bra and matching panties. While cocooned in the blanket, my head turned with a resigned smile. Her face sagged into a frown as she crawled onto the bed and sat on her heels. Normally, this scene would start my engine with no problem. She was so beautiful, not too skinny, smooth flawless skin and expressive blue eyes.

"No?" She pouted.

I turned onto my side and propped my head up on my hand. "My mind isn't here."

"Still? Ever since the shooting – I just thought that with your first day back, maybe things would get back to normal. Between us, I mean."

"I'm almost there, honey. It's just that today was like taking two steps back. I've been doing nothing but adjusting. This is the last adjustment. Soon, I promise."

"It would have to be a young woman, wouldn't it?"

"It's like a ringing phone that I can't answer."

She fell forward onto her side to face me, glancing down at her cleavage. "Not even a comment about my boobs popping out?"

"Hard to believe."

Her fingers ran through my hair. "Well, whatever you need, I'm here."

"I know." I kissed the inside of her hand.

"Cozy and her mother forgave you. They were appreciative. You need to forgive yourself, and maybe your nightmares will go away." Before I could open my mouth, she whispered. "And don't ask me how. I don't have the answer."

I nodded like a scolded child and turned back onto my side as Heather changed into a T-shirt for bed. She slid under the sheets and spooned me. Some primal instinct told me to push away, to decline comforting, but my arms wouldn't obey that command. How could I? Heather and Alicia were the only things that kept me sane. They gave me a reason to get up every morning.

FOUR

My morning started with an hour of *Muy Thai*, a kickboxing class that included elbows and knees, eight points of contact designed for close quarter fighting and was popular with the cops who liked to stay in shape. After five minutes of warm up, I paired with Frank Harvin, a cop from the Third District, who was considered opinionated in some circles and a dickwad in others. We traded rounds of pad holding while the other punched, kicked, and blocked.

So long as he stayed quiet and moved the pads where I struck, we'd be fine. Muy Thai required total focus or else you could seriously hurt someone or get hurt yourself, although with Harvin, I really didn't care.

"Heard you were at the range yesterday," Harvin whispered as I threw a jab-cross at the pads he held high near his shoulders.

The owner must have blabbed. I let out a breath with each strike, like the second half of a sneeze. *Screw you, Harvin.*

"Seems like your punches land about as good as you aim your gun." He shook the pads up near his ears.

"Who told you that?" I continued the routine of jab-cross-hook-kick under the supervision of our instructor.

"Word gets around. You sure you want to be carrying a firearm when you can't aim worth shit?"

My punches became harder. With satisfaction, I heard him give a small wheeze of effort as my kick knocked him off balance. "Maybe you should mind your own business."

"No one wants to work with you. You should retire for the public good."

"Thanks for the advice, douche-bag." My leg whipped into the pads at his hip.

"Who would want to work with a guy who shot an innocent girl?"

I threw another kick instead of a cross, catching Harvin in the stomach. When his pads came down, my glove landed on his jaw. He dropped to his knees. His glassy eyes wandered the room.

"Asshole." I left for the locker room under the stares of the remaining members of the class.

WHILE ON TELEPHONE hotline duty at Headquarters, I kept expecting a reprimand from the Captain at the Third District about pummeling Harvin at kickboxing, but none came. My day consisted of deciphering the real calls from the hoaxes pertaining to my River Doe. After writing down the name of the twenty-third caller, I dropped my pen onto the desk and leaned back. "You say your girl was abducted in Montana?"

"Yes, sir," the elderly female voice said. "When she was three years old."

"Missing since she was three?"

"The news said the woman has brown hair. My baby has brown hair."

"Yes, ma'am, the victim was a brunette."

"You need to check that this girl ain't my daughter. Sarah Mancini," she annunciated.

I jotted the name down. "I have all your information on file, and I promise to look into it."

"You'll call me back?"

"If it does turn out to be your daughter, I promise we will call you immediately."

I wiped my face, not knowing how many more calls like that I could take. Whether they were false leads, jokes, or optimistic family members, it drained my life force. My desk phone lit up yet again.

"Peyroux."

"Cozy Robicheaux is here with her mother," the downstairs desk clerk said. "She's asking for you."

Throat. Bullet. I squeezed my eyes shut. "Can you tell them I just left on a call?"

"They came all the way from Manchac."

"I know that, Rudy."

"Awright. No problem."

"Thanks. I owe you one."

Positioned on the second floor, I peeked through the window at Cozy and her Native American mother, Aponi, as they moved toward the parking lot. Cozy was a beautiful seventeen-year-old with flowing brunette hair and her mother just as striking. I watched them disappear under a cloak of oak trees.

Minutes later, the desk officer appeared on my floor with a gift basket of wine and cheeses wrapped in cellophane and a Mardi Gras colored bow of purple, green, and gold. He placed it on my desk, giving me the stink eye, and left without saying a word. The card on the basket read:

DETECTIVE LUCAS,
Avoid me all you want. I'll never stop thanking you.

IT HAD several hearts drawn on it. I fell back into my chair, rubbing my neck and staring at the brown, wicker basket. And I called Harvin the douche-bag.

FIVE

Manchac, sixty miles outside of New Orleans

The flimsy back door burst open and the cackling of familiar voices flowed in. Cozy Robicheaux backed up a step and froze in speechless awe as her boyfriend Ash, and his entourage of three sweaty yahoos, swung a fifteen-foot alligator onto the stainless steel table. They laughed in celebration, breathing heavily. This reptile would warrant a big payday from Ash's dad, the seafood-store owner.

"I thought you were going to see your detective in New Orleans," Ash said.

Cozy put her fingers on the small scar on her neck. "He was out on a case. We got back early."

"You haven't seen him since the hospital."

"I know."

Two of the rednecks exited to hose out the pickup bed, but beefy Tray and lean-framed Ash hung back. The smell of bayou and body odor filled the back room, overpowering the normal atmosphere of shrimp and crab boil. Ash disappeared in the bathroom as Tray took one final picture of their conquest. He pointed the cell's camera at Cozy, who shot the bird finger at him.

Tray's biceps rippled, causing the opposite of attraction in Cozy's mind. *Repulsion*. His sleeves had been ripped off a plaid shirt that clashed with a tight, discolored tank top.

His jaw jutted at the reptile. "Big, right? Biggest one I ever seen."

Cozy looked to the bathroom door for Ash.

"Things don't have to be weird between us." Tray scraped at his lips, then spit in the industrial sink.

She spoke through her teeth. "You raped me."

His fists clenched and his jaw tightened. "No one thinks it was rape except you, so stop saying it. If you hadn't been saved by that detective – *that* would have been rape."

Cozy secured the cleaver off the wall and held it by her thigh. "I was in no shape to say *no* to you guys. Doesn't mean I wanted it."

Tray's cheeks burned red. "Maybe if you remembered what happened, you'd know you liked it."

She charged into him, pushing the mountain of man against the wall with the cleaver angled into his groin. "You got no sense at all."

"Just hold still, Cozy. Things are getting out of hand, now." Tray attempted charm, but oozed sleaze, making a small effort to be sympathetic. "It's been two years. You're fine. Let it go."

She seethed, putting pressure against the thigh. "You ruined my life in high school."

"Before you dropped out, you mean."

"You don't know when to shut up, do you?"

Tray stared into her eyes. She absently stopped pressing the cleaver against his groin and let him fall to the floor, cupping his balls. She placed the heavy cleaver on top of the alligator and waited.

"You could have cut me for real, you crazy bitch."

"Get out of here."

He struggled to his feet, still eyeing the cleaver. "I'd call the sheriff, but I wouldn't do that to Ash."

"Please go." Without aggressive intent, she rested her hand a few inches from the cleaver, letting the imagined scenario of chopping off his head play out.

"Speaking of the string bean, he must be taking a shit, he's been in there so long." Tray laughed with weak breath, still pulling at his zipper.

Mr. Paul stuck his head through the swinging double doors with no clue as to what had transpired. "Stop bothering my help. You can go. I'll pay Ash later and he can give y'all your share."

"Sure, I'm goin'. Eric and Joe are probably going at it doggy style in the back of my truck, those *coon-ass* homos. Tell Ash he's gonna have to thumb it home."

After Tray left, Cozy unclenched and rolled her eyes for Mr. Paul's benefit. She then focused on the matter at hand, circling the reptile like an art critic at a gallery. Her fingers ran over the rough exterior, stopping at the magnificent head.

"Sorry for what I'm about to do, buddy." Her voice was soft and soothing.

The gator seemed more relaxed than dead. She lifted its front webbed feet, impressed with the weight and sheer strength. The claws would make an excellent necklace. It defied common sense, but Cozy imagined it could wake and scurry off the table. A creature this impressive didn't seem like it could be killed. The animal's belly spread wide, waiting to burst its bayou diet all over the floor.

Mr. Paul fully entered the room wearing his famous crawfish apron, the pattern stretched across his belly. He pulled off his latex gloves like he had come from the O.R. and stood in silence. His silver moustache twitched into an unbalanced smile as he pulled out his phone and snapped a photo.

"Facebook," he said from the left side of his mouth. "Where is that boy? Must be a hell of a shit."

"Ash's stomach ain't been right since I was shot." Cozy rubbed between the gator's eyes.

"He cares for you."

She nodded. "From this point on, this gator shall be known as Mr. Teeth."

"Mr. Teeth is the biggest one we've had yet."

"Normal slice and dice?"

"Yep. Just cleared a spot next to the shrimp. Just cut the tail and feet in chunks. I'll filet them."

"Can I have the claws?"

"Sure." He entered the walk-in refrigerator and came out with a box of boiled crabs.

"What about the head?" Her bottom lip curled under.

"C'mon, Cozy. You know I collect the heads. I'm going to put it right over the door. Besides, you know how expensive the taxidermist is."

"I've been saving up. Besides, I'll leave it to you in my will. Who knows when I might get shot again?" Cozy hesitated into a smile.

Mr. Paul glanced at the floor while his moustache drooped. "I don't like when you joke like that."

"Sorry. But you know, everybody's gonna die – natural causes or otherwise."

He slammed the crabs on a nearby chair. "Damn it, Cozy. You're just sixteen. What do you know about life yet? You haven't lived any."

"I'm seventeen now."

"You are. Shit. We're in April. I'm sorry. Happy birthday. I love you like my daughter. You know that."

Ash came out of the bathroom rubbing his belly. "Woo, those crawfish got me."

Mr. Paul stepped up to his son. "Why didn't you remind me Cozy turned seventeen? I forgot all about it."

"Sorry, Dad. With Cozy being kidnapped and shot and all. I didn't think."

"Right, you didn't think." He lightly slapped the back of Ash's head.

"You've been trying to marry her momma. Why didn't she tell you? You gonna' slap her in the head?"

Cozy smiled, liking Mr. Paul as a suitor for her momma. She felt the skin of the gator again as if it was cashmere, and then reached for the cleaver, allowing her eyes to become wet like she was chopping onions. Mr. Paul picked up the crabs with an apologetic expression and exhaled.

"Alligator autopsy," she laughed, pretending to hack at the base of its skull.

"You want the head, dawlin'? You got it. Happy birthday."

Cozy balanced the cleaver on the gator's back and stepped up to her boss. She was tall enough to easily kiss him on the cheek that still had muscle control due to the stroke. They both went flush and Ash glanced between them like he didn't understand or didn't want to. Mr. Paul then disappeared to the front of the store.

"Tray left me again?" Ash asked, looking around.

"Yeah." *That creep.*

"I guess I'll take my dad's car to go get cleaned up 'cause I smell like ass-cabbage." Ash kept a few inches between them, but leaned in for a peck on the lips as she held her breath.

His blue eyes glowed against his tanned, dirty skin. She exhaled watching him head for the back door. Cozy whispered, "Let's go out to our spot sometime soon, okay?"

"Whatever you want, babe." He let the door slam behind him.

SIX

While sitting on her bed after just waking, Cozy examined a black and white portrait of her parents on their wedding day. Her mother, Aponi Rainstorm-Robicheaux, bragged to be a direct descendant of the Opelousas Indian Tribe. Cozy's father had been pure bayou-mud Cajun. That combination instilled a fierce survival instinct in their offspring, evident from the night she had been born to the day she had murdered her father with a shotgun.

"Thought I heard you rustling." Her mother entered with a bowl of grits, butter melting on top, and a glass of orange juice. Her Cajun accent and Native American features were an interesting dichotomy.

"Tell me about when I was born."

Her momma beamed, handing over the bowl of grits. "Well, everyone involved tells it exaggerated flare, but I keep it truthful."

"I like your version best."

She sat next to her with the arched back of a British Royal. "I was playing *bourre* with Mr. Earl, his wife and Ms. Beverly and her sister when my water broke, ending the card game right there. You were three weeks early. Everyone had come in Mr. Earl's flatboat, so we tried to take your daddy's car, but it wouldn't start."

"He was too drunk to figure out the cable came off the battery." Cozy looked to the floor.

"Yes. Everyone helped me into Mr. Earl's flatboat, but by then it was too late. You were on your way. I gave birth to your right there."

"Born on the bayou."

"Born on the bayou." Her momma kissed the side of her head. "From your first breath, you were an indigenous creature of Manchac."

"Where you have to belong or move out."

Her momma stood. "Let's go into the kitchen."

She squinted. "You have coffee made?"

"Coffee? You want to try coffee?" Her mother paused in thought. "Let me make you a cup with sugar and milk so it's not so strong."

"I like it black. I had it at Ash's once."

"Black? Don't be silly."

Cozy squeezed her eyes shut. "Fine." She carried her breakfast, following her mother like an imprinted duckling while spying into the living room. Mr. Teeth's head would go perfect on the top shelf of the bookcase.

Her momma placed a cup of coffee on the table as they both sat. The brown cabinets hung over an 'L' shaped fake marble counter. Crawfish oven mitts hung from hooks along with other utensils. At the right end of the counter was the refrigerator covered with notes and magnets.

Cozy sipped the bitter-sweet, hot brew. "I miss Haley."

"I told you not to mention your sister in this house."

"But she's all alone in New Orleans and doesn't have me to protect her anymore." Her hands wrapped around the burning cup.

"Her choice. Besides, no one knows where she lives or works. So, until she contacts us, there's nothing we can do. Be best to forget about her." Her momma stared at the ceiling.

"Never."

"Paul called me about the gator. I can't believe your therapist would let you do that." Her disapproval came through.

"I can't believe I'm still seeing a therapist years after..."

"... don't mention your father, either. I just don't know about hacking up an alligator."

"As far as Dr. Clair knows, I just work at a seafood store. Besides, I killed and skinned lots of animals in the bayou before saving Haley from daddy. . ." Her voice dropped.

"Cozy," she blurted. "Stop it. We've gone through this too many times already. I don't want talk about it."

"Momma, you saw the cuts and bruises."

"Your sister hung out with thugs." Her hand slapped the table.

"No, that was *me* hanging out with thugs."

"I never once saw your daddy raise a hand to either of you. How your wild, drug-induced imagination cooked up that kind of sick scenario, I don't know, but I did not marry that kind of man."

"How come I didn't go to jail then?"

"Because that liberal D.A. believed those lies." She quickly added, "Lies that you believe to be true."

"Stop denying that he was a drunk."

"It's time for you to start acting like a proper young lady."

Cozy stopped talking to take a spoonful of grits. Her momma wouldn't even be happy living in a mansion with two daughters that attended Harvard. Dr. Clair had planted a seed that Cozy could be *tamed*, and now it was an excuse to keep her one remaining daughter under control.

Her momma had married young before learning there was much more to life than spitting out kids and serving a perpetually drunk Cajun husband. Her momma thought no one could hear from the bedroom, but she often whispered to the Spirits about being left widowed in virtual squalor in this remote part of the world.

But, that wasn't Cozy's problem to fix. Her own life was challenge enough. From a mere tot, Cozy had never been afraid of anything; teasing dogs just to provoke and avoid their bite, jumping higher than any boy on her bike, or swimming in gator-infested waters. As she grew bigger, she would explore the bayou a little farther, even more so when her father had finished a bottle. But after the State's Attorney ruled her father's homicide justifiable and after the court-appointed therapy sessions, her momma tried to lock the clamps down.

She topped off her coffee as a tiny show of control. "Careful. Coffee can be addicting."

"I've done worse than caffeine, Momma."

She placed the pot back on the burner. "I know about the drugs and I certainly know about the sex." Her momma cocked an eyebrow.

"You just want me to admit it." Cozy took a sip.

"I'm your momma." Aponi placed her hand against her forehead in defeat.

"You're Haley's momma, too."

"Can't be her momma if she's not here. You're here. I'll always take care of you . . . look out for you."

"You spy on me. I know the neighbors report to you."

Aponi kept her gaze in the coffee cup. "They're scared of you, dear."

"Scared? What, do they think I'm going to go on a murder spree?"

"It's just you've gotten so . . . aggressive."

"I want to talk about Haley."

Her Momma's rigid expression twitched as she inspected her fingernails. "Mr. Paul's bringing some crabs by for us to boil."

Cozy's hands fell hard on the table. "Momma . . . shit." She pretended to dig crust from her eyes and inwardly screamed as her momma turned for the sink to wash a bowl while humming.

After they finished the coffee in silence, Cozy changed into cut-off jeans and a Saint's half-shirt. Her biceps flexed in the mirror while twirling her hair into a ponytail. The scar on her throat looked cool – a real gunshot wound to add to her collection of battle wounds. They were better than tattoos; they told a *real* story.

She smiled inwardly, taking pride in her exotic symmetry, having inherited dark Native American features, but her eyes came from her father. They were a cool blue-gray metal color. Despite that, she despised having his Cajun blood coursing through her veins. She even considered changing her last name from Robicheaux to her mother's spirit name, Rainstorm.

Cozy Rainstorm. Cool and absurd at the same time.

She walked back into the kitchen just in time to hear the purring of a motor. "That's Ash's boat."

"You're going out?"

"Momma, I haven't been with Ash in weeks. I miss him."

"Put sunscreen on. Every inch of your skin is showing. And no bra? Honestly girl, you're too old for that now."

"Bye, Mom."

"Only 'cause it's Ashton," she warned.

The screen door slammed shut behind Cozy. Her beat-up Sketchers slid across the creaky planks to the end of the dock where Ash's pirogue putted to a stop next to a ladder descending into the water. When their eyes met, her feet halted well before the edge of the pier. He appeared freshly showered, which made him look like a college student.

"You want to go to our spot and talk?" he asked. "I know you've gotta be missing your big sister something fierce."

She felt the sting of tears rise, and swallowed them down. "You don't have to crab?"

"Motor froze up. Padre told me to check on you and I know you wanted to go to our spot. Speaking of gators, how'd the fifteen-footer go?"

She stepped to the edge of the planks and smiled proudly. "I brought a filet home."

"That gator's old. Younger meat's better."

"Still, you can tell people you ate a piece of the biggest gator ever caught in Manchac."

"Shit, I helped catch the biggest gator in Manchac. They should make a reality show about me." Ash's long, wavy hair lay flat in the heat. He had a couple of pimples, but on a handsome face, they weren't bad to look at. He was by far, the best thing she'd seen on this part of the bayou.

Cozy stepped wide into the pirogue as the bottom of her butt cheeks escaped her jean shorts. With a laugh, she tugged them down and gave Ashton a full-planted kiss on his lips. They departed to the center of the channel, wind flipping her hair as they passed each house built on pylons. Occasionally, the vigilant neighbors waved until finally they entered the tributary that had become their own private sanctuary. The mosquitoes tried to find their skin as frogs croaked in the distance under mossy Cypress trees. They motored to one huge Cypress that had fallen over. After tying up, they climbed behind it where several wooden pallets were laid out for dry flooring. Two cans of bug spray were still there.

They kissed for several minutes while the palate boards marked their skin. The surrounding weeds pushed to and fro in the breeze and the sounds of bayou insects floated around them.

"How you feeling?" Ash asked after a while.

"I'm still alive." She ran her fingers over the masculine bump in his nose onto his amazingly full lips.

He scowled. "Have you heard from Hales?"

"You know I haven't."

"How can she go two years without calling?"

"Haley wants us to forget about her."

"That doesn't sound like her."

"I know. It's like she's trying to erase us."

"That's assed up." His hand reached under her half-shirt and cupped her breast like a warm bra cup. His thumb ran over her nipple, pushing it left and right. It was his predictable first move, and she had once found it endearing. Now, she shifted away while maintaining a pleasant face.

The memory of that man holding a gun to her head hit her like a brick. He had been strong and smelled like a sweaty auto mechanic. She couldn't help comparing that psychopath to her father and how he had groped Haley in their hugs. But the image of Detective Lucas always washed that away. "I'm not in the mood. Not out here, anyway. I'm sorry."

"No, it's fine. It's just been so long."

"I know how you boys need your sex or you'll just *die*, like your balls will explode or something." She put her hand on his groin.

"Hey. Don't get it started if nothin's gonna happen."

"How about we smoke some weed?" She mimicked a toke.

"No weed – got coke."

"Then let's do that and maybe I can do something for *you* quick-like before the mosquitoes attack it." Odd that she would suddenly feel obligated instead of interested.

SEVEN

Since Forensics and the M.E.'s report were in progress, Captain Dobson told me not to rush into the station. Heather took advantage of my being home with Alicia by getting some shopping out of the way. My daughter was on the edge of finally trusting her to be alone. I sat in my sweatpants watching ESPN highlights and sucking down a third cup of warm coffee while Alicia slept off a late night of movie watching. My socked feet rested on the coffee table and my back pressed perfectly into a groove between two pillows. The house still hinted of Heather's perfume, a light, uplifting fragrance.

I finally heard my daughter stir, wondering what kind of day she had planned. I loved my quiet house, but I couldn't imagine it this way all the time. Alicia wandered into the living room in jogging shorts and a large, baggy T-shirt, with her hair a terrible mess. Her eyes were barely open as she fell into the recliner, legs outstretched.

"Morning." I offered. "Summer must be so nice for you."

"You don't have to work?"

"Going in late."

"Where's Mom?"

"Winn Dixie. You just missed her. What's on your plate today?"

"This and that."

"Which is it? This or that?" I studied my daughter as she inspected her belly button with her chin in her chest. Her shoulders rose in an answer.

A knock on the front door disturbed our non-conversation. Alicia barely took notice. Door- to-door charities and religious nuts came to mind, and I wanted to deal with neither. I carefully moved the curtains to the side, but saw a welcomed sight. I threw the door wide with a grin.

"Mr. Mayor, what do I owe this honor?"

He looked me up and down. "Damn, I didn't bring my sweatpants."

"I have an extra pair."

"I only wear designer sweatpants." He laughed.

Dressed to impress, he turned to his detail by the black Towncar and waved him away. Handsome as always, with a spiky brown tuft of hair, he flashed a set of perfectly non-perfect teeth. His thick, strong eyebrows would be bushy if not trimmed, and his square jaw and Roman nose were a perfect fit for a political career.

He stepped inside. "I miss you."

"Aww." We embraced in a brief man-hug. "Want some coffee? Anything?" I noticed Alicia had disappeared from the chair.

"Nah, just came from a power Champagne breakfast."

"My tax dollars at waste."

"Said the cop."

"Ouch."

"We haven't talked in a while, so I called Headquarters for you and found out you were still home. Thought I'd swing by for second."

We walked back to the living room, where I turned down the sports highlights and returned to my cup of coffee. Chance sat forward on the sofa, elbows on his thighs so as not to get any wrinkles or lint on his suit.

"You home alone?"

"Heather's at the store and Alicia's in the back. Got my first case, but I'm sure your sources are keeping you up to date."

"If you and I had dinner more often, I wouldn't have to call around."

"It's not like when we were kids, Chance. We've become busy people."

Chance glanced at the Saints football highlights on the television and pointed. "Hey, there's your brother. Brent's doing good, right?"

"Brent got his payday in the NFL. That's all he wanted."

Chance knew since the first day we met that I hated talking about my brother, but he always chipped away. "Spoke to him lately?"

"No, Fuck him."

"Alrighty, then. I want to talk about the girl in the river."

"What about her?"

"What are you thinking?"

I hesitated. "The only time you ever ask about a case is when it affects you in some way."

"Seriously? I can't be interested?" He almost smiled.

"How does this dead girl affect you, Chance?"

"My only concern is you." He appeared hurt.

"Do I have to go through the times you've meddled?" I pulled back one of my fingers. "There was Darnell Brown…"

He stopped me. "A dead white female doesn't bode well for our tourism."

"There it is."

"Never mind that I care about your first day back, then." He searched the room, aggravated he wasn't getting the information he wanted. "You visit Cozy yet?"

I let his inquiry into River Doe go, figuring he would come back at some point to reveal more. "Cozy came by the station yesterday, but I avoided seeing her. Chicken-shit, I know."

"You have to make a trip out to Manchac and see the girl."

"Heather keeps telling me to go see her, too."

"Then listen to those who love you."

My eyes shifted on Chance. After a few moments, Alicia skipped into the living room dressed in her nice summer clothes with brushed hair and a coating of lip gloss.

She stopped in front of us with a huge grin. "Mr. Chance. What a surprise. How are you?"

"Alicia, hi dawlin'. You're looking prettier than ever, a spittin' image of your mother." Chance reached out and my daughter hugged him like he had just returned from war.

"You don't come by enough." Alicia flipped her hair back. "Why don't you come to one of my soccer games?"

"Being mayor is a busy job, but I promise I'll try."

She giggled and fell to her knees, dimples out in full force. "Are you staying a while? I can get you a Coke."

"Who are you and what have you done to my daughter?" Asked and ignored.

Chance leaned forward to palm my daughter's face and then kissed the top of her head. "You're adorable, but I can't stay." He exhaled and then stood, as any further adult conversation would have to wait. "I'm going to make reservations at LaPlace on Bourbon for us. You, me, my date – to be determined – and your wife."

"That's four of us," I confirmed.

He threw his index finger at me. "I'll text you with the date and time."

"Bye, Mr. Chance." Alicia waved.

Once her crush shut the door, Alicia's alter ego vanished, and my lips parted to say something, but I couldn't find two words to put together. The sulking resumed. Needing a distraction, I jumped in the shower, so I could go into the station when Heather got home. At least Captain Dobson would be able to see my face and I could spend the rest of the day being productive.

EIGHT

For the most part, I twiddled my thumbs, occasionally watching one of the station's televisions. The news reports had moved on to a bar shooting near Tulane, where two college students were killed. This meant the desperate, misled, and weirdo callers would move on and River Doe's real family would remain in the dark or sadder yet, no one would miss her.

Tara had been scarce lately, working on other cases and informing me that my main job was to update her as the weekend cops went on about their business around me. No one had ever approached me about my little skirmish with Frank Harvin, so I could only assume he hadn't told anyone due to embarrassment.

Captain Dobson orbited my desk. Her polo shirt was crisp, tucked into her pleated slacks with a physique like a starving fashion model. She was once an overweight rookie, but had lost the pounds over years of intense dieting. She had taken several leaves of absence to have her excess skin removed. The stories of her throwing suspects around as a heavy beat cop were legend.

Her thin eyebrows arched. "It's Sunday. Why don't you go home if you're bored?"

"I've been sitting home for two months. Besides, Heather's doing some gardening and I don't feel like working in the yard today. If the M.E. wasn't so backed up, maybe I could make some progress."

"He's getting to it." Her shoulders slumped. "Two more autopsies with the shooting Uptown."

"What are you doing here?"

"I'm overdue on lots of reports and I tend to snack on anything I can find when I hang out at the house. It's good for me to be distracted." She smirked.

"I've been meaning to ask, how come I'm not getting any other assignments? Not that I don't know the answer."

She smiled patiently, like a mother. "Just get your feet wet on this one, okay?"

"You're worried about my decision making… about putting other cops in danger."

"I heard about you at the shooting range."

"Great."

"I'm not worried. It's like this; if you were a surgeon, I wouldn't give you three operations on your first day back, but I would totally trust you to do a heart transplant. You get me?"

"I get you. You want me to help Billy out with the autopsies."

"Ha ha. I trust our shrink. She says your mental health is fine. I'm good with that, but I need to make sure it sticks."

I bit my lip to keep more words from leaving my mouth.

Dobson went on. "Cozy Robicheaux called again."

"Yeah."

"Have dinner with them. The poor girl doesn't understand why her hero is avoiding her."

I mimicked stabbing myself in the chest. "Right through the heart. Okay, I'll do it. I'll call her."

Dobson nodded and straightened an overlapping belt she still wore as a reminder of her former weight. She looked over to yesterday's box of donuts that still had two remaining. "I totally get how recovering alcoholics feel." She shoved a stick of gum in her mouth and walked away.

I called a string of police departments north along the river, inquiring about any missing residents. River Doe's file sat cold on my desk, no different from a random gang execution or a homeless person's murder with no leads. I had a complete set of photos, a box of bagged and tagged garbage, and a few unhelpful witness statements. While waiting for lab results, I considered going back into older missing person's reports, ones that fell through the cracks because they didn't cause a public outrage.

However, my cell came to life with the name of Dr. Billy Phillips from the Coroner's Office.

"Peyroux here."

"Sorry to disturb your crawfish boil."

"I'm at the station."

"Brown-noser. I'm using my Sunday to finally get to your Doe from the river. You of all people deserve some expedience. You want to come down so I can go home and soak my feet? The dogs are barkin'."

Dobson glanced at me through her office window as if she heard the question. I stood. "On my way and I'll call Gray."

CAPTAIN DOBSON HAD ASKED Tara to help Frank Harvin question the neighbors in the Callio Projects since a white cop strolling in alone wouldn't receive such a great reception. I haven't told my partner about my episode with Frank yet, staying neutral about the whole thing. I just told her to meet me at the coroner.

Tara had said she didn't mind helping Harvin on a Sunday as she had nothing personal against him, and she had attended Saturday's Midnight Mass to free up her day. She joked with me that Frank Harvin wasn't scared with a trembling voice, imitating him. The truth was that Tara had built up a lot of good will in those projects and he needed her.

Peeking into the medical examiner's lab was like watching a jack-in-the-box, waiting for something to surprise the hell out of me. Tara had abandoned Harvin and arrived first; sitting perched on a stool near the body, rubbing her right hand. Maybe autopsies gave her weak knees, but she'd never admit it. I looked twice at her sparkling blue gym shoes that screamed disco.

Dr. Billy Phillips greeted me with a raised scalpel above that dreaded body, however my first priority was to smear a fragrant gel under my nose. It was strange that as humans, we were composed of mostly water, and yet this was the grotesque byproduct of what water could do. Doe's appearance wasn't any better than when I'd last seen her.

"Billy, how's business?" I asked.

"Busy with a broom up my ass. Hence Sunday." Billy looked to have a helmet of perfect, short black hair. His lanky body stood at six-foot-three with wire-frame glasses on a long face. His lengthy fingers manipulated the surgical instruments with precision. He was cool, but I suspected he was into some freaky stuff due to his sexually disturbing humor. Not much in this realm shocked him.

"Were you guys waiting for me?"

Billy cleared his throat. "Didn't want to start without you. She didn't drown. No water in her lungs. Asphyxiation."

"So, it's a murder. Great." I jotted it down in the small notebook I kept in my back pocket.

"Been in the river about four days. I'm ruling it a homicide. I've been going over the contents of her stomach."

I quickly wrote his comments. "No way to tell a dumping point, I guess."

"You're the detective."

"You would think." I glanced at Tara.

"Well, you're in luck. I saved the best for last."

"You know who she is?" I glanced at Tara.

"No, but almost as good. Just twenty minutes ago I pulled an iPhone from her vaginal cavity." He handed Tara the evidence bag. "You only get one joke, so make it good."

"No jokes." Wincing, I blinked the image away. "Do you know if she was still alive when the phone went in?"

"Yes, the tissue bled when it tore, but a suction had been created, so it didn't get wet."

"Let's see if it still works." Tara gloved up to handle the cell.

I watched the screen light up. "You said tissue tore. Was there a lot of trauma?"

"You asking whether she was a Catholic school girl, or one of those women who can take a fist?" His eyes smiled. "I venture to say it was painful, but under duress and the adrenaline of impending death, she might not have felt much."

"Like not knowing you were shot during an altercation?"

"Yes," Billy agreed. "Doesn't mean her killer didn't do it. Maybe she was unconscious at the time. Good luck with prints."

Tara looked up. "It's possible it's not her phone. Maybe someone else wants us to think the phone is hers, trying to fake their death?"

"Stupid way to fake your death," Billy said. "Of course there are people that stupid, but that's a question for you two. I have pictures. I found a mole on her inside thigh, pretty common, but nothing else to distinguish her. No scars or medical issues like rods or implants. No abnormalities. I'll need her dental records to get a proper ID. That, or some DNA to compare her to."

"It should be easy enough to track down the owner through the carrier." Tara motioned like Vanna White. "It's ready."

"We're not going to send it to Dr. Jerry for prints?"

Billy spoke up. "The way it was situated in there; it was like sliding it between two sponges and it came out slimed… sorry, there aren't gonna be any prints on it, in my opinion."

I lowered my vision until light flashed across the surface. "Don't see any obvious prints in the glare."

Tara pointed. "Our best bet for prints will be the inside cover and battery."

"Where it's been well-protected. But if the GPS is on, we'll be able to track her movements."

"That's right," Tara agreed, "these bastard phones know every move you make."

I pulled a pair of latex gloves from a box and swiped the screen. The wallpaper was a selfie of an attractive woman. Our luck held as her cell opened without a password. "The GPS is off. No record of where she's been."

"Figures."

"The account information won't show a name. Let's see her call history." It took a couple seconds to pull it up. "Hmm. Interesting. No contacts."

"That's freaky. Who has no contacts?" Tara extended her neck to see.

"New phone? There's only one call going out and it dropped."

"Has to be brand new. That's the only explanation."

"Maybe she deleted the call log. Can you do that?" I asked.

"Yeah, but why? Who was the call to?"

"Emergency 9-1-1. Four days ago." I glanced at her meaningfully.

"And it didn't go through? Remind me not to use her carrier. Find her picture gallery."

I scanned her sparse icons until finding the gallery. "Five pictures."

"You're kidding me."

"Has to be her first iPhone, maybe days old. Nothing carried over from a previous card and she didn't have time to fill it up or know to turn the GPS or lock screen on." I touched the first thumbnail and the picture blew up on the screen. It portrayed a bored, but attractive girl-next-door.

"Anything other than her?"

"Let's see, a kitchen, and a door with a 'B' on it, probably her front door and praise Jesus," I turned the phone so Tara could see. "A picture of an apartment building. I know this balcony. It's on Dauphine. Oh, man, there's a video here."

"Well, play it."

I pressed the arrow and a black, shadowy image bounced around until settling on a hulking figure heading toward the camera operator. It was too dark to see details, but there was a snake pit of humans around her. The view spun to bright penlights on the wall like twinkling stars. The screen became black and the video ended.

"No audio. She was probably too afraid to say anything. We have to get this to tech so they can blow this video up and maybe lighten it, so we can make out details," Tara said.

"Check this out. The time stamp of the video is a minute before the 9-1-1 call. She took the video hoping to get her killer on camera, dialed emergency and then…"

"...And then inserted it, probably thinking the 9-1-1 call would be traced and she'd be found."

"But the call didn't go through." I played the video again. "Had to be a place with little to no bars. There are other victims in the video, too, like a trafficking ring. God, and then to stick this phone in? She was brave."

"I'll dial her carrier and get a name. At least we have a place to start."

"And we definitely keep this tidbit out of the press."

"Damn straight. Can you imagine?" Tara walked away from me, dialing the number.

"A print on the inside cover would be nice." I saddled up to the body. "Preferably her killer's."

"It's possible," Billy mumbled.

A few minutes later, Tara dropped the cell back into the evidence bag and faced the body as if exhausted. "The account's only been active for five days. Makes sense with the number of photos. The name is Haley Robicheaux."

"Oh, God. No." I wiped my hands down my face.

"Wait, Robicheaux – as in Cozy Robicheaux?"

"Haley's her sister. *Was* her sister. She told me about her running away in the hospital. Damn."

"Now you *have* to go see her."

"To tell the girl I shot that we found her dead sister who might've been caught up in a human trafficking ring. Fantastic. Of all the fucking coincidences." I paced around the room, letting my head tilt back. "In the hospital, Cozy had asked me to remember her sister's name in case I ever ran across her." I came back to the body, which had been cut open vertically. My eyes focused on Phillips' work.

"That from her stomach?" Tara asked, pointing.

"Last meal was an assortment of shrimp, crab, roast beef, vegetables, some possible caviar. Some items digested more than others."

I wrote in my notebook. "Like she was having little bit of everything. Like appetizers or hors d'oervres."

"A cocktail party," Tara added.

"That video wasn't at any cocktail party."

He presented a tray that looked to contain little red buttons. "Her nails had been manicured."

I glanced at them. "Either at a party or a fancy dinner. Probably drinking alcohol."

Billy stopped tinkering with the food. "We'll have to wait for the labs to see if drugs were involved."

I touched Tara's arm. "Let's check out Haley's apartment to at least get some DNA to compare. Then, we'll inform the Robicheaux family."

"You want to call Dobson?" Tara asked.

I moved toward the door while scrolling for Dobson's number. "Yeah, she can check out Haley Robicheaux's history while we head over to her place."

"Tell her to have CSU meet us there."

"Right." I followed my partner out while explaining our findings to Captain Dobson. We stepped out of the building where I noticed Tara's hand had swelled a bit. She had just been with Harvin questioning the Callio residents. Could she have decked him, too? I put my arm around her shoulders and gave her a quick squeeze. "Thanks."

"For what?"

"For adding to my artwork on Harvin's face."

"Your artwork? You gave him that black eye?"

"Yep. Why did *you* hit him?"

"He was talking shit about you. Said I'd get a bullet in my back if you were covering me. How do you know I hit him?" Tara questioned.

He cocked his head and smirked. "I'm a detective."

NINE

Cozy laid in a ball on her twin bed, staring at a silver-framed picture of Haley taken five years earlier. Haley's mouth was wide with genuine happiness at her seventeenth birthday. Ash had his arms around her sister's waist from behind as if surprising her, a picture of two people in love. Having sex with Haley's ex-boyfriend was either a way of lashing out at her sister, or being closer to her. It should've made her feel guilty, but it only made her numb.

The bedroom was barely cool, despite the window unit. She wandered to the refrigerator, cracked open a beer and poured it down until her throat burned. After a quick breath, the rest of her Abita Amber vanished with one last large swallow. She pushed the bottle deep into the trash, and then watched through the screen as her Momma dragged the ice chest along the pier, stopping at the large pot and burner. Cozy meandered outside and leaned against the metal pipe that acted as a railing. Her momma offered a comforting smile while pouring salt into the tap water to purge the crabs in the cooler.

"Those are big," Cozy said.

"Paul just dropped them off. He's such a sweetheart. I told him to stop by later tonight with Ash."

"Mr. Paul likes you. He gave you crabs." Cozy giggled and blushed.

"Cozy, ew." She rolled her eyes. "I told you, *hawt*, the man who wins my hand isn't going to be anyone that lives here."

"But you're stuck here. Kind of a catch-22."

Her momma wiped the sweat on the back of her neck and gave her a kiss on the forehead. "You are so smart. I wish you would change your mind about college."

Cozy deflated. "You need to get the police to find Haley and talk to her."

"You need to concern yourself with the here and now."

"I am. Haley should be here... now. I don't know why I don't just go and search for her myself. I could do it every weekend."

"You most certainly won't." Aponi slid a rogue hair away from Cozy's face. "The Spirits can guide you if you choose to let them."

"Do you think the Spirits are upset that the Indians who once honored them are mostly gone or stopped searching for them altogether?"

"Interesting question. I never thought about it. Hypothetically, would the Christian God be less powerful if there was only a handful of worshippers?"

"I guess not." Cozy gave her mother a rare, genuine smile.

Her momma inhaled like a bloodhound. "You drinking beer?"

"I had one."

Instead of a speech, her momma surprised her. "Go get us two more, would you, dear? We can set up the boiler together."

"Sure."

Cozy ran into the house, grabbing onto the counter as the room spun. With a splash of water on her face, her equilibrium balanced, and a wave like being upside-down passed through her eyes. Something was wrong – she could feel it.

Steady again, she opened the refrigerator and let the cool air even her out. Enjoying a beer with her momma? How odd. She pulled out two ice cold Coors Lights.

The squat, middle-aged landlord wore a wretched, powder blue tank top, shorts and sandals. The thinning hair on his head looked like a hot spot that a dog can't stop licking, but it might've been his only sympathetic quality. With a thick beard and crossed eyes, he impatiently rocked as Tara and I spoke to our captain on my cell's speaker.

"We're right outside Haley's door." I tilted the cell next to Tara, standing far enough away so the landlord couldn't pry.

Dobson continued, smacking loudly as if chewing gum, "I ran Haley Robicheaux's name. Robicheaux is like the Cajun version of Smith. Still, she is definitely Cozy's sister."

"Anything else?"

"Nothing on Haley. Completely clean record. You already know about Cozy killing her father. Got the address out in Manchac for you, if you don't already."

Tara backed away. "Can't wait to get to the bayou. Yee-haw."

At the hospital, Cozy had invited me to visit her home. All I knew of Manchac was passing the exit on my way to Hammond in I-55 and seeing some of the camps situated on pylons. It looked like one of those small towns Stephen King wrote about, a town you grew up in, but never moved to.

Tara sucked on a mint as she spoke. "Now we have to deliver the news, but with the caveat that it might not be her. How messed up is that?"

"We can hold off."

Dobson's voice shot out of the phone. "Go talk with them after you go through the apartment and see if they can fill any holes. Dr. Jerry's on his way with his team."

"Thanks, Cap." Tara said to the phone. I ended the call not telling our Captain that had been the plan all along.

"You say she was hardly ever here?" My attention returned to the landlord, Mr. Porter.

He rattled the keys in his hand. "Sometimes I saw her leave in the afternoon and usually she'd come in sometime before dawn. Like she worked a night shift."

"You know this how?" Tara asked, folding her arms and shifting her weight.

"My place is right at the entrance so I can see what kind of characters are coming and going and I'm a light sleeper. My ma' said that's because I'm a worrier. I worry a lot."

"She bring any friends over?"

"Only two I know of. There was this little black dude that came over a few times and there was this white loser that came by once that I saw."

"Little black dude? Like a kid?" I asked.

"Like a drug dealer. I saw a deal go down right outside the gate one day. I'd never invite that dude inside."

"And the white kid was a loser? Why?"

His head swayed as if it got his brain moving. "Raggy, baggy clothes. Didn't get a look at his face. Can't help you there. It was dark, but he was young, brown hair. They hugged and kissed like they knew each other. Like I said, though, she was hardly ever here."

I turned to the door with my partner. "Open it up, please."

DOBSON and I discussed tracking down this supposed drug dealer Haley knew. She gave that task to patrolling uniforms. Haley Robicheaux's miniscule apartment lacked any meaningful clues. It had none of the charm of an intimate French Quarter residence. A flophouse actually came to mind. After inspecting each drab room, we quickly ruled it out as being the location of her murder, considering the voyeuristic landlord and where the body was disposed. The landlord Porter had said she only moved in with a suitcase, using the furniture of the previously evicted tenant. At least Tara and I could stop saying River Doe, small comfort as it was.

Dr. Jerry arrived with his crew of two: Julia Sawyer his assistant and Freddie Boucher, the photographer. The small apartment suddenly became cramped.

"Hey y'all." Julia's blonde hair hung in a ponytail covered with a Saint's cap.

"Did Dobson threaten to pull you off the case, being that girl's sister and all?" Dr. Jerry surveyed the place.

"Not yet. And she better not." I watched Freddie take general shots around the room, disinterested since nothing would come of it.

Dr. Jerry put on a pair of gloves. "Don't give her a reason. You didn't touch anything in here, right?"

"I vaguely recall that from my procedure manual."

"Leave my man alone, Jerry," Tara held up her fist and shook it comically.

"What you guys got?" he asked, switching gears.

"A messy twenty-something that didn't spend much time here. Not much in the fridge. Some beer and take out. Basic toiletries in the bathroom. This wasn't a home, it was a place to sleep. We still need to talk to the family out in Manchac. There's a hairbrush in the bathroom. You're going to run DNA off it to compare to the body?"

"I seem to remember that from forensic school."

I held up both palms to him. "Just had to say it for my own piece of mind."

He ignored me and spouted off instructions to Julia. Tara and I left forensics to do their job and headed out the door. Manchac was our next destination. We preferred not to invite the State Troopers to accompany us on this one. The fewer cops seeing me power through this, the better.

It took an hour and ten minutes as we traveled over calm water and tree lines full of moss worthy enough to be painted. Getting to Manchac was one thing, finding the physical address proved to be another. Tara had checked the paper map every time the GPS voice told us to turn, thinking we'd end up in the bayou. She loved technology, but always expected the glitch.

"You're nervous." Tara stated.

"No. I'm just dreading this. I can't imagine their reaction."

"I hope I don't hear any banjos," Tara said.

"Same old bayou jokes. Listen, try not to be too black out there, okay? No *shizzle my nizzle*."

Tara cocked her head, and then spit flew with a burst of laughter. "Alright, Peyrizzle. Let me get my jar of mayonnaise. I can be as cracker as the next cracker."

"You're more like a Trisket."

"Shit, your last name's Peyroux. You got some coon ass in you. I hope you speak Cajun. You gotta protect me."

"You better hope you can run faster than me."

I parked where the grass met road. My stone legs pounded up the gravel path with a folder in my hand. The immediate front of the house was on land and the rest extended over the water. I took my sunglasses off, making sure my firearm was holstered and our badges were visible. The locals were sure to be armed with shotguns and suspicion. I knocked and seconds later an extremely attractive face peered through a crack in the door. It was hard not to imagine a red stream flowing from her throat.

Her eyes lit up. "Detective Lucas!" The door swung open and Cozy latched her arms around my waist. "About time you come see me."

"Cozy. You look good. How are you?"

"Great, now." She let go. Her scar made my stomach pinch. "Detective Tara, I remember you from the hospital."

"Good to see you again. Is your mother home?"

Her eyes looked from Tara to the folder. "Wait, this ain't about seeing me. Is this visit about Haley?"

"Maybe you should get your mother for us."

"My momma's right inside. Come on in."

The front room was decorated for function and comfort. Native American items occupied shelves. Old Pictures of ancestors hung on white and gold fleur de lis wallpaper, an eclectic clash of cultures. Small, Indian-patterned throw rugs covered most of the floor and the occasional alligator head kept watch over the room.

She led me into the kitchen. "Here, sit," she said, offering us chairs at a chrome-rimed Formica table. Tara and I didn't sit just yet, which made Cozy frown.

She yelled towards the screen door leading out back. "Momma. Detective Lucas is here about Haley."

Aponi Robicheaux stepped through the flimsy screen door with a single glance toward us and then leaned over the sink to wash her hands. Cozy sat on her knees with her elbows on the table, staring as if I was going to burst into flames. Her mother turned, dried her hands and then approached, assessing us from under lazy eyelids.

She shook my hand with confidence. "How are you, Ms. Robicheaux. This is Detective Gray."

"I've told you before, call me Aponi. Please sit, Detectives. Can I get you some tea? Water?"

"No, thank you." I inhaled the intoxicating aroma of crab boil.

"That was a long ride," Tara said. "Can I use your restroom?"

"That way to the left," Cozy pointed.

Aponi sat rigid with her hands on the table while watching Tara disappear into the hallway. A tilt of her head told Cozy to sit properly in the chair. Aponi addressed me. "I imagine it can't be good news."

"I'm afraid not. Maybe we should speak in private."

"That's quite alright. You go on."

I hesitated. "But, Ms. Robicheaux - Aponi…"

Cozy stood, and the chair kicked out. "I'm not leaving."

Aponi motioned for her to sit back down. "Whatever happened, she's going to find out anyway."

My eyes fell on Cozy's and I couldn't protect her yet again. "We pulled a female from the Mississippi River. Haley's cell phone was found on her person."

"Oh, God," Cozy said.

"So, Haley drowned?" Aponi never flinched.

"Actually, the victim had been killed prior to being left in the river."

"Victim?" Cozy repeated.

"We're not a hundred percent positive it's Haley. The body is unrecognizable."

Cozy's voice cracked. "Then, maybe it's not her. You could get her address from the phone, right?"

I nodded. "We did, but Haley hasn't been at the address for days."

"So, it's likely my daughter."

"No, Momma."

"Did she have any tattoos?" I asked.

Aponi and Cozy both shook their heads. Tears drew to Cozy's eyes. "She hated tattoos. She made me promise never to get one. She said if I was in a room with six friends and they're all tatted up and I'm not, then who are the followers? I liked the idea of being a rebel by not conforming."

"Any scars?"

"I don't know of any," Aponi said.

"Me, either," Cozy agreed. "She wasn't a risk-taker, so no scars like me. My father used to give her bruises and small cuts, though."

Aponi slowly turned her head to face her daughter.

I broke the tense silence. "Bodies have been found with different identification on them before. It would help if we could get her dental records and any personal items that might help us."

"We have nothing left of Haley's here. I threw it all away."

"You didn't box anything up in case she came back?"

"You kidding me?" Cozy interrupted. "Momma was fixin' to burn it all until I told her she'd have the fire department out here."

"I will not apologize."

"Take me to her," Cozy demanded. "I can tell if it's her."

"We need more than a visual for this one. I have photos, but they're quite graphic."

"I don't need to see those." Aponi never faltered.

Cozy's arm shot out like a Cobra strike and snagged the folder. Her fingers rifled through the pictures, then suddenly stopped. She ran out the back door with her hand covering her mouth. Aponi's entire face folded into an exhausted, disappointed look while following her daughter. I watched through the screen while she held Cozy's hair as she threw up into the bayou. Steam rose from the boiling pot behind them. After several minutes, they came back inside and Cozy disappeared into another room.

Aponi continued, "Haley doesn't have any dental records. She hadn't seen a dentist in over five years."

"I guess we'll just have to wait on results from the hairbrush we found at her apartment."

"Anything you find you can just throw away."

I made an effort to keep my voice even. "Is there anything you can tell me about what she may have been into in New Orleans?"

"It's been over two years since she left."

"I know this must be really difficult for you, but…"

She pushed the folder of pictures toward me. "Haley made her choice and it wasn't us."

"Aponi." I reached out to touch her arm as Tara ventured back from the bathroom.

"I have to prepare supper. You're welcome to stay for the crab boil, Cozy would like that, but there will be no further talk of Haley. Otherwise, please see yourself out." She left quickly.

Tara leaned to me. "Stay for the boil?"

I collected the pictures, watching as she returned to a large pot outside with a face of stone. The fact that she wasn't comforting her one remaining daughter shocked and saddened me.

"Go out to the car for a minute. Let me check in on Cozy, see if she can offer anything else we can use without her momma around," I said.

Tara smiled and lightly slapped my face with a squeeze. "I don't know why Dobson was worried. You're going to be alright."

"Tara." I held her hands and leaned into her ear. "I think I hear banjos."

"Bitch." She backed away to leave. "Good luck with her."

Watched by several gator heads, I entered a short, dark hallway decorated with oil paintings and portraits. Soft crying emanated from the back room, so I approached the doorway slowly. Cozy was lying in the fetal position, her face wet.

"Cozy." I waited a minute while she sniffled and straightened herself. "That's an interesting name. I wanted to ask you about that at the hospital."

She dabbed under her eyes and sat upright, cross-legged on the bed. "My mom's Native American. She said when I was born; I looked cozy in the blanket. They went with it."

"Are you okay? Your mom…"

"She may seem cold, but she doesn't show emotions…" Her blue-gray eyes found mine. "…she thinks you swallow it down and continue on no matter how bad you're hurting."

"You sure she's not Irish?" I took an unobtrusive look around the room.

"I know, right? My father used to drink like an Irishman."

"I could tell from the pictures on your wall that you and your sister loved each other."

"Momma wanted to throw those pictures out, but that was the last straw for me. I told her I'd leave if she did. I threaten to leave a lot." Cozy laughed through her tears. "Haley was all I had. I feel so alone here. Everyone in town already calls me *snut* behind my back."

"Snut?"

"Nut and slut. A couple years ago, I got drunk at a party and was raped by three guys. I don't remember it. Hell, if they had dressed me and kept their mouths shut, I probably wouldn't have been sure about it. But the traumatic part for me was that they told everyone."

"You know them?"

"Yeah, Tray, Joe, and Eric." She rolled her eyes.

"Are there pictures or video?" I sat on her bed with a few feet between us.

"Not that I know of, and believe me, I'd know. They're too stupid to keep that under wraps."

"If you can prove anything, get any witnesses, the statute of limitations hasn't ended on it yet."

"I can't prove it. I can't even be sure I didn't start it all. I always got a little touchy-feely when I drank, but I've never blacked out before. It's really just my word against theirs and everyone at the party says I was dancing with Tray." Her eyes waited as if searching for something poignant from me.

"At this point, it would be a tough case to win, but at least you would have a moral victory."

"Moral victory? Get real. I'd get labeled a liar and have to live under the stares and accusations of these hypocritical Catholics who judge me despite living under God's rule of 'thou shall not judge'."

"Those kinds of people are ignorant."

"Thanks, but they're my people."

I nodded. "Anyway, I'll help you if you ever want to go forward with that."

"Maybe one day. You still feel guilty about shooting me?"

I sucked in a breath. "Your mother is pretty stubborn about Haley."

"Yeah, things were weird between them even before Haley left. She doesn't believe that my father used to beat her. Did she invite you to stay for the boil?"

"Yeah, she did."

"Manners and appearances are very important to her. Even out here." Cozy broke down again and buried her face in her hands. "I'm sorry."

"I was hoping you could give me a recent picture of her."

She regained composure and opened her dresser where a picture presented itself. She handed it to me with a slight smile.

"Can I get one of Ash, too?" I pointed to one.

"Sure. Why?"

"We're going to question him and want to scan it for the file."

"You're lying, Detective Lucas." She wiped under her nose.

"I think you can just call me Lucas." I leaned against the door frame.

"Lucas." She almost smiled. "I know Ash has nothing to do with this."

"We have to check so we can say so in court." I slipped the pictures into the folder.

"What's going to happen to her body?"

"If it turns out to be Haley and she isn't claimed, she'll be cremated and put in storage, unless I intervene for you."

"I'll talk to momma about bringing her back here. Was she wearing an alligator pendant when you found her?"

"No. No jewelry or clothes." A half-second too late, I cringed at my mistake.

"No clothes? She was naked? So, where was her phone?"

She was quick. I swallowed hard and felt the room become pressurized, or maybe it was my head. "You don't want to know."

"Oh. Oh, my God." A fresh stream of tears cascaded down her cheeks. "That's sadistic."

"We think she may have done it herself, so she could be identified. That would make her very smart."

"That's her, pretty smart."

"We kept that fact from the press because it helps us weed out the crackpots who claim they have information."

"Can I follow you to her apartment? I can collect her things." Cozy stood with renewed vigor.

"Sure. It's near the station. I can drive your car and Tara can follow us."

"Okay, but it's a piece of crap Civic from the stone age."

"That's fine. What about your mother?"

"She wouldn't want to come."

"No, I mean will she let you go?"

She looked to the side as if she could see through the wall. "She won't want me to go, but she knows she can't stop me. Wait for me outside."

Cozy was seventeen and didn't need her mother's permission, so I waited on the porch as she instructed. Ashton Bergeron, who I remembered meeting for a brief second from the hospital, could wait to be questioned. Bringing Cozy to Haley's apartment seemed like a much better idea at this point.

TEN

My partner extended a fair amount of trust in letting me handle Cozy, but maybe that was the plan to get me over the hump. Tara also understood that Cozy was more likely to open up to me than anyone else. We drove out of the bayou and into Kenner as if changing a channel. The unremarkable city turned seamlessly into Metairie until passing over the beautiful Metairie Cemetery and the New Orleans skyline came into view. We switched cars at Headquarters in order to drop Tara off, and Cozy followed me into the French Quarter.

Cozy and I arrived at Haley's apartment located three blocks off the infamous Bourbon Street. I let Cozy dial in Haley's four-digit code to enter the confines of the gated courtyard, inundated with plants and uneven bricked walkways. I lugged Cozy's empty suitcase up a rickety wooden staircase that hugged a brick wall with bad tuck-pointing. The short, damp hallway leading to her door smelled of mildew.

"Here it is," I said.

Cozy's hands trembled as she inhaled. She nodded to indicate she was ready, and we entered a room that appeared meager and abandoned. Worn, outdated furniture depressed the ambiance, but no personal touches were attempted. Her rigid body remained still like a statue just two feet inside the doorway. I put my arm around her shoulders to gently guide her further inside.

"There's still a chance she's alive, right? She wasn't killed here, right?" Her voice was thin as a worn thread.

"This isn't a crime scene, but you have to prepare yourself when the results come in. All the evidence points to Haley."

"I know." She wiped hard at her face as if mad. "I don't know where to start."

"Just look around."

"I guess you've already been through her stuff," she said.

"Yes, but it was like this when we arrived. We took her hairbrush to compare DNA. There's also a storage area on the first floor, but all she has in there is a really old computer monitor, a vacuum cleaner and a few other items. Nothing of real value."

"I'm surprised she has a vacuum cleaner. She was always a slob." She gave a shaky laugh, touching a lampshade.

"We didn't find anything we needed to take as evidence."

"I wish I could tell you something. Being apart for two years kind of dulls the memories."

"Take your time."

Cozy crossed the floor as if avoiding landmines. "Except for her clothes, I can't spot anything that says Haley. It might as well be a stranger's apartment." She floated about, randomly touching things. "She must have been so lonely. So, if she's not dead, she's at least missing."

"I'm sorry you had to see those pictures."

"I've seen what water can do to dead animals."

"I guess you have." We stood for a moment in an awkward pause. "And then with your father. I'm so sorry about all that. Child abuse is the one thing that gets a cop right down here in the gut." I touched my stomach, feeling it churn.

Her expression never changed. "The last time I saw my father, he had grabbed a bat and went after Haley. I grabbed the shotgun. The very last second I saw him alive, he was bleeding to death. Long before that day. Long before I pulled the trigger, I imagined doing it."

"You planned it?"

Her eyes snapped to mine. "Of course, not." She turned and wiped her hand under her nose. "What makes me sad is what Haley was thinking in her final moments. How scared she must have felt. I wonder if she thought of momma and me."

"I'm sure she did." I took a seat on the arm of the sofa.

"I'm glad it was you who told us about Haley. I could tell you were uncomfortable. You've been sweet."

"Not a word that usually describes the NOPD."

"I guess if you hadn't found Haley, I'd still be chasing you down, huh."

Cozy slid between my legs as I sat on the arm of the couch and wrapped her arms around me into a deep hug that lasted longer than normal. I stood for support. Her body heaved and bucked as the side of her head snuggled into my chest. Every noise possible escaped her nose and mouth. I gave her minute, then my hands found her elbows as I stepped away.

She wiped her face with her shirt and cleared her throat. "I guess you have to go. Go on, then. You don't have to hang around. Maybe I'll see you again after my momma dies."

"Cozy, this isn't the time to discuss that night."

"When is? When do I get to talk to you?"

"Let's get through this first and I promise we'll talk. Just you and me over a cup of coffee. I promise."

"Promise?"

"Promise. You're right, though. I think you should do this alone, but I'll wait in my car downstairs in case you need me."

"Don't make me feel bad about wasting your time. Just go home to your family. Just remember your promise."

I pretended to acquiesce. "Okay. You have my number. Call for anything."

"I will."

I sat in my car near the apartment, with a beer acquired from a corner bar. Cozy's hug had seeped all the way to my bones, like a hot shower. I can't remember the last time my daughter had embraced me in a genuine moment like that. A nice memory of Alicia sleeping on my chest after watching a late movie came to mind.

Twenty minutes later, Cozy came out with the suitcase and spotted me. She waved with no surprise, as if knowing I had lied about going home. I felt for the girl… Smart, charming, resilient. It seemed the poor thing couldn't catch a break.

ELEVEN

Cozy sucked in a breath from her Civic's open window while admiring the decaying architecture of a city that had been built in the middle of nowhere. She learned in school that it had been the only major port city in the 1700's. Why hadn't it ever grown into a metropolis like New York or Chicago? It had to be the fault of Southern politicians. She quickly returned to the curb in front of Haley's apartment after circling a few minutes.

Lucas had been kind, but she could smell bullshit a mile away and knew he was going to wait for her to leave. She skirted through the gate and up the scary steps to contemplate her sister's total and utter violation. New Orleans had chewed her up and spit her out, right into the Mississippi.

When she was ten years old, she had wandered into the kitchen at three in the morning to get a cup of water, only to find her father sitting at the table in the dark with his hands around a tall bottle as if having a conversation with it. His shiny eyes had turned to her and he said, "I love your sister. You know that, don't you?"

"Yes," she had squeaked. In that moment, getting a glass of water suddenly lost all importance. She turned right around and went back to bed. Just minutes later, she heard Haley's door open and she prayed that her sister wasn't going into the kitchen. She'd been too naive to realize her sister had probably never left the room.

She picked up the cheap plastic phone, still connected to the landline. "Hello, Momma? I'm in New Orleans at Haley's apartment."

She rolled her eyes and tapped her foot as her momma lectured about responsibility, carelessness and lack of respect. She held the phone away from her ear. "Momma… Momma… Don't be mad. No, do *not* send Ash."

The discussion was one-sided as Cozy tried to spew halting syllables and broken half-words while her momma was in a state. In the end, she promised to return first thing in the morning, hung up and then fell into the lumpy, purple sofa.

Not having eaten since the grits at breakfast, she found a stack of fast food menus and ordered a pizza. They knew the address from the number. She then grabbed several trash bags to begin separating the trash from what she might keep and what might offer a clue as to why her sister died. Haley had to have made friends. If only she could find the name of one.

One bag ended up stuffed with tacky clothes Cozy would never wear, and she finally stopped when her fingers shook too much to continue. She splashed cold water on her face in the bathroom and swallowed an Ibuprofen tablet from the medicine cabinet. An abrupt buzz from the intercom made her to jump.

She cautiously approached to press the speaker button. "Yes?"

"Papa John's."

"Upstairs. Apartment B." She held the button for a few seconds to let him in the gate.

Footsteps echoed through the hall and she cracked the door a bit to make sure it was the delivery guy. The money-pizza exchange with the dumpy, middle-aged woman went quickly and she settled back on the couch, taking a few bites out of a slice while checking her surroundings again.

The cracked plaster walls were void of pictures, unless discolored patches resembling images such as the Shroud Of Turin could be considered art. Haley hadn't settled in to make this a home, yet. That was why she didn't decorate or have personal touches around the place.

Cozy stretched and attempted to hold down the rest of her slice of pizza. She didn't want to live or have children or grow old without Haley. It was an empty feeling to only have one thing to live for, to avenge her sister's death.

What the hell, Haley? What the hell?

A rapping on the door forced her head jerk up. "Yo, Haley. You in there? I saw your light on." He sounded like the black men in rap songs. How'd he get in without buzzing, unless he knew the code?

Cozy put her eye to the peephole. Sure enough, a short, skinny black guy with a Saints cap was on the other side. She spoke through an eighth inch of seam. "Haley isn't here. Who are you?"

He looked confused. "Who you? Haley on vacation or sumptin'?"

"She's not here."

He wiped at his lips and tried to look through his side of the peephole. "Listen, here. Me and her – we friends. I ain't seen her in a while."

Cozy opened the door as far as the chain would allow. "What's your name?"

The black man checked her up and down. "You her friend?"

"Her sister."

A gold tooth appeared in a smile. "You don't look much like her, but you got that same crazy-ass accent."

"Name?"

"Titus."

Must be the guy Lucas had said came by a few times. "You her drug daddy?"

"Drug daddy?" He mused. "What, 'cause I'm black?"

"I ain't a racist, but I ain't stupid, either." Cozy dipped her head. "Haley's dead."

"Dead? Get the fuck. What happened?"

"I'd rather not talk about it."

"Listen here. I ain't her drug daddy. I get her shit. She pay with green. That's it. I liked that girl, but she was running with some bad dudes."

Cozy zeroed in on the chains around his neck. One of them was Haley's alligator pendant. "Can I ask you a couple of questions?"

"You inviting me in?"

Cozy hesitated, needing to make a quick decision about her safety. But, why would he be looking for Haley if he had killed her? "Awright. C'mon." Cozy closed the door, and then swung it open after the chain dropped.

Titus instantly dipped his shoulder as he strutted inside. "Shit, you got balls. A white girl inviting a nigga' like me in. I guess all you Cajun bitches crazy."

"You saying Haley was crazy?" Cozy noticed the butt of a gun sticking out of the back of his waistband.

"Nah, figger of speech. Serious shit, Haley was awright with me."

Titus walked straight to the couch and sat as if that was his normal spot. He threw his Adidas covered feet onto the coffee table and watched as Cozy took a position on the armrest.

"You fine, girl."

"You ever do anything else besides get her drugs?"

Titus seemed taken aback, as if no one ever questioned him before. "We ever do it? Yeah, I got in it."

Her throat constricted. "Are you a pimp, too?"

He laughed. "Pimp? Yo, I guess I gots a few girls. Haley wasn't one of them, you hear me? Not that I didn't try. She was spoken for."

"Spoken for? Haley was a prostitute?"

"She was no busted corner ho' if that makes you feel better. She too fine to get fucked up on the curb, you get me? I set her up in the bigs. I gets me a finder's fee when I bring in the phat ho's." His attention turned to her chest. "Crackers with money got with your sister by appointment, like some Uptown escort bitch."

"Yeah, Titus, that makes me feel better."

"I ain't nothin' if not real."

"Haley wouldn't do that shit."

"Listen here, your sister was desperate. And she had the goods to make top dollar. She did it all right."

"Let's say I believe you. Who was her manager?"

"Now, what the fuck you want to know that for?" He leaned forward, exposing his weapon.

"How'd you get her alligator pendant?" She pointed.

He fingered it. "I helped her with some fast cash a long time ago."

"Or maybe you took it after you killed her."

His amusement waned. "Sounds like you investigatin' shorty's murder."

"She's my sister. If you didn't kill her, then give up her pimp."

Titus mildly chuckled and fell back into the couch. His eyes molested her again. "Now, I can't give that info away for free."

"So predictable. Is that what it's going to take?"

"Listen here. If I'm going to take that kind of heat, there's a price."

Cozy sized him up. He was small, maybe 140 pounds, but cute in a boy-band kind of way. He probably grew up in the projects having to establish his street-cred every day, which would make him cocky and aggressive. Should she go down this road? It was possible that the name of Haley's pimp was written somewhere in the apartment, but not likely. She doubted that Haley would admit to prostitution.

"I just found out my sister is dead and you want me to fuck you?"

"I like that. You fuck me. That's rich, girl."

She smirked back at him. "I ain't nothin' if not real."

Titus tilted his head with a grin. "A man's gotta take it where he can gets it. We each want something here."

"What you got on you?"

"On me? Gun? Drugs? Dick? Can you be more specific?"

"Weed, Titus. What say you and me relax a little?"

"That's good. I don't do anything stronger than weed. See these teeth?"

"Braces?"

"Damn, right… my clean eyeballs… my liver, although you can't see that… I'm not messing with this pretty package. I'd be happy to smoke what Haley liked if you get me a beer out the fridge."

"She's got Coors Light."

"Now, we're talking. I gots some powerful weed that'll knock you on your ass."

"Good, I'm going to need it."

She walked on stiff legs to the refrigerator and pulled out two Coors Lights. Not even one day in New Orleans and she was already in over her head. Cozy stared him down as her feet slid forward, the bottlenecks numbing her fingers. Handing him the beer might as well be signing a contract. She braced herself to do the unimaginable. But, Haley deserved to be avenged.

"She was one of Molly's girls," Titus said as she took the beer.

Cozy grabbed a pen and wrote it down real quick. "Molly. Where can I find her?"

He laughed while drinking. "Oh, she's around the Quarter."

"I'm surprised you told me before we do it. What if I back out?"

He put the empty beer down and exposed his teeth in a wide, gummy smile. "Oh, ain't no backing out now."

Cozy had talked Titus into having a second beer, but that empty bottle now sat next to the first one on the cheap coffee table next to his gun. His hands made a show of grabbing at his belt buckle, which flopped to his hips once undone. "Get yourself undressed, girl."

"I don't feel that good. That pizza…"

"Power through it." Titus let his jeans drop. His shirt came off, revealing ribs and stringy muscle under several dark tats.

She shifted her weight while undoing her shorts. Her skin felt dirty just standing that close to him. Her stomach flopped and she fell onto the sofa with her arms around her torso. "Seriously. I think I'm going to be sick."

"Fuck you are." Titus back-handed her and she almost flipped over the arm of the couch. "The time is now, bitch."

Cozy appeared frightened on the outside, but Titus would never know the rage she felt on the inside. A plan needed to be formulated while reacting to the pain of his slap. She pushed down her shorts as Titus allowed his underwear to fall, his large dick wagging, stiffening and aggressive like its owner. She felt the blood trickle down her chin as Titus came near.

TWELVE

Cozy stirred to the smell of stale beer and weed. Her nose sucked in air through a sour-smelling pillow while one arm hung off the side of the bed. Her other hand scratched at the panties riding up her ass, a reminder of the night before.

The advancing drug dealer invaded her memory and she pushed it away like an evil daydream. *Shit.* She lifted her head with a moan, releasing a pulse of blood to her brain that almost rendered her unconscious. However, she had to piss.

Blood tinted the majority of her body, with streaks staining the sheets. She wiped away drool residue and looked at the nightstand where she left the note. The paper next to the alarm clock gave the promise of a trail to follow. She reached out, unlocking stiff joints and stretching tight muscles. She read the note softly while rubbing her eyes. "Molly."

Titus hadn't clarified, saying that she'd have to ask around on Bourbon Street and that way he wouldn't get any heat. Little did he expect that retribution from the higher-ups would never transpire. Haley's alligator pendant sat near the lamp. She kissed it and then secured it around her neck.

Her eyes snapped to the bathroom door as last night's events clicked, making her stomach knot again. She balanced her weight onto each foot and stepped onto the chilly tiled floor, but only glanced at the tub. Just a few hours ago she had stood nearly paralyzed on that cold floor as Titus' blood dripped to her toes. That same blood now dried to her skin.

She crept forward to look at the horror again. Titus was sprawled in the crimson-stained tub with the knife planted deep, sticking out of his chest like a vampire stake. Her body went numb and her eyes rolled back, but she fought away the lightheaded feeling.

The sight of his dead body immediately brought back that afternoon with her father, when she had basked in the relief his death had brought. She remembered fragments of sitting on the bed next to her father with her legs crossed, watching his blood glimmer as it stopped pulsing out onto the mattress, his surprised expression frozen in time. She could still see Haley cowering in a ball after having scurried from her bed where the beating had started. Her balance faltered and her knees gave out. She fell next to the toilet in a fit of hyperventilation, only calming herself with the thought of preventing her own rape.

Oh, Titus… Titus… Titus.

She closed her eyes to force out the tears. *Get the crying over with,* her clinical side thought. She turned onto her butt in order to ease her pounding headache. Clear thinking would be critical. *Clear thinking. Breathe. Think. Breathe.* There was a dead drug dealer in the tub.

"Gut you like an alligator. I warned you, didn't I?" *Alligator – drug dealing pimp, not so different. If either one gets a hold of you, you're fucked.*

Saliva buckshot from her mouth in a full sob. She put her head between her knees for ten minutes. At least she had enough sense to push his legs the rest of the way into the tub. His dick wasn't so hard anymore. She imagined mounting Titus' head above the apartment door.

She used the toilet to pull herself upright and opened the medicine cabinet for more ibuprofen, downing three capsules with a cupped hand of water. She had taken a human life… again. But, he was a bad man, a rapist. Titus contributed to Haley's demise and got what he deserved. A towel saturated from the faucet did a fine job of cleaning the blood off her skin. But that was just the start.

A drug dealer like Titus would need to carry cash. Cozy pulled at the right pocket of his jeans as his body lay contorted in the tub. His shocked face seemed to be made of wax. She slid her fingers deep within the tacky wetness when a loud ring tone from his pants sent her reeling backwards. Some rap song echoed in the tub until cutting off a few seconds later.

"Jesus Christ." She held her heart as she approached the tub again. Her face grimaced as her hand quickly slid into the pocket and pulled out his phone. It needed a code for entry. She smashed it on the sink, and then pulled out the battery and memory card for good measure. Closing her eyes, she entered the other pocket and discovered a huge wad of hundreds, fifties, and twenties, mostly unaffected by the hemorrhaging.

She left the bathroom to find a pen and paper and scribbled a list. *Bleach, plastic wrap, scouring pads, gloves, duck tape.*

THIRTEEN

The sliding of Heather's slippers filled the hallway as I ate my cereal at the kitchen table. Her thick, brunette hair teased her face in a way that stopped my heart. She crossed behind me, but I could still feel her stare. Her hands slid over my shoulders and ran down both sides of my chest as she bent to kiss my neck. Her right hand went even further south into the hole of my boxers, pulling it out. The sensation was so intense that if a nail were driven through my foot, I wouldn't have felt it. Maybe, that was an exaggeration.

"Out here? Really?" I whispered. "Alicia?"

"No, we're not going to do it out here. I just want to do this for you. It'll be quick. Alicia will sleep to ten at least."

"That feels too good to argue."

"Just relax. You need this. Your hard-on in record speed makes that obvious."

I put the spoon back into the bowl and stood, signaling the bathroom door slamming in the back the house. I laughed in frustration as Heather kept hold of my erection as if on pause.

"I forgot." Her bottom lip curled under. "I'm taking her to soccer practice this morning. This will be going on all summer."

"Of course."

"We can do it. You know she always showers before leaving the house." She squeezed. "We can shoot for virgin speed."

Alicia yelled from the bathroom. "Mom! Can you come here a second?"

"Damn," Heather said, and shouted back, "Give me a minute."

"You've been patient with me. Thank you. I think I'm ready." I *flexed* it for her.

"It's good to have you back." My wife didn't want to let go. She gave it a final tug. "Till we meet again."

She left me standing alone as my little man pointed north. I pulled the hole of my boxers back around my erection and returned to my soggy cereal, enjoying the fading sensation with guarded optimism about our sex life.

My phone rang. It was the medical examiner. "Peyroux here."

"You with Detective Gray?"

"Not yet."

"You at the station?"

"Not yet."

"Don't matter. I have some info on Ms. Robicheaux."

"Is it the caviar?" I took a spoonful of soggy cereal.

"You're incredible."

"I do have superpowers, you know. My other senses have been heightened ever since I lost the sense of sex."

"What?"

"Nothing. Go ahead."

"It's Almas Caviar."

"How do you know that?" My spoon hovered between my mouth and the bowl.

"Process of elimination. I actually did some of your legwork on this one last night. I shot a close up and sent it to Chef Chagnard at Naquin's. Friend of mine. Once he got over the fact that it came out of a dead woman's stomach, he was quite helpful."

"So, Almas Caviar? There must be lots of restaurants and caterers that have it."

"No, they don't. It's the most expensive caviar in the universe."

"Really? There's caviar on other planets?"

"Anyway, Chagnard says it comes from Iran and distributed through England. There's a website you can order it from."

"Something that rare and expensive should be easy to trace."

"You're welcome. I'll take a case of Abita Amber – cold."

"I'll send Gray right to the Winn Dixie. I'll even throw in some moon pies."

I took my cereal to the laptop in the living room and searched for Almas Caviar on the Internet. Almas meant 'diamond.' It came from the Beluga Sturgeon fish, common to the Caspian Sea. The Caviar House & Prunier in London's Picadilly was the sole outlet, selling a kilo for over $27,000 a pop. Plus, according to the Caviar House website, the only restaurant that served it was the Seafood Bar at the JFK Airport, of all places. No US distributors. However, you could order online, and they shipped anywhere.

Once we found the person who ordered the caviar, we'd find out what party Haley had attended. And once we found the guest list, we'd find the killer, who was possibly involved in a trafficking ring. How this bayou chick from Manchac ended up eating the most expensive caviar in the universe was certainly an intriguing puzzle.

FOURTEEN

Titus had bankrolled the cover-up of his own murder. The items on her list were easy enough to locate at the Walgreens and Ace Hardware. It felt like everyone was watching her – *everyone knew*. She arrived back to Haley's apartment building just before noon, spotting a man in the window of an apartment near the entrance. Did the landlord know Haley well? She smiled and continued on as if she belonged there.

The strong aroma of something she couldn't place filled the apartment, and her nose led to Titus being ground zero. Decomposition had started the second she punctured his heart. She opened all the windows, then lit up another joint needed for this project. After a few tokes, she slipped on latex gloves, closed her eyes and pulled the knife out of his chest with a grunt and little sympathy. Titus wasn't in the human classification. This was a predator.

First thing before cleanup was to handle the smell, and he was already in a container of sorts... it just needed a lid. The cellophane edge of the first roll was taped onto the rim of the tub and wrapped around its belly, which hovered above the floor on four ornate claws. She continued this process with three rolls until Titus was sealed in airtight, like a bowl of fruit salad. She drew the shower curtain, inhaling like a bloodhound to be certain that no funk would escape.

It made no sense to clean everything if she wasn't going to dispose of the body, but she planned on staying there for a while. A generous spreading of the bleach quickly overpowered the room. In between deep breaths at the window, Cozy took the bathroom to task.

Two hours later, she found herself on the sofa with her head in her hands, her one puffy cheek stinging a bit. Her eyes burned, lungs struggled to take air, and her elbows and knees were spent. Her strong fingers were swollen and tingly, but her heart and stomach had settled. The crime scene was no longer an obvious one.

Having rested long enough, she stretched her sore muscles and inspected the entire bathroom with satisfaction, but she still couldn't handle the toxic smell. The living room was bare now, except for the junkyard furniture. She couldn't wait to leave. Cozy took three more ibuprofen. Her headache was almost gone, but Titus would be with her for a while.

Once dressed, a thought crossed her mind. Lucas would be getting a frantic phone call from Manchac if she didn't check in. Despite wanting to have a friendship, she'd rather not have him in her hair just now. She left the apartment, planning to drive home to show her face and then come back in the evening when the bleach smell had cleared. However, when she stepped out the gate, she saw an empty spot where her car had been. Shit. Stolen? Towed? It didn't matter. It was gone, and she couldn't report it.

She rang her momma at the corner bar to say that she was taking care of Haley's release papers, but she would instead spend the rest of the day scouring the Quarter for Molly. This woman needed to be found fast, because there was no turning back. The next time her momma would see her would probably be on the news.

FIFTEEN

The morning's erection Heather had created wouldn't leave my mind as I drove into work. My wife thought it silly to refer to it as *morning wood* or my *breakfast burrito*, but I enjoyed annoying her. Every time I replayed the scene, it would start to grow all over again. The police therapist would probably say that was a sign of healing, to be free of this anchor of guilt keeping me down. However, I probably just needed to stop being so selfish. My wife deserved better. Luckily, it didn't take long to reach the station where other distractions would abound.

Tara accosted me as soon as I hit my desk, laying down a stack of files. "These are unsolved murders of women, some prostitutes."

"You think there might be similar autopsy reports?"

"What if Haley Robicheaux isn't the first? Charles cleaned up that video the best he could and emailed it to me. It sucks. His team's been going over it. Too low res… too grainy to blow up. I know *I* can't see anything. But one thing for certain, there are other women in that video."

"Mind if I look at it?"

After examining the seventeen-second video to no avail, I moved on to the cold case homicides. Tara sat beside me catching up on paperwork and her eBay sales. When I grew tired of getting nowhere, I meandered to my Captain's office.

"What can I do for you, Lucas?" She didn't look up.

"You mind calling the FBI field office to see if they can initiate contact with the proper officials *across the pond*?"

"The Picadilly caviar?" Dobson finally looked up.

I leaned against the doorjamb. "Making a British contact should facilitate a dialog with the local magistrate who could get a list of the purchases delivered to New Orleans." My eyebrows popped up several times at her.

"Wow. You know your shit. You got it."

"Nothing came from questioning the local drug reps?" I asked.

She made a noise of incredulity. "What do you think? Although, one admitted to seeing he around."

"No shit?"

"Titus."

"I know him, I think I'll follow up with that."

While Dobson handled my caviar request, I met Tara back at her desk. "I got a loose end to tie up. The black kid the landlord Porter mentioned could have been Titus, the dealer."

"So, have a uniform pick him up." Tara's eyes stayed glued on the laptop.

"C'mon, princess. We can both use some air. Some nice humid afternoon air."

She reluctantly stood, looking around her desk. "Okay. It wouldn't hurt to see if this was her guest."

Tara and I drove around asking business owners the whereabouts of Titus, but they hadn't seen him since the day before, which was strange because he always made an appearance, as regular as a street performer. "If he couldn't make the corner for any reason such as jail, he'd have a replacement at the ready," Tara offered, fanning herself in thought. "We're wasting time." She kept her eyes peeled as I drove down Burgundy Street. "Let's just get some uniforms to keep an eye out for him."

"Give me one more shot." I turned a corner. "Let's go to the Marigny."

"You want to start canvassing the neighborhoods outside the Quarter?"

I pointed. "It's right down there. There's a guy I know."

We criss-crossed through the crumbling streets and broken-down homes of the Marigny until seeing a BMW pull to the side of the road. A slouched black man drew to the driver's side and took money in exchange for a small packet. I let the Beamer escape, then crept up to the dealer with my grill lights flashing. His frayed jeans were too baggy for his frame, and his white T-shirt had all the stains of a short order cook.

"I know this guy," I told her. "Just back me up and let me lead on this, okay?"

"It's your show."

When the car halted, he stomped his foot and put his hands behind his head as if on reflex. I casually got out of my car and pushed him against the fender. His hands slapped down on the sizzling hood in excessive drama. Tara smiled through the windshield and saluted while I patted him down.

"Nice of you not to run, Percy."

"You should be arresting the bitches buying that shit, yo."

"You telling me how to do my job? You should try out for the academy."

"You just watched my last bag drive away, cop. What you gonna arrest me for?"

I held the gun from his waistband in front of his unshaven, oily face. "Got a permit?"

"Damn, bra. The gun I found in the ditch? I was just about to turn that in. Thought maybe there was a ree-ward."

"Shut up, stupid mother fucker." I slapped his head and cuffed his wrists before shoving him into my back seat. Curtains moved in the nearby houses, but no one came outside. An Audi crept towards us, then turned left before reaching this block. Business was good out here. I got in the car and made a show of kicking up rocks as we left.

"What up, sweets?" Percy greeted Tara.

"Well, aren't you husband material." Tara kept her eyes forward. "I think you'd have a better wardrobe, being so enterprising."

"My shit gets invested. Ain't going to do this shit forever, dig?"

"You wanna tour Esplanade?" I asked Percy.

"Sure, Peyroux. Whatever. Where you been? Ain't seen you in months." His razor bumps stood out like mountains when his face hit the sunlight.

"How's your *Mom an 'nem*?" I asked.

"Don't fuck with me. What you need?"

The car started to smell like ripe armpit and bologna. I pulled over next to a fire hydrant under a Magnolia tree. I propped up Haley's picture up on the backrest. He leaned forward to see it, and then fell serious.

"I know the bitch," he said. "She taken care of."

My voice lowered. "What do you mean taken care of?"

"I don't mean kilt. She taken care of. She gots somebody to keep her pretty, you hear me?"

"Her pimp?"

"Not pimp, Peyroux. This girl ain't street; she an escort. She get bank for that pussy."

"Eloquent as always, Percy. I need a name."

"Shood. All I know is that bitch gets her shit from Titus. He told me she kept, but the nigga' wouldn't tell me who."

"When did you speak with Titus last?"

"Last week. Why? The mother fucker dead?"

"He's missing," Tara said.

"Missing? You can't find him in jail, then he either kilt somebody or he dead himself. Now, let's talk the bis-nez side of this transaction. My time is worth money."

"You would be getting a taste, Percy… If I hadn't drove up on you in mid-deal. Your payment is not going to jail."

"Damn." Percy shook his head. "Let me out this bitch."

I grit my teeth and gave Tara a serious stare she knew all too well. Haley was murdered and now Titus was missing… This was growing more and more interesting.

It was end of shift. Tara stood in the partition next to me at the gun range, like bathroom stalls separating us. Shots rang out down the line, but we could still hear each other if we spoke loud and clear.

She projected her voice. "This was a good idea, Lucas. Have you been back here since you took leave?"

"Yeah, once. Surprised you didn't hear about it."

"Cops are a bit reluctant to talk to me about you. Hold on a sec." Eight shots fired in quick succession. After a pause, she knocked on the thin wall. "You gonna fire or what?"

"Or what. Let's see what you did."

The target rushed towards us and I stepped into Tara's space to see her cluster, which all hit true to the head and chest. "Check it, bitch."

"Alright, I'll go. Tell me what you make of this."

I went back to my spot and put on the headphones. Taking aim, I let the rounds fly without thinking too much about it, six shots in all. The silhouette came to me.

Tara's eyes widened. "Your cluster is three inches to the right. What the hell, Peyroux? *Trying* to give the guy a shoulder graze?"

"I started off drifting to the left. Now, I'm compensating right, but a hair of an adjustment ends up being exponential on the other end. I can't seem to work it out."

"Cozy was to your right when you fired and the fucker jerked her up at the exact same time. It's in your mind to go left."

"Right. How do I fix that when I'm aiming where I should be aiming? I aim center, they land left, and I over adjust right."

"Alright, calm down. I can tell your muscles are tight."

"I can't try to compensate when it counts. Maybe that douche Harvin is right. I can't aim worth shit."

"We'll fix it. We'll come here every day and fix it. Consider me Mickey to your Rocky."

"I'll drink some eggs, but I will not catch a chicken."

"Good. Keep your sense of humor. That's how I know I haven't lost you. Now, you reload while I go get a Coke."

SIXTEEN

Dusk settled on Rampart Street as Cozy walked out of the corner poboy place, full from a bowl of gumbo and a latte for dessert. She was glad to have been out of the apartment all day. The coffee tasted sweeter than her momma's. She had found her second wind with the night rolling in. Despite being tired and her senses amped with caffeine, she kept her wits about her situation. She figured to have a few days at minimum before the landlord interfered and found Titus. However, her dark road to discovery and vengeance would continue on.

A car pulled behind her and tapped the horn, not causing much alarm until she saw the driver. It was Lucas and his partner Detective Gray. She bent slightly to look inside the car. "Lucas… bet you're surprised to see me."

"I am."

"You still on duty?"

"Just bringing Tara back to her car before heading home. You?"

"I decided to come back. Funny, you roll up on me like this."

"Quarter's a small place and everyone walks. We know most of the residents by sight."

"Like Manchac."

The car shifted into park, but they stayed inside. "Your cheek's red. Did someone hit you?"

"No." She touched her face. "I had this crazy idea that maybe Haley had used her secret hiding place for the alligator pendant, so I came back. When I looked under the sink, I slipped and hit my face on the toilet." She laughed with fake embarrassment. "It was late, so I ended up staying the night. Don't worry, I called my momma."

"I see you found it."

She held it up from just above her cleavage. "Yeah, sure enough it was taped under the sink where she's hid lots of things… joints, money and whatnot. This must've been the last thing from home she had."

Lucas scratched his chin. "Under the sink. I'll have to tell the boys at CSU, embarrass them a little. You mind if we come back up since we're right here? Maybe there's other hiding places we missed?"

She glanced down at her shoes. "There aren't any. I looked in every corner."

"No doubt, but you're also not a cop. We missed that, we might've missed something else."

Cozy looked back at the apartment building. "I, uh… I was uh… trying to get the deposit back from the landlord, so I cleaned the place. I wiped down everything and even bleached, so it smells up there. Unbearable, really. I've had to stay out all day."

The engine shut off and they both climbed out of the car. "Let's just take a quick look around anyway."

Cozy swallowed hard as she walked toward the steps with the two police officers. She fought her wobbly knees to continue going up the stairs and into the apartment. Once the door opened, she waved for the cops to go in first in case she had to run.

"Oh, Jesus, you weren't kidding." Detective Gray held her nose.

"I left the windows open."

"You went ape shit with the bleach." Lucas coughed. "Couldn't just use window cleaner?"

"My momma always says bleach works best." Her forehead turned red hot and she pressed her fingers against it, trying to cool it quickly before they could notice.

The cops walked into the bathroom and Cozy perched tensely just outside the door, watching. Lucas went straight for the sink, bending to get a good look under it and searching with his fingers. "Wish there was a diary somewhere."

Detective Gray looked up at the shower curtain that hung from a rod and reached up, about to expose the tub.

"Detective Tara," Cozy shouted. "Can I talk to you?"

"Just Tara." The detective ran her hand down the length of the curtain, but didn't let go. "What is it?"

"What are the odds of finding out who really did this?"

"There's no answer to that. Let us do our job and you focus on grieving and honoring your sister's life, okay?" Tara tugged the shower curtain to one side, exposing a clean, empty tub.

Cozy felt the world flicker darkly for a second as she almost passed out. *What the fuck?* What had happened here?

"I love these old tubs," Tara commented. "So much character."

It took all Cozy had to close her jaw and look away from the tub. She nodded at Tara's statement. Lucas searched the seam behind the medicine cabinet with a tiny flashlight and then behind the spindly white Ikea cabinet that held the towels.

They left the bathroom and Tara said to her, "We did catch a lead… Maybe. You alright? You look like a ghost."

"Just trying not to breathe."

"We think Haley might've associated with a drug dealer named Titus. We're looking to pick him up – see what he knows."

"She cleared her throat. "Weird name."

"Jeez, my eyes are watering." Lucas came out of the bathroom to join them. "Let's check the kitchen and get out of here. Look inside the oven under the grease pan and the freezer's ice cube trays. The nooks and crannies."

Tara nodded and continued speaking. "There was also a visit by a young, brown haired, boy according to her landlord. Ring any bells?"

"I don't know anyone she knew out here." Cozy felt her strength come back.

Tara's cell phone jangled, forcing her to stop opening and shutting cabinets. She answered it. "Gray. Really? Damn, I thought I was going home." She ended the call. "We got a possible Titus sighting, let's roll."

"You okay here?" Lucas asked as they headed for the door.

Cozy nodded.

"I'll call you soon and keep you updated. If the landlord gives you any trouble, call me."

The door clicked shut and Cozy grabbed onto back of the sofa and finally unclenched, running to the open window to close her eyes and gulped a breath of air. Her wet underarms felt as if she had run a marathon.

The landlord.

It had to be.

COZY RUSHED to Bourbon Street to get a grip on the situation. Stumpy, thick metal pillars rising from holes in the crosswalks kept cars from turning onto the crowded street. Tourists laughed and drank, and trashcans were already overflowing. People on balconies dangled colorful beads and thankfully, no one paid any attention as she sat in a corner bar.

She assumed the only other person with a key to Haley's place would be Porter, the landlord. But, why on earth would he dispose of Titus and clean the tub instead of calling the police? No, that didn't make any sane sense. Haley could have given the key to someone else, but again, who would want to clean up that mess? Why? And could do it in half a day for that matter? Maybe someone was protecting her? That would mean she had been followed and this same person might know Haley, too – if not loved her enough to clean up her little sister's mess.

After several hours of getting nowhere and watching an old man nurse a drink, she headed back to the aired-out apartment to wait for this person to be exposed. Her limbs and back protested free-range movement. Her leg muscles wanted to lock with each step, but at least she would be able to rest in a Titus-free apartment. Without seeing

Porter in the window, she entered the gate, slowly ascending the stairs. She stopped at the top: her suitcase sat outside the front door. That middle-aged balding man came from inside Haley's place, wearing shorts and a football jersey. He stared cross-eyed at her.

She didn't know if she'd be able to run very fast. "What are you doing?"

"Kicking you out." He pointed at her stuff like she was in trouble.

"You went through my shit?"

"This apartment needs to be vacant so I can show it."

A bell sounded in Cozy's head. "Do I know you?"

"You waved at me that time in my window. I'm the landlord."

"No, that's not it." Cozy tried to let it go.

"You bleached the fuck out of the bathroom. You got the windows open and I can still smell it."

Is he messing with me? "I want to make sure I get the deposit back. I guess I used too much. But this was my sister's apartment. She just died."

"I know that. You don't think I know that?" He spoke fast and hard.

"What's your problem?"

The whites of his eyes glowed. "You can't stay here. Her lease is void, including the deposit."

"You can't do that."

"Fuck, I can't. Do you want to take over her rent?"

"C'mon, mister. What happened to Southern hospitality?"

His eyes tilted back as he gazed down at her for several seconds. She thought his head might start spinning. "You want it or what?"

"How much?"

"First and last month's and security deposit. Twenty-five hundred dollars."

"I know for a fact that you can't keep her security deposit."

"It's in the contract she signed. She signed it." He blinked hard. "She signed it."

Past arguing, there was nothing else she could do. "I can give you five hundred for the next week. Let me get it." She bowed in order to snag the bag and pulled a few feet away. With one eye on Porter, she fell to her knees and opened the bag, pulling out a pair of jeans. She dug into the pocket, but came up empty. She swore under her breath. "I had five hundred dollars in that pocket."

"I wouldn't know anything about that."

"It was there." She shoved her hand in the bag, feeling around.

He huffed. "All I did was carry all your stuff out here instead of throwing it away 'cause I'm nice like that. I don't know nothin' 'bout five hundred dollars."

Liar. "Empty your pockets."

His face turned red and his fingers tapped at his thighs. "No."

"I had a policeman's permission to be in there. He's not going to like hearing this."

"Call him. I'm sure they'd like to hear about that gun in your bag. Call him. Call him."

Titus' gun. She stared the twitchy man down. Her eyes found a small circular scar on his forearm and she fell onto her butt, still staring. "What'd you do with Titus?"

"What?" Porter followed her eyes to the red mark at the widest part of his forearm and he covered it up with his hand. His brow furrowed. "Are you okay?"

"I'm fine." But she wasn't. The feel of an arm around neck caused her breathing to halt. Her eyes finally shot up to his.

"Why are you staring at me like that?" He dropped his arms and clenched his fists.

"You cut your long hair. You have a beard now. It was you. *It was you.*"

"Are you on drugs?"

"I know who you are. You killed Haley and you tried to kill me, you fucking scumbag."

"That's crazy." The kidnapper's act wasn't convincing.

"I recognize your voice. It's you." She snagged the gym bag, scrambled to her feet and shot down the stairs as she yelled. "I'm calling the cops."

"Stop," he commanded from the summit of the staircase. "You call the cops and I'll give them Titus. You want that!" She heard him taking huge steps down the stairs, then the thud of tumbling bumps. He had fallen.

Cozy made it out the gate and down the street without anyone on her tail. She had done it. *She found Haley's killer.*

SEVENTEEN

With all her possessions hanging in the bag over her shoulder, Cozy ducked back into the corner tavern where she had just been sitting moments ago. The old man had a fresh drink. She consciously controlled her breathing and wiped the sweat from under her hair on her neck. No one had followed her, and she had a nice view of the street. Should she call Lucas or just kill Porter herself? She knew the answer.

Once calm, she got change and called her momma on an ancient payphone. "No, I'm not coming home tonight, Momma."

"Why on earth not? Haley is dead, Cozy. There is nothing there for you. Come home now."

"I can't Momma. I have some things to take care of." Her eyes scanned the bar.

"You are coming home, now. Now, girl." Her momma's voice boomed, vibrating the receiver.

Cozy felt the tears return. She almost screamed. "I'm not coming home, Momma. I don't know if I'm ever coming home."

"Where are you? Tell me where you are!"

Cozy put the phone down on the little shelf as her momma's

muffled voice lost strength. With wet eyes and an awkward smile at the bartender, she sat on a backless barstool.

"She still yelling at you?" The bartender motioned to the receiver still off the hook.

"I can't hang up on my momma. Better to just let her ramble. Tequila and Abita Amber, please." Her voice shook.

"I.D."

The old man spoke up, "Aw, Jesus. Give her a drink. You ain't gettin' raided."

The bartender nodded like he lost a debate. "Never going home again, huh?" He repeated from Cozy's call. "This is on the house."

"Thanks."

With a quick flip, the Tequila fell down her throat and she swished the beer afterward like mouthwash. The old man with a cane turned toward her several times, just two stools over, admiring her drinking style. It took a minute, but he eventually found his own drink again.

Moments passed while some familiar Zydeco music eased from the speakers.

"I'll have what she's having," the old man said, leaning with a leer. "I overheard that fight with your momma."

"Sorry about that."

He waved it off. "Ah, parents don't always know best. You Cajun?"

"Straight from the bayou."

"Boyfriend hit you?" He pointed.

Cozy looked away as if ashamed.

"You just getting here or just leaving?" He waved at her bag.

"It looks like I might need a place to stay for a few days, actually."

The man smiled and slapped the bar with his palm. "You may be in luck. I'm Sal."

"Cozy." She squinted at this character as he held onto the bar while his other hand extended in greeting. He looked like he just won a scratch-off ticket. "What do you mean? You have a place?"

"I got a room for rent. Better than any damn hotel."

She called the bartender over. "You know this guy?"

The bartender nodded without any subtle warnings. "Oh, yeah. That's just Sal."

"Good guy? Not a rapist or anything?"

"He used to be a cop. Comes in here most days. Never causes trouble."

She spun on the barstool, trying to contain her anxiety. "How much per day?"

"Let me think."

"I'd be interested if you can wait a few days until I get my paycheck from the place I just quit."

"How you gonna get your check if you don't have an address?"

What was it with cops trying to figure everything out? "A friend is going to pick it up for me and bring it here. It's just a two-hour drive from my hometown. Once I cash it, I can pay you. If it's cheap enough."

"That is an exquisite diamond pendant you got."

"Not a shot in hell." She put her hand over it.

"Just admiring it, dahlin'. So, you quit your job and just up and moved to New Orleans? Oh, to be young."

"Like you said, sometimes parents don't know best."

"So, I'm being nice and all, but how can I trust you not to rob me blind?" His question seemed irrelevant, as she had him hooked.

"How can you trust me? Two-way street, mister."

"Shit, look at me. You could whip my ass no problem."

"True, Sal. Very true. I'll take the room if the price is right."

"Cozy is it? That's nice. Cozy, I think you should hold on to your money 'cause you're going to need it. I have an idea for a barter." His voice gained vitality.

"What?"

"Not everyone in the world is infatuated with money."

Something in his eyes made her cringe. "I got nothing to trade."

"Don't be so sure. How familiar are you with the Mardi Gras custom of getting beads?"

EIGHTEEN

No curtains allowed any of the morning's light entry into the old man's spare bedroom. A crack in the window meandered up from the bottom left corner, its origin hidden behind wood with a spotty paint job. After staring at the abandoned spider webs hanging raggedly off the sill, Cozy wiped goo from her eyes, her mind paralyzed with uncertainty. Did she expect to go kill Porter today? Just walk right up to him and blow his brains out?

Why not?

Surrounded by Sal's ancient, beat-to-hell boxes, she peeked into a few hoping to find something of value, however musty old clothes and magazines weren't worth the effort to steal. In one box was a stack of photos taken during Mardi Gras. Each picture had Sal in full uniform posing with different females showing their boobs and beads. She flipped through hundreds of photos like a deck of cards, eliciting a full body shake. Some of the pictures dated back to the seventies.

She closed the box and surveyed the cramped room. On the walls hung dusty plaques, award certificates and portraits of a young, odd-looking cop with his entire life still ahead of him. He had a triangle face with straight black lines for eyebrows and thin lips. Sal definitely wasn't ugly, but his looks had to match a woman's particular tastes. He had a huge grin in all the pictures, proving that Sal once seen far better times.

Cozy fingered her eyes again, brushing the residue off her face. Her rims burned and she had to piss something fierce. The old man hadn't imposed on her last night as she'd imagined he would. Seeing her boobs for a few seconds apparently merited enough for a free overnight stay. Maybe letting him take a picture to add to his collection would be enough to get two days. She let a single laugh escape. It wasn't like the locals had never seen boobs before.

Sal had gone on most of the night about how New Orleans' glory days had long since passed and now it was nothing but crime and tacky tourist shops and delusional residents. They had gotten drunk; the scrapes on her hands and forearms from falling off the curb was testimony to that. Thankfully, Sal was old and couldn't walk that far, especially intoxicated, so his favorite bar was right down the street from his house.

She was still in wrinkled clothes that stunk of alcohol. Her shoes by the door were caked with Bourbon Street filth. In her bag between the dilapidated boxes, she found a clean pair of Haley's shorts and a tank top, tucking them under her arm. When she stood, something fluttered to the floor from the shorts. A business card. She picked it up, seeing in bright red letters: Molly's Girls. It was a gentlemen's club. She worked there.

Titus, you asshole.

She put the card back in the pocket of the shorts. She opened the door, and it creaked on rusted hinges.

"Good morning, Sunshine," a gravelly voice said from the front room.

Cozy detoured to the entrance of the den, spotting the old man in his recliner still wearing pajamas. He was just elderly enough to be non-threatening and just virile enough to be annoying. She was certainly surprised to find him awake. "You're up early."

"I might be what you call a functioning alcoholic. Been doing this for most of my life."

"Even on the job?"

"I was a damn fine policeman."

"Sal, I need to shower." She backed away.

"You want to stay a while longer for free?" he yelled.

She stopped, thinking she might have to. "You want to take a picture this time?"

"Yeah, I think I'd like a picture. You want some *lagniappe,* too?"

"Lagniappe… a little extra? What you got?"

"Let me feel them and you get a few extra days."

She rolled her eyes, then turned to face him. "You got a set of balls on you."

"At my age, I can't dilly-dally or apologize. Besides, I know desperation when I see it. You got nothing else."

Her eyes found the stained, buckling carpet. "How long?"

"A few minutes would be great."

"No, how long will I get to stay?"

"Three days," he said as if he thought it through.

"You know I'm only seventeen, right?"

"That's what I like about you… and the fact that you don't want to do it."

"Ew. Give me a minute to think."

"Think about this; I can get a whore off the street to let me do it for twenty dollars. I'm offering you a deal."

Cozy staggered to the refrigerator to cool her face in the freezer and instead, excavated a chilled bottle of vodka to help sort her moral dilemma, which couldn't even compare to hiding a dead body. Her mouth puckered at the first swish of Vodka. She had gotten used to Moonshine, so this was nothing.

"Let's go already." He tapped his cane on the hardwood.

She appeared again. "One week."

"A week? You hear what I said about the whore?"

"A whore ain't no conquest. You like me because I *don't* want to do it."

"Five days. And you have to let me feel them until I'm done, if you know what I'm saying." He picked up a packet of blue pills and waved them at her.

Her empty stomach heaved. "Six days and you aren't touching me.

I'll let you watch me shower. What you do outside the tub is your own business."

"Watch you shower? Like, with no curtain?" His face soured.

"You're not putting your hands on me. I'd rather leave."

He fingered his pills. "Fine, but you can't turn your back to me and you have to keep showering until I say so."

"You seriously have no shame."

His shaking fingers secured a pill. "You have to wait a half-hour." He popped the pill into his mouth.

"I'll be in the room."

"I can still get a picture?" He asked before she retreated.

"Yeah, Sal. You have quite a collection."

"Oh, you found those? Some people collect stamps or baseball cards. I collect boobs, so to speak. You'll make a fine addition."

If Cozy didn't look directly at him, she could get over having someone watch her shower. It was worth it, to get the time she needed.

NINETEEN

London was six hours ahead of New Orleans. I found myself on the phone with a Mr. William Burrell, VP of sales and distribution for the Almas Caviar; a very polite and cordial man with a clean British accent, who I imagined wore an ascot and sipped brandy. Making me feel linguistically inferior, he probably imagined me stuffing a Big Mac in my mouth, wiping the sauce off with my sleeve. With a fine 'cheerio,' I had my pen and paper at the ready while Tara caught up on neglected paperwork next to me.

He said, "No problem, Detective Peyroux. I have to request the list of sales for the past year on my car and shooter."

"What?"

"I'm sorry, my computer."

Gotta love the British. "Take your time. I know my car and shooter is slow as hell."

Tara's confused face turned to me.

"Right, these transactions are routed through Switzerland, so bear with me. I'm narrowing down my search for New Orleans, Louisiana, USA or ex-British Colonies as some hard-core Brits would say. Yes, brilliant, here we are."

"You have something?"

"I have a contract for a company called Winning One Incorporated. The contact is one Mr. Harry Winslow, Esquire. The last delivery was two weeks ago. Delivery address the same. I would assume Mr. Winslow has adequate refrigeration at his company."

"He must like to show off for clients. We love our food."

"Your city is world renowned for its food among other things… I do so want to holiday there someday."

"It's unique. Let me know if you ever do. So, can you email that or fax it over?"

"I'll save everything in a PDF and send you an email. How's that?"

"Perfect."

While I waited, I did an Internet search of Winning One, Incorporated. There was no website, but from what I could gather from miscellaneous web pages, it was a consulting firm. If it didn't advertise, then they must have clients in the upper crust. My friend the mayor came to mind.

Chance wanted to dine at LaPlace on Bourbon. I can ask him what he knew about Mr. Harry Winslow, plus I've heard nothing but great things about the restaurant. It had opened nine months ago and has been booked solid since its inception. In other words… impossible to get into.

I printed out the email and filled Tara in during the drive to Spring-Love Square located in the Central Business District. I had been in this particular building on several occasions to question witnesses, but didn't remember this company name. The elevator hummed to the fifth floor, releasing straight into a glass wall with Winning One, Inc. etched on the door. A bombshell receptionist greeted us with professional courtesy, eye-candy for potential clients. She sat behind a crescent shaped desk made of beveled glass. I guess all the glass meant to show transparency. Behind her to the left and right were two hallways of offices.

I tilted my badge on my belt. "I'm Detective Peyroux and this is Detective Gray. You are?"

"Amy Schultz." She tilted her nameplate in the same manner with a smile. There wasn't any *ditz* in her twinkling eyes.

"We need to speak to Mr. Harry Winslow."

"Esquire," Tara added under her breath.

"Harry's in Washington D.C. with the partners right now."

"Mr. Esquire lets you call him Harry?" Tara asked.

"Esquire was an inside joke when he was in law school. Those who know him appreciate his good humor in keeping the title. It's really not meant to be pretentious, but just the opposite. He's very informal. He insists on being called Harry."

I nodded. "Does Harry have an assistant here now? A right hand man?" I rested my hands on the desk, but lifted them quickly realizing I'd leave prints. As Tara made a tour of the surrounding artwork on the walls, I conjured up the proper charm for a twenty-something.

"No. Office is cleared out. I'm just here to answer the phone and be a physical presence."

"Must be nice not to have the boss around. What exactly does this company do?"

"We manage political careers, hold fundraisers, do consultations. Harry gets people elected to office from Texas to Florida." She flipped her blonde hair back with just the shake of her head.

"Ah, you guys are the man behind the man... or woman, of course."

"Yes, girl power." She flexed her arm in the air.

"When does Harry come back?"

"He'll be back tomorrow."

"Did Harry throw a party about a week ago?"

She bit her pen. "Are you investigating something?" She asked with a high inflection. "Maybe I shouldn't be talking to you."

I brushed it off with a laugh. "You're being paranoid. Why would Harry want to keep a party for a client secret?"

"Sometimes there are reasons. Never criminal, mind you. That's why I'm telling you I don't know of any party recently. The last fundraiser Harry threw was about two months ago. Senator Folsom... Held at the Hyatt."

"So, you wouldn't tell us even if you did know."

"No. Yes. You're trying to bait me. We only leak information when it suits us. Confidentiality. That's a mantra around here."

"We just want to ask him about one of his guests, so anything you can tell me about the riverboat cruise would be helpful."

"Riverboat cruise? You *are* persistent."

"We have to be. You seem like a loyal employee."

"Careers are at stake here."

"If you're as smart as you are attractive, then you should be in MENSA."

"Smooth… but, we're not in a bar. Sorry, I can't help you."

I looked at Tara. "You were right, we should have got the warrant." Then turned back to the blonde. "Better get your records in order, because we're moving in for the next few days."

She stood, her blouse form-fitted to her thin waistline. "Look, just come back when Harry's here, please. I'm sure he'll answer your questions."

"Sure. But, I got one more question for you, then I'll let you get back to work. Do you know if Harry imported special caviar for this party?"

Her mouth opened, then she shrugged. "Harry does have an account for Almas Caviar to use at fundraisers and special dinners, but that's all I can say about that."

I stood straight as if everything was casual. "I understand. We'll try back tomorrow."

"What about leaving your card?"

I slipped one out of my back pocket like a pro and she took her time pulling it from my fingers. "Just tell him not to leave the office tomorrow or he'll just have to do this at the station at our convenience."

Her pen scratched notes on paper as we walked out.

TWENTY

The bathroom mirror had fogged, but Cozy cleared a drippy path with her hand. Watching the girl in the mirror, she combed her hair, feeling its cold, damp tips on her shoulder blades. She had just earned six days stay in the old man's spare bedroom; all for letting a voyeur get his shriveled rocks off. Her eyes had been kept closed for most of the shower, only catching a curious glimpse of what a seventy-year-old dick looks like. Instead of her feeling repulsed, Sal had actually gained her pity.

The alligator pendant went on first. An inverted tattoo on her left breast of a tiny crawfish with its claws extended reflected back. It was close enough to her areola to be hidden under bras and bikinis. It was the one secret she'd ever kept from Haley. The swelling in her cheek had gone down enough for her to appear normal. Ash was probably wondering why she didn't just ask him to come along on this adventure. Why? Because Ash didn't need to get ass-raped in prison. She would kill Porter - if he weren't already on the run – plus, she would check out Molly's Girls unless the cops found her beforehand.

She pulled light pink shorts up her sore legs. Her red tank top fit snug over a black push-up bra that excelled at its job. More of her father's drunken worldly advice was to *show the cleavage, you never know when it will get you out of a jam*. Haley had never shown her assets. Just the opposite, she always wore baggy clothes, especially when hanging around the house. Maybe not so strange, after all.

She hoped Sal had fallen asleep after his eventful morning, but she wasn't that fortunate.

"Where are you off to?" he asked from the den as she stepped into the hallway. "Just curious." The CIA must have made the man's hearing aid.

"To look for someone." She clutched the purse that held Titus' gun.

"What's the name? Most lifers here in the Quarter are familiar with each other."

Cozy stepped into his line of sight. His eyes scanned her like airport security. "I'm looking for someone that owes me something."

"If you gotta go out looking for them..." The old man picked up the remote and shot it at the television. "...maybe they shouldn't be found."

She shrugged. "Can I use your washing machine?"

"Leave your stuff right there. I'll throw them in with mine."

"Thanks. Can I make a sandwich or something?"

"Sorry, sweetheart. My groceries are regulated to feed me a week at a time. I'm bare bones and if you noticed, I ain't got a lot to begin with." He gummed a smile. "You got money, right?"

"Right. Yeah, I'm good. Okay." She started for the door.

"Wait a minute, dahlin'. I know you see me as a dirty old man and that's fine, but you... look. You made me feel young again... alive. One day if you get to be my age and end up alone, you might understand." He picked up a note pad and wrote something down, and then held it up for her to take. "This is the number to a burner phone a cop friend got for me."

"Burner phone?"

Sal held it up. "Can't be traced. Call if you find yourself in trouble and I'll know it's you, 'cause no one ever calls me on it. I still have connections, and can maybe help you out of a jam."

She took the paper and folded it up. "Cool."

She walked out the front door, down three steps and turned onto

Dauphine Street. She meandered into different sections of shade, light-headed from hunger. After spending all her money on alcohol that first night with Sal, buying his drinks because he looked so sad sipping at his watered-down cocktails, her options for food were shoplifting, the dine and dash, or garbage picking. She wasn't going to do an O.J. and stupidly get busted for burglary after getting away with murder. She'd be too easy to describe if she ran out of a restaurant without paying. Garbage picking and dumpster diving was the only option. If gutter punks can do it, so could she.

Two blocks into the journey, she spotted a McGriddle wrapper, like a diamond sitting on a pile of coal. She casually snagged it as she passed, happily feeling the roundish form of a partially eaten breakfast sandwich inside. What did she care about what went inside her body? She stopped in front of LaPlace on Bourbon's and gazed through the window at all the beautiful place settings waiting for the lunch crowd. It would be nice to eat there one day, dressed to the nines.

Out on the Bayou she had consumed unusual wild game to fuel her active lifestyle. Besides seafood and gators, she had eaten deep-fried snakes, live bugs, and even the beaver-like rats known as *nutria*. A discarded breakfast sandwich held no challenge. She devoured the stale breakfast in four bites, but it would only satisfy her for a couple hours and she didn't even know how long it would take to spot Porter coming or going from the apartment complex.

TWENTY-ONE

While staring at the file of a woman who had disappeared two years ago, my thoughts turned to the firing range and the cluster I had created earlier with Tara. The session ended with one of my shots hitting the target, but the other five ended up to the left, next to the ear. It was progress, at least according to Tara.

My cell rang and Chance's name lit the screen. He spoke immediately. "I pulled some strings and got us a table at LaPlace tonight."

I pushed away from my desk and rubbed my face. "You suck."

"You're welcome."

"Heather and Alicia are going to the movies tonight. I told them I was working late."

"That's fine. Just you and me. I've had yes-men yapping in my ear all day and I need someone to tell me how much I suck."

"I'm your man. What time?"

"Leave now, I'll be there in a few."

"I'm in jeans, but I do have my dress Nikes on."

"It's fine. I know the owner. We'll be tucked away in a corner – and don't say that stupid movie line or the dinner's off."

"Nobody gives Baby an ultimatum." I tapped my pen on the desk as my buddy chuckled. Tara had already left along with most of the day shift. "What the hell? See you there."

THE STAINED-GLASS double doors opened to a simple, gold-plated oak podium where a sophisticated high-school girl in a black bow tie and white shirt stood by a computer screen. No one was waiting as you might find at an Applebee's. The bar was full, however. She took inventory of my wardrobe through bloated, black-framed glasses and smiled.

"You must be Detective Peyroux, the Mayor's guest?"

"Yes, I am."

"This way, please."

She led me to a smaller side room, meant for privacy. I felt like a peasant worker that had been invited into the royal palace. Brilliant white tablecloths hung low to the tiled, marble floor, but the dim lighting made it hard to tell if it was real or laminate. Chance was already seated at the back table, the lone patron.

The hostess backed away and was replaced by our waiter, a sturdy young man with a pronounced jaw.

"Bring us a couple of Abita Ambers, will you, Darren?"

"Of course, Mr. Mayor."

I sat in front of a small, white plate and a glass of ice water. Purple flowers in a tiny vase were centered perfectly. Chance waited for me to make one of my smart-ass remarks about the swank accommodations.

"Nice," I said, letting him down.

"I know what you're thinking."

"What am I thinking?"

"You'll get a half-dollar sized medallion of steak for fifty bucks. No. Good sized portions. Fantastic blackened redfish. Or maybe the seared scallops... unbelievable."

"I think the experience here is a little lost on me tonight."

"What do you mean?"

"Part of the excitement of coming out to place like this is the anticipation, and the getting ready with a shower and nice clothes and not having to wind down from a stressful day at work. This just feels awkward."

"That's why we'll partake in their finest mead and ambrosia first and take our time."

Darren and our beers came right on cue and after a perfect pour by our waiter, we toasted. It would just be a matter of time before Chance laid the cards on the table.

CHANCE LET me unwind by talking Saint's football through the savory crab cake appetizers. I stayed away from grilling him about Harry Winslow, Esquire, and why he chose this restaurant. He stayed away from asking about my brother Brent. And after catching up on each other's lives and the mandatory small talk, our dinner came. That's when I brought up an issue that had been bugging me: the way my daughter always went goggle-eyed when he was around.

"What can I do about it?" Chance said. "I don't want to break the girl's heart."

I took a scallop in my mouth. "And I don't want you to break her heart. We've all been there. You've handled her crush perfectly. I just didn't know it would last this long."

"She's becoming a very beautiful lady. She looks just like Heather."

"It's just so weird."

"Ha… it creeps you out that she's into me. That's hysterical."

"Don't say *into me*. Let's stick with crush." I shifted took a piece of bread.

"Wow. Talk about Daddy's little girl."

"When did you stop being 'Uncle Chance'?"

"I don't know. When did she get her training bra?"

"Watch it, Heffner." I pointed my fork at him. "So, have you ever tried Almas Caviar?"

He fixed his eyes on mine. "They don't serve it here."

"You're pretty quick to know that."

"I know the whole menu."

"But, Harry Winslow, Esquire has some over at Winning One."

He frowned. "Harry called me about your visit."

"Boom. There it is."

He put his elbows on the table in order to crack his knuckles, one by one. "I want to know what's going on with your investigation."

"Did you know from the onset that my River Doe was connected to Winslow? Is that why you came by my house?"

"Like I'm some crazy, French Quarter psychic? Get real." He scowled.

"Fine." I didn't push it. "I didn't even get the chance to question Harry Winslow, Esquire, yet. He cried to you already? How you know each other?"

"He said you harassed his receptionist."

"It's only harassment when they got something to hide."

He casually sipped his water. "I'm eventually going to run for governor of Louisiana."

"I figured that, Chance. Everyone knows you weren't stopping at mayor."

"Harry is going to run my campaign. We've been working very close together, so of course when you and Tara go into his company and grill his staff about some imaginary party, he's going to tell me about it."

"You better not be telling me to cool it."

He pointed toward me with his fork. "I'm just not sure you're looking up the right alley."

"Consider it a proper vetting. You don't want to be involved with a criminal, do you?"

Chance wiped his mouth and then threw his napkin on the table. "I'm concerned. You associate a murder with him and his company, you'll ruin his credibility."

"It was bound to happen, eh?"

"What?"

"You're the mayor. I'm a detective. There was bound to be a favor to be had somewhere. We couldn't just be friends and leave the politics out of it. You are actually sitting there inferring that I leave your pal out of my investigation."

"I'm not suggesting you stop or alter your investigation. Go on and question the shit out of him for all I care. Our being friends is exactly why I'm warning you."

"Warning me?"

"Harry's political arm reaches far beyond me. Let's just say if you irritate the wrong people, they won't be inviting you out to dinner."

"Is that what you do, Chance? Crush your enemies? Victory at any cost?"

He made a sour face, offended. "That doesn't deserve a response."

I finished the last of my beer. "You're a good guy, Chance. You can only swim with sharks for so long before they realize you're not a shark. Then what?"

Chance's body slumped. "You know how New Orleans politics go. You run, you're elected, you're indicted. I'm going to break that cycle. And for the record, if I wanted you to stop your investigation, I'd tell you that plainly in a direct sentence."

I nodded. "I know you would." *And he would.*

"My concern for you extends to people I can't control."

I stared at him. For the first time, I saw Chance as a politician.

TWENTY-TWO

Night approached and the Quarter breathed a little deeper. And like a vampire that wakes at dusk to suck the blood from its victims, so too, had Bourbon Street.

After walking life back into her numb buttocks, Cozy stood alone near St. Peter Street, having walked past Molly's Girls three times. She figured it would be easier to maneuver around the inside while the club was filled up, so she waited until after the dinner rush when the real partying began.

On the opposite corner of where she stood, The Cat's Meow drew the crowd's attention to its huge open windows and packed balcony. It was the Quarter's most famous karaoke bar and a landmark in which to give directions. Her stomach rumbled and tugged at her in waves. She could beg for more food, maybe show her boobs again. Lucky Dogs were cheap and filling and the corner vendor appeared to be straight. She cast her gaze into the crowd if only to make sure those cops weren't around. If she appeared to be a local expecting someone, drunk tourists and college kids looking to get laid might not bother her.

Neon lights under balconies radiated adventure, beckoning wallets and purses to be opened for food, loud noise called music, souvenirs, or a sexual experience. Sal had said take Bourbon Street out of the equation and New Orleans could possibly return to her former glory. She saw his point.

As the music and the crowds grew rowdier, Cozy thought that perhaps it was time to enter the lion's den. A cheesy car salesman type stood in front of Molly's Girls trying to solicit anyone who would look at him. On both sides of the open door were large posters of extremely attractive women wearing lots of makeup and little else. And inside the doorway was a fantasy world colored in muted red light.

"Hey, dawlin'. C'mon in. Ladies drink free."

"Free drinks?" Cozy strained her neck trying to see past the dark wall just within the entrance.

"Hell, yes. Female patrons classy up the joint, ya know?" His eyes disappeared in a wrinkled smile.

Cozy pushed his hand away as he tried to guide her in. Heavy Metal music blared from within, peppered with some cat-calls. Her stomach shrunk. "You have snacks? Like pretzels?"

"Nuts and pretzels and popcorn. We got a kitchen. You can order food from a menu if you want. Go on in."

The man only waved his hand this time, showing her the obvious path. She stepped in like it was a ride for a haunted house, expecting half-naked ladies with clown makeup to jump out of the shadows. The room opened to an expansive space, much bigger than she would assume from outside. The stage was a large T-shape with a pole at each end. She hugged the wall for a few feet until she hit the bar. A bowl of mixed nuts prompted her to scoop a handful.

"Something to go with that?" An appealing man who reminded her of Thor was one of three bartenders, all with porno actor looks.

"Coke?"

"Excellent choice. I'd hate to have to ask you for an ID." He winked.

"It's free, right?"

"Right."

He pushed a tall, narrow glass towards her. It had six ounces of Coke at best. She drank it down in two swallows and took an ice cube into her mouth. The man refilled the glass.

"First time?" He asked.

Cozy dipped her chin.

"Sit back and enjoy. It's really more harmless than most prudes think." He smiled and walked off to fill an order from a waitress.

She propped one of her butt cheeks onto the bar stool, leaving one foot on the floor in case she needed get-away traction. In the distant glow, a gorgeous, curvy woman wearing Victoria's Secret type underwear wedged herself between a man's knees. His middle-aged friends cheered her on as she whispered in his ear. He agreed to something and they both walked hand-in-hand to a back room closed off with a curtain.

Her vantage point allowed a partial view of the couple through a seam. He sat on a small couch and the show immediately started. Her ass found his crotch and she gyrated in circles. It didn't take long for her to unhook the bra, exposing her tits just inches from his face. He raised his hands to caress them, but she caught his exploring fingers with swift rejection. Instead, she placed his nose in her cleavage and her thigh massaged the inside of his.

After the song ended, the man shook his head in answer to a question and the attraction drained from her face. He handed her money; how much Cozy couldn't tell. She knew what strippers were about, but this was Haley's work environment. Tease a man, show your wares and get paid for it. That was basically how she got her rent with Sal. Did Haley work here as a dancer or waitress? Did she massage men's cocks for a living?

She took her drink and a bowl of peanuts to an empty table in the darkest corner. The rotation of women flirted for private dances, with clientele bellied up at the edge of the stage, inserting bills into G-strings. Bouncers with earpieces had been strategically placed around the room like giant Roman eunuchs ready to mess someone up. She was a fly on the wall.

Talking to a dancer would be the easiest route to go, but pick the wrong one and she could sour the entire crew against her. Most of these girls were probably a tight-knit bunch like the cliques she had experienced in high school. Was she being paranoid? All she wanted to do was find out if her sister worked here. Find out if she was well-liked. Maybe she'd even had a best friend here.

A hall with offices in the back caught her vision. Perhaps Molly was in there, if she was even a person at all. Cozy should talk to the owner of the place, but how do you bring up the subject of one of their murdered dancers who, according to Titus, sold her body?

Or better yet, she could get a job here and make some quick cash. What if it was days before Porter showed his face again? What if he left town? She might just have to tell Lucas after all. Screw the job application. Go big or go home.

The pendant hanging from her neck needed to go in her pocket. Two songs later, after working up the courage and while no one paid attention, she forced her butt from the chair and let her shorts fall to the floor. She wasn't wearing a G-string, but her panties were sexy enough. The bartender Thor had left his station and the bouncers stood bored as she pulled off her tank, sporting a lacy powder-blue bra.

With a deep breath, she rounded the table and entered the mix like a car entering traffic. She touched a well-dressed, middle-aged gentleman on the shoulder and he smiled as if porn had magically jumped out of his television. He wanted a dance and to her amazement, the bouncer never looked twice as she led the gentleman behind the curtain.

Cozy snapped her bra cups together in the front before taking the money. Her dance routine wasn't much different than dirty dancing with Ash. The man adjusted himself before pulling out forty dollars and stuffing it into her cleavage, letting his touch linger. She had found herself turned on at this point, not by the man, but for having the power to give an erection. He exposed large, overlapping teeth in a smile and she ruffled his hair, pushing him back toward his seat.

The two twenties scratched her boobs as she entered the floor rotation to scan her next prospect, but someone tapped her shoulder instead. "Excuse me, young lady."

He was a dark-skinned man in his forties, well-built in his tailored suit. His hair strived for perfect uniformity and he wore the same earpiece as the bouncers. She took him to be the boss, but getting his attention had been the intention all along.

"Need a dance?"

"Come with me."

"I was planning on it." She combed her fingers through her hair with the most dignity she could muster, and then weaved between tables to retrieve her clothes. The man returned to the rear hallway with the arrogance of expecting her to follow.

She felt the stares of the room, like space aliens who knew she wasn't one of them. Again, doubt about this plan crept in. Screw asking about Haley tonight. This was just a lark. Learning about Haley as just another dancer was the best way to go. But, first she needed to get hired.

They entered his office two doors down where the man sat in an impressive cushioned chair behind a decrepit desk. The walls contained an array of photos of men and women she didn't recognize, although one man looked like George Bush. A Saints bobble head occupied the corner, probably used to set his employees at ease.

Two scars on his forehead became apparent in the harsh light. Cozy wondered if he got cut in a bar fight. His eyes were narrow and sunken with dark circles, like he might have been European.

A tall, sexy woman with long dishwater blonde hair with bangs also entered, closing the door. The guy swiveled, leaned back and brought both his index fingers together at his lips. Cozy quickly dressed, glancing at them like they were a principal and teacher.

"You called the cops?" She asked in jest.

"What's your name?"

"Keri Sullivan."

"Love the accent. How old are you?"

"Eighteen, but I lost my license."

"Eighteen's legal to enter as long as you don't drink."

The woman exhaled as if bored. Cozy relaxed having the presence of a second person, and a female for that matter. Cozy said, "Your bouncers should pay better attention."

"I saw you on surveillance the moment you entered." He swiveled his laptop to face her. "The bouncers acted on my orders to let you dance. You don't think we know who all our girls are?"

"Okay. Did you like what I did out there?"

"Believe it or not, strip clubs become monotonous. People like you make things interesting."

"Don't fuck with me."

"We're just getting to know one another. I'm Raymond Corondelet. Call me Ray." He looked at his laptop screen and spoke into his collar. "Vince, table twelve. Keep an eye on him."

Cozy made up for lost air with a very deep breath. "You're in charge here, right Ray? You look like you enjoy power, whether it's firing someone or just ordering a poboy."

"I do like my sandwiches made correctly."

"Jeez. I feel like you're going to take me out back and smack me around." Cozy glanced at the woman. "He's not going to smack me around, right?"

"Why did you undress and dance for one of my customers?"

"Looked like fun."

"Fun if you were wasted, showing off for your sorority sisters. You wouldn't be hard up for cash would you?"

She shrugged. "Not hard to fathom."

"You seem intelligent. What's your story, Keri?"

"Kicked out of my house."

"Where did you call home?" He inquired.

"Empire, down south."

"Homeless?"

"I'm not on the street. I got a place."

The man had fierce coyote eyes. "So, you want to dance?"

"I want to make money."

"What if I offered you a chance here?"

"I'd do my best."

"Well, normally I'd want an audition, but I think you'll do fine. This nice lady behind you is Tabitha Wheelhouse."

The woman bit at her cuticles. "Nice to meet you."

"Talk about liking power? She's the boss when I'm not around. Hell, she's pretty much the boss even when I am here. Anything you want, any problem you have, you go to her. You guys go talk, but not in here."

The lady pushed off the wall. "C'mon, Keri. There's a probation period before we officially hire. You can get your hands on proper ID?"

"Sure."

"Let me show you around. Tell you how things work."

"Good luck, Keri," Ray said as they left.

Cozy followed the confidently bored woman into the main room where strobe lights popped and the bass thumped. They sat at the very table Cozy had found earlier and faced the action. Tabitha held up two fingers to a waitress, then pointed down at the table like a mob boss. That was so cool. Her eyes finally relaxed.

"You're extremely beautiful, Sugar… for this kind of work."

"I'm not sure what that means."

"Well, you got your different types that work here… hot body – bag the face, plain face, exotic face, androgynous, black, brown, pale, ethnic, with curves or showing ribs. What's common between these women is that they're sexy, but flawed. Your face has nice symmetry. You're beautiful in a *shouldn't be here* way. Your body is tight. That's rare."

Cozy pointed. "That one on stage is beautiful."

"Velvet? No, she's stripper hot. Paint on the makeup and do up the hair and she'll turn heads at a party, but her family tree grew in a trailer park. Believe me, I make my living as a talent scout. How are your tits?"

"What do you mean?"

"Real? Fake? Let's see."

"They're real." Cozy lifted her shirt and Tabitha gently tested each one from underneath.

"Amazing. The men are going to empty their wallets for you."

"When do I start?"

"Knowing your financial situation, I won't put it off. Come in tomorrow night. We'll start you off on the stage until you get used to the kinds of customers we get. Plus, you have to come up with a name. Something dirty, dangerous, provocative or intimate."

"I have no idea."

"Spitfire came to mind when I first saw you."

"I like that."

"Oh, yeah. I can see a girl and pen her name in seconds."

"There's rules about touching, right?"

"That's right. You'll learn about what's acceptable and what's not. There's a difference between a creep putting his hand on your ass during a personal dance and a lonely husband."

"I get it."

"And you do not make arrangements to leave here with a customer and take money for sexual favors. Believe me, it's the easiest thing to do, but if Ray hears about it, you're gone. Got it? We don't want any trouble from the cops."

"Where do I get my stage clothes? I don't have any money, except for this forty dollars I just made."

"No money?" She paused for a moment. "Normally, here's where I'd say that's your problem, but Ray has never taken to a girl so quickly."

"You took that as liking me?"

"Sugar, half of these girls have never heard word one from him until he says *pack your things*. He wants you here and it's my job to make sure you are. Meet me in front of the Cathedral tomorrow for eleven. We'll get you an outfit and have lunch. You can owe me. For now, why don't you sit here, have a burger on me, watch the girls and learn. You do good and Ray will take good care of you."

"And if I suck?"

Tabby's face finally softened and became feminine. "Sugar, I have no doubt you can do the job. It's the politics offstage where I worry for you."

"I can take care of myself."

"Famous last words, Spitfire."

TWENTY-THREE

Morning came quickly. Cozy spent no extra time in bed, and snuck past Sal in the recliner. She stopped at a local cafe for a Danish and coffee before her second day of staking out Porter's apartment. Things appeared to be quiet, with empty sidewalks that made her nervous for potential muggers or rapists, even with the sun shining bright. She kept her hand on her weighted purse.

Where are you, Porter?

THE FIRING RANGE represented anxiety and frustration. I almost convinced myself it was the building itself that was the problem. The pulley spun and the rope snapped, rushing the target toward Tara and me.

"Bloody hell."

Tara pulled the sheet from the clips. "Your issue is that your mind is not trusting your body."

I crushed it into a ball and chucked it at a nearby trashcan. "I hate when that happens."

"Trusting yourself is the main issue. I don't think practicing is going to do it. There's a wall in your head and psychologically, you have to jump over it or knock it down before you can move on."

I put away my gun and headphones and stepped from the partition. "A shrink?"

"Or – you can have that heart-to-heart you promised Cozy Robicheaux."

"Thanks, Mick."

"Hey, if Stallone had seen a psychiatrist, he might have stopped with Rocky III." She gave a quirky smile. "Go see if she's still at the apartment."

THE WALK from the station cleared my head. As I turned the corner, I saw her. Cozy focused on the apartment building like a terrier that found the foxhole. I sat on the opposite stoop and watched her for a moment without her noticing. She turned at the sound of my sipping coffee and nearly fell to the sidewalk. "Lucas! Shit, you scared me."

I handed her a coffee. "What's going on here?"

She took the cup. "What are you doing here?"

"I wanted us to have our talk, so I called your house and your mom took ten minutes to tell me you hadn't come back. I figured you were still at Haley's apartment."

"Oh." She took a sip and glanced at the building.

"I know a stake-out when I see one."

"Landlord kicked me out. I'm just wondering if I could sneak back in. I'm really not ready to go home yet."

I leaned back to get comfortable. "So, let's talk... about that night."

She squinted, seeming to choose her words. "You saved my life and then avoided me."

"I may have saved your life, but I almost ended it, too."

"Can't live thinking about the *what ifs*. That's fantasy, not reality."

"This is actually a huge step for me."

She closed her eyes. "If my sister hadn't been killed, you'd still be avoiding me."

"Maybe, maybe not. I'd like to think I would've gotten my shit together sooner or later."

Cozy moved to my stoop and sat to face me, taking my hands. "I've thought long and hard about that day of the shooting and I've come to one conclusion… you need to stop being such a baby."

I reared back. "What?"

"You're being a baby – a cry baby. Stop it." Her intense eyes willed her message into my brain.

"Wow."

"Everyone's tap dancing around you and you're just not getting it. That day when you found me and he had his arm around my throat… I knew the moment I saw you that you would save my life. I remember fighting for a moment, but then I just went limp."

"I remember."

"I was waiting. I had never seen you before, yet I trusted you and I was right. Man up. Own it. Be proud of what you did that day. Can you do that for me? Huh, you little baby?" She poked me in the ribs playfully.

I laughed and felt tears welling at the same time. She clutched my hands as if to keep me from running, waiting for me to answer. "Okay. You make a great argument."

She raised one of my hands to her throat and brushed my fingers over the scar like a blind man reading Braille. She held it there. "Say this for me. *I saved your life…* Say it."

"I saved your life," I managed under my breath. My fingers felt the ridges of her skin that had healed. What I felt was the pulse underneath.

"*Mean* it."

"I saved your life."

"Make me believe it."

"I saved your life," I announced as if speaking to an audience.

"There you go." She put my palm against her cheek and closed her eyes with a sigh, but for only a second. She stood up beside me. "Now give me a hug like you're happy not to be visiting my grave."

"I can do that." My arms wrapped around her and for the first time, I could feel relief overtaking the guilt. For the first time, I smiled while thinking about her and actually meant it. "Cozy, I can't tell you how badly I want to catch that guy. I dream about nailing him and putting him away for life. I want to do that for you."

"I owe you my life, so I think I owe you this." A tear ran down her face. "I should tell you something."

"What is it?"

"I'm sitting out here waiting for that landlord, Porter. I'm waiting to kill him."

I TOLD Cozy to wait outside the gate. If she was right about Porter, and he was her kidnapper, then it couldn't be a coincidence that he was the landlord of Haley's building. No, Cozy had been targeted. I'd be willing to bet there were other victims, and some of them were probably single women with no family who'd rented in this place.

Porter didn't answer the doorbell, or when I pounded on the door. I did smell something sour, however. According to Cozy, the man who liked to peep out his window hadn't been seen in days. With my gun at my chest, I entered the unlocked door and stepped into the living room, inhaling the decomposition right away. There were no signs of a struggle.

Cozy appeared at the front door in my peripheral. "I told you to wait outside."

"I know that smell. Is he dead?"

I continued forward to the hallway. "I don't know. Wait there."

My nose led me to the main bedroom where I saw Porter lying on his bed with a portion of his head missing and a gun by his side. I bent to see that his eyes were still open, staring at the light fixture. By all accounts, it looked like a suicide. Cozy had found him out, and he might've felt he had no other option. Sure enough, his forearm showed the scar from my bullet. With hair and no beard, it could be him, but I wasn't sure.

"Oh, my God," Cozy said behind me. "Did he kill himself?"

"Looks like it. Don't come in here, Cozy." I pushed her back through the doorframe. "This is a crime scene. Go wait outside and don't touch a thing."

"Okay." An expression of surprise and glee flashed across her face, like she had spied her Christmas present before it got wrapped.

I turned back to the scene. The mass of blood on the bed and the splatter against the headboard told me CSU would come to my conclusion, but it seemed too convenient. The expression on Cozy's face and the fact she had been waiting for him told me she was innocent. I stepped outside to call dispatch, and Cozy was nowhere to be found.

TWENTY-FOUR

Cozy ran the first block, then power-walked the rest of the way, panting. She still had to meet Tabitha at the St. Louis Cathedral. When she had seen Porter's body, she figured he wasn't the only one involved. If Porter hadn't killed himself, his bosses would have. He just avoided the torture. The strip club was the only other connection. Lucas would probably have every cop in the Quarter searching for her, so she had bought a Saint's cap and sunglasses.

Tabitha was waiting, and they began to hit the stores. It only took an hour of shopping for Tabitha to find the right items. When her adrenaline had subsided, she found herself enjoying the experience. Cozy's bag contained a slutty Catholic high school girl uniform and a hot pink, glitzy bikini. She and Tabby strolled through the French Market next to the river. Tables in the Market displayed an eclectic assortment of cheap merchandise that fit into the category of local, knock-off, or Made In China. Tabby predicted that Cozy should make enough money tonight to buy a month's worth of costumes, but using that money to get another place to stay was first priority.

They crossed over to the sidewalk and stayed parallel to the river, coming to a restaurant with outdoor seating and a chalkboard menu containing a varied list of fried seafood available on French bread. The glare prompted them to lower their sunglasses as they fell onto metal chairs with groans.

Tabby emphasized every word. "I love to shop."

An attractive waiter with a ponytail came to take their order, keeping his back to the sun. His attention stayed on Tabby like a magnet needing a place to stick. She flirted effortlessly and with class. When he retreated, Tabby watched his ass. A nearby jazz band set the mood.

"You warned me about the club politics. Anything specific I should watch out for?" Cozy asked out of the blue.

Tabby pulled down her glasses to expose her eyes. "Number one, dancers can't date the bouncers."

"I'm not in a place to date anyone. You dating?" Cozy asked, but retracted. "I'm sorry, that's none of my business."

"Are you kidding? I miss normal girl talk."

"So, spill." Cozy slid the metal chair across the concrete to get closer.

"Well, it's strange. When I was the number one dancer at Molly's, I was with Ray. When he saw I had a brain, he made me manager, and we stopped. It was like I wasn't bimbo enough for him. The weird part is he doesn't want anyone else to date me, so I'm kind of still his in a way."

"That is so Alpha Male."

She grimaced. "He fucks whoever he wants, of course."

"Of course."

The waiter brought two sweet teas and they raised their cups. "A toast. To the absence of men."

Tabby stopped drinking to focus on something from behind her glasses. "Hey, that's a nice alligator pendant. Funny—it looks familiar."

Cozy screamed in her head. How could she be so stupid as to wear it in front of Tabby? "Thanks. I've actually seen about ten of these since I bought it. There's a whole box of them at the Market."

"Yeah, I know I've seen it around." She leaned back and took a drink, searching for that waiter with the cute butt.

"Any personal advice you give to the girls you like?" Cozy primped her hair for effect.

Tabitha laughed. "I do like you. You remind me of another girl that used to work there, but…"

Cozy froze. "But, what?"

"Don't freak out, but one of our girls was found dead in the Mississippi last week. Right over there by the Moon Walk, in fact." She pointed through the shops blocking their view. "From what I understand, no one claimed her body." She shook her head and lowered her gaze to the table. "Sad."

"What'd you tell the cops?"

"They don't know she worked for us. She was off the books, like a contractor."

"Like I am right now."

She nodded. "Ray doesn't want the bad publicity or have the cops scaring off the customers." She nodded at me. "But lots of our customers are off duty cops, mind you."

"So, none of these cops recognized her?"

Tabitha laughed. "Like those drunk bastards look at the face. These girls wear so much make up. And if they add a wig, they're practically in disguise."

"Makes sense." Cozy bit her nail, then stopped as if Tabitha wouldn't approve.

"It's a shame about her. Haley was her name. I never heard about a funeral, but I wanted to pay my respects. She was a really good friend, and I can't say that about most of these girls."

"What do they think happened?"

"Well…put it this way. Regarding that advice you wanted, I'd stay away from Vince. Even though we don't condone dating the bouncers, they try to poach the girls behind our backs. He's a bit… overbearing."

"You think Vince was involved in that girl's death?" Cozy leaned sideways in the chair.

"I didn't say that. They dated without me knowing when she was first hired, but they broke up long ago. And then Jeanie…"

"Another dancer?"

"Vince and Jeanie were chummy. Jeanie quit a couple weeks ago."

"Vince did something?"

"She just quit without telling anyone. Dancers tend to do that. Just… don't fraternize, okay? Vince can be a cliché, you understand?"

"You can't fire him?"

"He's Ray's favorite, loyal and good with the customers. It's his career. He's not just passing through."

"Thanks for the advice. You don't know how much that means to me."

"I survive on my instincts. There are some girls that you just know will do this until they're sagging and can't pull a buck anymore. I don't think that's you. I see you figuring things out and leaving at some point."

"I would like to think that."

Tabby stirred her tea with the straw. "Your gears are spinning."

"What does that mean?"

"You're thinking about something."

"You've just made me think of where I might be a few years from now. I've never thought that far ahead."

"This becomes the life for some girls. It's hard to watch, but it's kind of like running a dog shelter; you just know some of these girls aren't leaving until they have to, and you can't save them all."

"How many well-adjusted girls do you hire?"

"Ha." Tabitha agreed with a toast. She tilted her head and swung around to pat the waiter's ass.

TWENTY-FIVE

Tara and I stood outside the door of Porter's apartment while CSU collected the scene. I had recounted my reunion with Cozy and what led up to finding the landlord. His DNA would be tested against the samples from the abandoned house, so we wouldn't get results for a week or two. I called Captain Dobson to have someone check the addresses of any missing persons to see if they ever lived in the apartment complex and to find out who owns the building.

"The way Porter killed himself," I started, "doesn't sit right."

"You wanted to get justice for Cozy for so long, you don't want it to end like this. He killed himself. That's good."

"But, consider Haley in all this. The trafficking. I think these apartments could be a half-way house for these girls."

"But they're free to come and go." Tara said.

"What I'm thinking is, they work as strippers or escorts for someone who picks certain girls to sell at a hefty price. Quality over quantity. They offer the apartment at a discount or maybe for free and when the time comes, they just get taken – like Haley in that video."

"And Haley let someone know she had a younger sister, maybe

showed a picture, and then they set out to kidnap her. If Haley was going to be sold, she must have really pissed someone off to be killed."

My cell rang, so I put it on speaker. "Peyroux."

"A Russian company owns the apartment building." Dobson blurted. "*Grom* Holdings. I have the Feds looking into it."

"So, dead end for now."

Dobson's voice crackled. "And Edgar Porter is not in the system."

"We have to find Cozy, Cap."

"We've got all available on it. What's your next move?"

I looked at my partner. "Tara and I are going to talk to Harry Winslow. We'll search for Cozy after that. Maybe she's gone back home."

"Keep me posted."

IT FINALLY SUNK in that the kidnapper who forced me to shoot Cozy was dead. I felt good about that, but unfulfilled that I hadn't caught him. At least Cozy and I would have closure and after our little talk on the stoop, the clouds had parted. That twinge of anxiety while holding my gun had left for good. My decision to shoot had been the right one.

We made our second trip to see Harry Winslow. Chance's warning at LaPlace on Bourbon about irritating the wrong people made me want to do it all the more. We stepped off the elevator toward the glass walls of Winning One. This time the secretary, Amy Schultz, spoke into her headset after spotting us. She announced our arrival with cheer as her wide blue eyes locked on mine, reminding me of Alicia's crush on Chance. Tara would tease me about Amy's flirting after our interview.

Ms. Schultz escorted us down a bright hallway with a shiny cherry wood floor. Black-framed pictures of important men and women spied on us with permanent smiles on their faces. Harry Winslow naturally had the corner office. She tapped the door twice and opened it wide. "Detectives Tara Gray and Lucas Peyroux."

Mr. Winslow stood and extended his young secretary a cursory glance before she shut the door. There was something behind it, extending past a paycheck. "Have a seat, Detectives, and call me Harry." He offered an animated smile as if he was always on.

We sat on thin, chrome, black-cushioned chairs, and then he eased into his larger leather chair. Two potted plants guarded each side of his desk and behind us were a sofa, three chairs and a coffee table lit up with slivers of light from the window blinds.

I examined the surroundings. "Very nice office. That painting… is that a real Blue Dog or a print? And is he inside the Dome?"

"It's real. I commissioned this painting a year before George died. Blue Dog in the nose bleeds of the Superdome; how can you go wrong? So, how can I help you?" His hands were clasped on the desk as if this was his interview, making a show of being relaxed.

Tara sat like a statue. Only her eyes and mouth moved. "Last week, you hosted a private party somewhere close to the banks of the Mississippi, right?"

"Last week? No. I hold fundraisers for political figures and yes, the occasional party for my clients, but I don't know what you're talking about."

"All roads lead to you, Harry," Tara said. "You and your company, Winning One."

"Roads? I can't admit to a party I didn't host."

"Cut the bullshit, Harry," I said, chomping at the bit to show him a picture of Haley. "We know you ordered Alma Caviar for the party two weeks ago."

"Almas," he corrected.

"Almas. Excuse me. We know it was served at the party and we know this dead girl was at that party." I placed the picture on the desk with a hard *thwak*.

He gave it a glance. "I served Almas two months ago at a fundraiser for Senator Folsom. The order from two weeks ago was for my own personal use with my own money. A bonus I pay myself, if you will." Harry licked his lips and glanced at the phone. His eyes returned to mine and he exhaled.

I slid the picture toward him. "Do you recognize her?"

"Pretty, but no."

"Did you and her have a private party with this personal order of Almas?"

"No."

"Really? 'Cause you're turning pale."

"I'm on blood pressure medication. This matter is making me nervous for the mere fact that you don't believe me. Yes, I order Almas caviar. You got me on that. I'll show you the damn invoices."

I pushed the picture an inch closer. "This girl was found floating in the Mississippi River with Almas Caviar in her stomach. You can deny it, but we know for a fact that it came from you."

"Have you tossed around the hypothetical that the Almas came from a different order out of state?"

"Sure, but we'll follow the most likely scenario first, if you don't mind."

"I'm a lawyer, detective. I know you're fishing. You can call my Blue Dog painting a Picasso all day, but it will never be true."

I nodded. "Having ordered the caviar doesn't mean you spoon-fed her, but you're linked. Look again; see if it jogs your memory."

He didn't look. "Sorry."

"It's just a matter of time before I interview one of your guests who will place her there, so if you know anything…"

"You don't have guests to question if there was no damned party."

"What about your partners here? Would they have taken some of your caviar and had their own party. An array of appetizers was found in her stomach at various stages of digestion. It was a real catered party, Harry."

"No one here touched my caviar. But, ask for yourselves."

"We will. We'll have a guest list once we get our warrant."

He laughed, and then stopped abruptly to lean forward. "A warrant for what? You act as if there is a list to be had. The most you got is that I pass around caviar."

"So far." Tara added.

"This is a waste of time. My company caters to very powerful people, including the judges that sign your warrants. Feel free to stick your noses where they don't belong."

"You hear that, Detective Gray? He's going to get us fired."

"Are you that naïve?" Harry spun a quarter turn in his chair, admiring his Blue Dog one more time.

"Are you that arrogant?" I shot back. "Forget the guest list. Maybe we should start at the top of your client list and work our way down."

His pores opened as a sheen of sweat took hold. "That would be a clear-cut case of harassment and for that, I can sue."

"Maybe we run into a few of your clients at their favorite bistros. Maybe we chat about things. We don't have to ask a single question."

"Do you know what it will do to our credibility if you link a murder to this company when you're not even sure about the facts? Just the assumption…"

Tara let her folded arms drop. "I don't get what the big secret is. What the hell kind of party was this? You guys wearing masks like Eyes Wide Shut, goats and shit?"

Harry scoffed at that with a sneer. "Is there anything else, detectives?"

I stood and inspected the Blue Dog up close, blocking his view. "Let's say you're innocent, Harry. What if I told you this Blue Dog was painted on top of a Picasso? Would it be true then… that this is a Picasso?"

"I'm not protecting anyone." He was quick-witted.

"Harry, we're trying to wrap this up right here in this room." I returned to my seat. "You shut us down, and then we have to go elsewhere for information. That will be when your clients start to call you with their own questions."

"Fine. Let's do this. I want to help."

"Your caviar gets shipped and stored here, correct?"

Harry's eyes glassed over. "I guess you've done your homework."

"Let us interview your employees today. We'll do it right here in the building."

"I have no problem with that. I'll set it up."

I looked at Tara with a nod. "Did you take any of this personal order home? Did your wife or kids have any?"

"No. I can show you where I store the caviar, but the refrigerator is empty at the moment." He paused. "I suppose you're going to question my wife, too."

"If we still have our jobs in the morning," Tara said.

Harry's attitude took a dump. "On second thought, my employees are really busy today, so unless someone is under arrest, we'll have to do this another time."

"Fine. We can play this game."

"Look at the time. It's way past lunch and I'm starving," Harry poured his attention into his laptop. "I'm thinking soft-shell crab at LaPlace on Bourbon. I have a standing reservation." His eyes darted to me for a split second.

Why would he stress that? I pushed out of the chair. "Make sure you tell the mayor we were gentle."

"You have a sack, I'll give you that." Harry tapped away on the keyboard.

"I got nothing else. You, Tara?"

"Not a thing. Just know, Harry, that this was the nice visit."

He stood and walked to the door, making a broad show for us to exit. "When you come back with your warrant, if you come back, consider me, how do you say in cop-speak, lawyered up?"

We left Winning One knowing that Harry wasn't clean in this. *Dirty Harry*, I chuckled to myself. Tara called Dobson to have the company's financials opened up. I only prayed that Chance was in the dark to his activities. I figured my cell would be lighting up with Chance's call at any moment.

TWENTY-SIX

A platinum-blonde dancer showed Cozy to a locker and a spot at the chipped Formica counter to put on makeup. They were less catty than she imagined, but maybe that came from a perceived sisterhood, or misery loves company. Just like high school, all the lockers had padlocks, which Tabby hadn't mentioned. She undressed and put her clothes on little hooks near the top of her cubby, having to trust her stuff wouldn't get stolen.

Cozy fiddled with her costume while pondering Porter's death. He had cleaned up the Titus mess. That could have been so he could continue his sinister activities, knowing she wouldn't say anything. And then he kicked her out with no money, telling her she could keep the apartment if she paid the rent. He had balls. But, did someone give him those orders? They wanted her out on the street. And lastly, this job fell into her lap. She didn't believe in fate, but she did believe in manipulation.

She held confidence that if they wanted her dead, she'd be dead.

Where did Haley keep all the money she had made? Detective Peyroux would have mentioned a bank account. Haley wanted to stay off the grid and if her sister was a top earner, then she stashed it someplace. A secret place where there may be tens of thousands of dollars. It certainly wasn't in that dump of an apartment, unless the cops had found it. Could Tabby be the one who had it? Would Haley have trusted her?

Could Ray know her real name? If he did, the charade would continue as long as it had to. Keri Sullivan was the name of her childhood best friend who had moved to Empire and pumped out a kid with a fifty-year-old Denny's cook that refused to marry her. If they tried to look her up, at least there would a record of a female her age with that name.

The dancers checked out her body as she squeezed into her bikini – or maybe they noticed her scars. The main ones included a two-inch jagged line across her thigh from a close encounter with an alligator, a four incher across the small of her back from when she crashed into a bayou tree while knee-boarding, and a small vertical one on her stomach from falling through a pier of an abandoned camp. Most guys liked the scars. The bullet to her neck was the best one yet.

She finished dressing with a plaid skirt, white blouse and double ponytails sprouting from the top of her head. Her abdomen felt like she had done a hundred sit-ups and her nipples hurt. She had eliminated a cancerous, drug-dealing drain on society, and yet she had to close her eyes and take a deep breath, feeling light-headed in anticipation of her stripping debut.

Several girls pranced around on stage, which jetted out of the rear wall like a giant phallus. Portions of the lighted platform expanded into a dancing circle at the base, middle, and tip, all complete with a pole. Cozy was to do three ten-minute sets an hour, but no rotation on the floor for lap dances just yet. That suited her fine, as she felt exhausted just watching.

THE NIGHT WENT BETTER than expected, even with wearing the same outfit for every show. Initial count put her at three hundred and twenty-two dollars. Her mind spun with the possibilities of continuing this line of work. Her makeup-caked face looked slutty in the backstage mirror, but that was part of the package. Haley must have entertained the same thoughts of getting rich quick.

Ray surprised Cozy as she wiped off her glittered disguise, placing his large hands on her bare shoulders. The warmth felt comforting in a decadent way.

"You did as well as any first-timer. Congratulations."

"It was so surreal, like I was somebody else. And the money – wow."

"How would you like to make a little more before you leave?"

"What? Go back out again?" She tried to turn to face him.

"No. We have a VIP in the audience, one that was very taken with you."

"Who is he?"

"A VIP, which means he's a spender. Are you up for the challenge?" His hands smoothed her hair back.

"Give him a dance?"

"Yes, but in the Emerald Room with total privacy. The rules can be bent with this VIP. Do you know what that means?"

"He can touch my boobs?"

"Not exactly. In this case, what the customer wants, the customer gets." He took his hands off and spun the chair around to face him. "I'm giving you an out. The girls that do this extracurricular work… they want to. They're experienced at it. I won't hold it against you if you decline. For legal reasons, I'll tell you this has nothing to do with your job or getting paid. There have been girls that have refused. I've never fired a girl for saying no. I promise you this."

She waited a beat. One of these people killed her sister and once she hesitated, she would be done. It was just sex. It was just skin touching skin. The degradation and humiliation would be worth it if she dealt out justice in the end. She swallowed hard and squinted at him. "Morals are great for people with a bed and food. Can I do a couple of shots before I go in? Tequila?"

He clenched his jaw. "I'll have Diana send them back."

"Thanks."

"Five minutes," he said before walking away.

Moments later, Diana arrived with four shots and a beer. She looked down at Cozy through her nose, holding out the drinks for her to take. Her hand found the counter as if it kept her from falling. "You're the first girl who has ever been allowed to drink without a customer at their side."

"Is that a good thing?" Cozy imagined Ray would pounce on her like a panther once she blinked.

THE VIP WASN'T TOO horrible to look at, but Cozy's vision blurred with the shots of Tequila taken with the beer backer. Her equilibrium started to falter as her head buzzed. The dim room closed in on her, but she focused on the task at hand.

The older gentleman's casual attire still looked expensive. The dance in the Emerald Room started normal enough with him watching through dim lighting as her hands massaged her body to a slow Journey song. But things changed when he took her by the hips, pulling her G-string to her ankles without warning or hesitation. A wave passed through her stomach and she fought not to throw up. *This was real.*

His hands streaked up her thighs and around her ass. She almost bit her tongue when his finger penetrated. It took several minutes of clumsy foreplay before he suggested she return the favor with her hand. If she could just get him to finish before anything else happened…

Two minutes into the hand job, she felt something hard tap her head. She hadn't noticed that he had pulled out a gun and placed it against her temple.

"What are you doing?"

"Does this scare you?" His hard expression reminded her of a mad drill sergeant.

"You don't need that. I'm doing what you want." Cozy's head tilted with the pressure.

"Maybe you need incentive to do a good job."

"I'll do a good job."

"Maybe I want to blow your brains out as I cum."

"You're scaring me."

"Good. I want you scared. I want you to act like I'm forcing you. Are you a good actress?"

"Yes."

"Then act like this gun has bullets. Act like I just broke into your bedroom. Cry if you can."

That wouldn't be a stretch. Cozy snapped into the character he wanted. Her eyes watered. She bit her lip and cringed at the sight of the gun. He pulled her fingers away from his erection and smiled, commanding silently to go down on him. His erection blurred and the room swayed.

"No, please. Not my mouth." This kind of acting wasn't a problem.

"That's good," he hissed.

With a small Tequila belch, she closed her eyes and pictured Haley's bloated corpse in the river. With that anger, she found the strength to guide her lips to the target while leaving her own body to join her sister back in the bayou. The tear that rolled down her cheek meant nothing to her, but she sensed he was pleased.

The man clawed at her hair, bringing her back into the room. He… it… was smaller than Ashton, clean and manicured and smelling of fresh soap. She thanked God for that. After ten minutes, he finished in spasms like an epileptic, the gun pointing skyward. He collected himself as if he had lost his dignity. Cozy held her lips tight while searching for somewhere to spit. His hand found her shoulder.

"Swallow it." The barrel of the gun touched her nose.

She closed her eyes, already having built up a pool of saliva. With a deep breath and a single flex of her esophagus, she sent it down, hoping it wouldn't come right back up with the Tequila. As her eyes dried, she stood, but he caught her wrist.

"Wait. Open your mouth."

"Why?"

"I want to make sure."

"Okay…" Her mouth opened and the VIP used his fingers to search inside, checking as closely as a dentist. Once satisfied, he handed her a beer to drink as if a reward. He nodded and then pulled up his pants, barely having smiled through any of it.

"I have to be careful about leaving traces behind, you understand."

"You don't have to explain."

The man finally cracked a grin and exited without a farewell. Cozy entered the backstage bathroom to vomit with the urgency of having a terrible case of diarrhea. Opening the stall door triggered the upchuck reflex and her stomach evacuated. She flushed, pushed her hair from her face and then rinsed her mouth out with Scope, coming to grips with the world she had entered.

She dressed like a sloth to hid her anxiety, placing her stage clothes in her bag. She left the other girls with flimsy goodbyes. It was early morning and the main room was mostly cleared. She stopped at the bar.

"Tequila me again, please. Make it two."

The bartender didn't move. "Mr. Corondelet?"

Ray stepped up to the bar. "Pour."

Cozy turned to face him, wiping under her eyes. "Am I fired?"

"Fired?"

"I don't think he liked me."

Ray kept eye contact for a moment, holding out a fold of bills. "Keri, Keri, Keri. He loved you. Loved the tears. Makes that kind of man feel powerful. This was a big test. Not all the girls pass. Do your shot."

"Test?" Cozy tilted the glass into her mouth, welcoming the stinging effect. She slapped it down onto the bar and did the second shot while staring Ray down. With her eyes watering again, she flipped through the money.

"This is five hundred dollars."

"You may have just invited yourself into a higher income bracket."

"He seemed… I just thought…"

Ray touched her chin and then returned to his office.

She had over eight hundred dollars from one night alone and she hadn't even been on the main floor. Money was a great incentive to hook these girls. Little do they know they're being indoctrinated to be slaves. She shouldered her bag and walked for the exit where a bouncer stood guard. She kept a poker face, something she had become adept at.

"Hi, I'm Vince." He held his hand out.

Jesus. Will this night ever end? "Hi, Vince." *Tabby thinks you're a dick.*

"Hell of a first night," he said. "Going in the Emerald Room with that guy. He doesn't come in too often 'cause he likes to see the new girls. A couple times he just walked in, took a look around and just walked back out. He's very picky. Might not be a coincidence he came in tonight."

Vince was a solid-framed Italian and ruggedly so, not lacking in confidence. He had the bad-boy stubble and large hooked nose. His black T-shirt fit over a well distributed layer of fat on muscle, telling her that he was cock-strong. There were many like him in Manchac. He probably was a wealth of information, but she remembered the warnings.

"I did pretty good," she said noncommittally.

"You're straight from the bayou aren't you? We used to have a girl here with that Cajun accent. I dig that accent."

She pointed at the door. "I'm going to go."

Vince stopped her, but gently. "Let's get a drink. I get off in fifteen."

"I'm not supposed to see you socially."

"What, are we in friggin' Nazi Germany?"

Cozy paused. She couldn't help a grin. "I have to go to the Moon Walk."

"This late?"

"It's something I've been meaning to do. It's personal."

"You can't go alone. That place is deserted at night and it attracts creeps who'd love to get a hold of chick like you."

"I can take care of myself. Been doing it my whole life."

"I'll bet."

"So, I'm going."

"To the Moon Walk." He stepped aside.

"To the Moon Walk." She gave him a second glance while straightening her Saints cap.

Dressed in jeans, ratty K-Swiss, and a plain T-shirt, Cozy zipped through pockets of die-hard tourists under a near full moon until hitting St. Peter Street. She acquired a Lucky Dog on the corner, and devoured it while heading toward the river. The Jackson Square psychics and performers would be setting up for morning in a couple of hours. Stragglers and other service industry workers meandered in front of the St. Louis Cathedral. Cozy made it point to avoid cops or look anyone in the eyes.

Once over Decatur, she journeyed around the side of the vacant stadium steps used for talented public performers and followed the sidewalk to the pay parking lot. A few feet further brought her to the decorative sign commemorating the Moon Walk, named for the ex-Mayor Moon Landrieu.

The Moon Walk was deserted like Vince had said, not a soul in sight. The Crescent City Connection hung over the Mississippi with red and white lights flashing between beams. With clenched fists, she found the steps leading into the murky depths of the Mississippi, the place where the locals toss the ashes of loved ones at the end of the St. Anne's Parade during Mardi Gras. Did that make it ironic or just appropriate that her sister ended up here? The black water moved with impossible momentum, shimmering and bubbling against the banks, just as Haley must have.

"Quite a view," a deep male voice said.

Cozy turned as if a cold beer had been placed on her back. "Oh, God. Vince. You scared the shit out of me."

"Sorry." His beefy hands came up in surrender, however, one held a bottle of Jack Daniels. "Right when you left, Tabitha let me off, so I lifted this bottle and tried to catch up. I'll admit I did follow you for a few minutes 'cause you got one hell of an ass on you."

She faced the river as Vince warmed to her side, offering the bottle. His body seemed to take up the entire walkway. Already in a fuzz from the Tequila, she took a stiff belt from the bottle and handed it back. The pier felt like a cliff, high up over a gorge and she was just inches from falling. All it would take was a push… a tap. She wrapped her arms around her body, despite the warm night air.

"Yep, nice view."

"This is what was so important you had to do? I don't get it." His fingers brushed her hair over her shoulder.

"My momma took me here when I was a little girl. I promised myself I'd come back and see it in her memory. After tonight, I was feeling particularly low and I wanted her with me in spirit. Now was the time."

"That's deep. You know, this is right where that dancer's body was found."

"Oh, yeah?" For the first time, Cozy thought her voice sounded different… like a woman's. "What you know about that?"

He took a pull from the bottle and passed it on. "I know she must have done something wrong to end up there."

"Why does it have to be her fault?"

"Oh, no. I just mean being in the wrong place at the wrong time can be doing the wrong thing. I don't mean she deserved it."

She carefully kept her face neutral. "I guess."

"Bodies turn up all the time. It's so easy to dump a body in the river."

"I was told about you and Haley." She slipped her hand inside her jeans pocket to feel the end of the switchblade.

"Let's not talk about her." Vince put his arm around her shoulder. His nose inhaled the scent of her hair and he pecked her cheek.

"Vince. I can't."

He turned Cozy to face him. "This is a romantic place, isn't it?"

"At the right time… with the right person."

"What? Something wrong with me? C'mon, you're a stripper."

"So, that makes me easy?"

"Easier, maybe." He winked, showing his dimples.

"Funny, asshole."

Vince stared at her with the same dead eyes see had seen on Tray the day she confronted him about the rape; the same eyes of her father as he stumbled through the house looking for Haley. She imagined jumping into the water, letting the current take her away without a fight. That, or bashing the bottle over his head.

She pushed his arms away from her body. "Vince, I just swallowed and threw up the load of our special VIP and then replenished with Tequila and a Lucky Dog. You don't want to kiss me and I don't want to kiss you. At least not right now."

"When you put it that way."

She rested her hand on his shoulder, taking control. "Look, let's go sit on that bench over there and talk and drink a bit."

Vince lit up. "Talk? What a novel idea."

They sat about a foot apart, each taking a swallow from the bottle. Despite this adventure, as Tabitha put it, she wouldn't be around long enough for Vince to become abusive. He had that cat and the canary stare. If his forehead was a movie screen, it would be playing the two of them having sex. He took large drinks, completing each with some Italian phrase - *Il buon volte roll* - and a smile.

Cozy copied him, phonetically repeating his phrase. "What does that mean?"

"Let the good times roll."

"Ah, the Italian version. That's cool."

"I forgot how nice it is out here."

She decided to push a little bit. "It's kind of creepy to know that girl was right over there... having worked at the same place as us."

Vince played with the cap on the bottle, screwing it on and off. "Yeah. Nobody wants to talk about it at the club. Like it's a jinx or something."

"Have the police been around asking questions? I'm not exactly good with them."

"No. Haley was what you might call an independent."

"So, there are no records of her working?"

"Ray told us not to lie about it if asked, but not to volunteer anything, either."

"Tabitha said you dated her."

"Yeah, but we broke up like a year ago. When Ray started having her do the private parties, he didn't want her with me and I understand that. It's a business. Oops. Just burped up Jack. I think we need another bottle."

"Private parties?"

"Yeah, big parties with political types. Just an excuse to have sex." Vince inspected the remaining inch of whiskey in the moonlight. "What kind of trouble you in with the cops?"

"Petty shit. I'm sure I'm on surveillance shoplifting and stuff like that. I'm broke. The cops chased me down Pirate's Alley after I stole a beignet off a woman's plate."

"That's hysterical. You probably gave that woman a story to tell for the rest of her life. If you're worried about cops, you should be aware that some come into Molly's when they're off- duty."

"I'm more or less in disguise at that point."

"True, dat."

"So, how do I get Ray to invite me to these parties? I need the cash."

"You blow me first, then I recommend you to Ray." His cheeks inflated with a grin.

"Right. I was warned about you."

He laughed. "I figured. But, I guess you like to live dangerously."

"Up to a point, Vince. Up to a point." Cozy started to feel warm, but still in control. She waited until he spoke again.

"Tabby's protective of her girls. What'd she tell you about me?"

"Something about you making one quit."

"Ms. Wheelhouse has a way with words, but it's not always the truth. Sometimes that shit is two-sided. It takes two to tango, you get me? That dead Cajun chick…" He pointed at the river. "…she liked to argue and knew how to push my buttons."

"She asked for it, is that what you're saying?" Cozy jerked away involuntarily. She didn't want to give too much away, but at the same time she could feel her face blanching as the blood drained away in horror. Could he have done it? Could it be that simple?

"No." Vince let out a defeated breath. "Did I set out to hit her? Was it premeditated? No, of course not, but in the heat of it…" He clenched his fists up near his chest like he was belting out a song. "…in the moment, when words are flying back and forth… hurtful words… it happened. That bitch said some things she shouldn't have."

She recovered quickly, shrugging and looking into the black water. "Like some bitches do."

"You get it." He slurred a bit. "I did like her, though. But, she could be mean, too. That is the honest truth."

"We are who we are, right?" Cozy asked.

"Right. And we all regret something."

"What do you regret, Vince?"

"Things." His head dipped.

Cozy thought he was right at the drunk-honesty threshold. "Are you sorry you hit women?"

"Not women… wo-man. Just the one. Because she had a mouth. And yes, I'm sorry she made me hit her."

Bastard. "Did you kill that girl?" Her voice stayed light, teasing.

"Like I'd tell you if I did. Am I sitting on the magical confession bench here?" A moment passed and then he laughed, building to a cackle. "No, I didn't. Fuck, no. I can tell you some things, though. I can tell you just what she was into."

"I wish you would, because you're two for two with scaring the shit out of me."

"Get real, Keri. We don't work in no office with cubicles, making investments and crunching numbers before going home to a family and two-car garage. We're types."

"Types? Like I'm a slut and you're a bad-ass?"

"We're not nuns and priests." He cackled. "You notice violence and economic status go hand-in-hand?"

Cozy closed her eyes instead of joining Vince in his laughter. Vince could have killed Haley, but her instincts said not. Still, he had information she needed. For a moment she envisioned stabbing and pushing him in the river, but instead, she quickly stood. "Listen, I got in with an old guy for a place to stay because I had no other choice. Now, I can get a hotel room until I make rent money. You want to walk with me to get my shit?"

"As long as I don't have to walk a straight line, I'm with you. And you don't need no hotel. You can stay at my place."

"Bad idea, Vince."

"Sleep on my sofa." He belched and blew it out. "Crappity-crap-crap. That Jack just hit me."

"And the next thing you know, I'll have a black eye."

Vince spun to face away from her. He head dipped below his shoulders. "Fuck. Knew I shouldn't have said anything."

"Vince?" Cozy circled to face him again.

His cheeks were wet. "I can't believe I hit her." He wiped his eyes. "I hit a woman. My mom would disown me."

Cozy took him by the wrist and led him across a set of old streetcar tracks and back onto Decatur. He didn't know how close he'd come to floating in the same spot as Haley.

THE COUPLE ENTERED Sal's dark, stale apartment in silence. Voices moved in a low bubble, but Cozy realized from the vibrating glow it was the television. Sal didn't percolate, so he must have been in the middle of his two hours of sleep.

She was careful not to bump anything as she collected her possessions. Not a significant sound was made, but Sal's radar was on. He stirred.

"That you, Cozy?"

"*Cozy?*" Vince asked, "Where do I know that name?"

Shit, another stupid mistake. "I gave him a fake name. Just go with it."

"I swear I've heard that name before. Wait a friggin' second. Haley's *sister* was named Cozy!" Vince grabbed her by both arms, almost pulling her off the floor. Her biceps screamed with pain.

Her knee shot into his groin. "Let me go."

"I'm getting my gun, you bastard." Sal's body shook with urgency.

Vince shrugged off the pain, and pushed Cozy down. She landed on her knees on the floor while Vince checked to see what Sal was doing. "I came with the lying bitch, old man. I didn't force my way in."

"Get the fuck out of my house." Sal pointed a shaky gun at him. "I used to be a cop."

Vince rushed Sal, knocking him to the ground. He slurred while sweeping his foot across the old man's butt. "Don't ever point a gun at me."

"Cozy, what's going on?" Sal questioned.

"What'r you doing with her, old man?" Vince grabbed the collar of the pajamas. His fist reared back, but paused when Sal raised the gun to Vince's nose and pulled the trigger.

Vince's head came apart as if from the inside. His limbs went stiff as he fell sideways off of Sal. She expected some kind of animated recoil from Sal, but like Vince, he wasn't moving. With a gasp as if she had come back to life, she jumped to Sal's side, but his mouth was open and his eyes were glassy. Did he have a heart attack or an aneurism? A stroke? She knew those blue pills fucked with blood pressure.

"Oh, Sal. I'm sorry." She inhaled until her lungs filled and ached.

Her time as a free woman grew short, but she balled her fists hard, remembering that the situation was still hers to control. His neighbors had to have heard the shot, but hopefully just rolled over, thinking it a dream. The burner cell Sal had mentioned sat near the lamp on the end table. She pocketed it, already having the number, and then ran a rag over the bathroom faucets, reminding her of the Titus clean up. Her analytical approached scared her. All the death she had experienced in her life had left her desensitized. She couldn't worry about her prints anywhere else, as an immediate exit was mandatory.

TWENTY-SEVEN

Dobson's call jolted me awake at 5:30 this morning. "Yeah?" I croaked into my cell. My dry mouth barely worked.

"You got a homicide in the Quarter." Dobson sounded sprite.

"A second case? Great."

"Nope. It's related to the Robicheaux case. Got a pen?"

I rushed to the address where a uniform stood guard at the door. He let me in where I met the CSU team already in action. Salvador Santiago had killed an intruder, or so it seemed. At six in the morning, the tenacious Forensics team worked nearby as I flipped through four pictures of Cozy printed from one of those home printers. Her breasts were on display, as if exploited by someone in the flesh trade. Her name and date were scribbled on the back. Were these two deaths unrelated to the pictures? I put the photos down and stood by the bodies.

Tara had told me to start without her, but her raspy voice and delayed responses told me she might've had a date last night, tied one on and gotten to bed very late. Good for her, she deserved it. Actually, I imagined the guy to still be with her.

Dr. Jerry had pulled out the wallet of the gunshot victim, one

Vincent Dean. I reenacted the scene in my head, considering there was no sign of break-in.

"Did Mr. Santiago open the door for Mr. Dean?" I mused, thinking aloud, but internalized my thoughts when Dr. Jerry glanced at me. The old man used to be a cop, so they could have known each other. But he sported a Molly's Girls shirt, which could have been bought as a souvenir, but he's big enough to be one of their bouncers. Would he be stupid enough to try to rob someone's house while identifying where he worked on his shirt? Or, old Salvador could have been a patron and Vincent walked him home. They argue, and Mr. Santiago gets in a scuffle he has no chance of winning. When Vince thought the old guy was out of commission, he got shot and the neighbor called the police.

I paced around the room, taking it all in.

Another scenario – Cozy tracked her sister to Molly's Girls, which was ground zero for the trafficking ring.

I walked the possible path they took, stopping by the recliner where Sal pulled the gun from the open drawer. Vince probably thought he could move quicker than Sal and that was a fatal mistake. Santiago shot him point blank, but what caused the old man's death?

"Looks like cardiac arrest." Dr. Jerry looked up at me from his knees. "He was old. Went quick."

"He shot him and then had a heart attack," I said, dismissing Cozy for a moment.

"Seems that way."

Seems would translate into *allegedly* in court of law. I hated that.

The spare bedroom looked to be used for storage and the occasional sleepover, due to the mattress and blankets on the floor. However, the dust on the boxes and furniture had been disturbed. Mr. Santiago had a recent guest—either Cozy or Vincent. The Viagra on the coffee table came to mind and the pictures of Cozy would indicate that Sal wasn't homosexual. My biggest question was if the crime scene had been staged by Cozy, or if she ran after the scene transpired.

I rejoined the crew and put on a pair of latex gloves. "Jerry, can I get into his cell?"

He glanced at my gloved hands like an afterthought. "Go ahead."

The cell sat atop his wallet, a thick leather tri-fold deal. A cell phone contained more info than a wallet ever could. The Samsung Galaxy came to life without needing a password. I checked his recent call history, but the last call was outgoing to his mother at two in the afternoon yesterday for forty-three minutes… a momma's boy. The picture gallery contained many photos of women, some I would guess to be strippers, but some were just headshots. I scrolled through, stopping at the sixth girl – there she was. Haley Robicheaux.

BACK AT THE STATION, Tara confirmed what we had assumed. "Vince was a bouncer at Molly's Girls." She put her cell down.

"Aponi claims Cozy still hasn't come home," I said.

"You think her mother's protecting her? Hiding her?"

"I don't think Aponi would do that. Cozy has the same line of thinking we do. If her revenge stopped with Porter, she wouldn't have run."

"Probably."

"So, Cozy finds ex-cop Sal, who gives her a mattress in return for some naked pictures. She tracks down Haley to Molly's Girls and hooks up with Bouncer Vince to see if he had anything to do with her sister's murder." I jotted down quick notes.

"Why take him to Sal's?" Tara stared at me for answers.

"Good question. She knows Sal has a gun?"

"So, once there, Sal doesn't like that Cozy brought home a boy, grabs his gun, and hilarity ensues."

"And Cozy runs."

"Yeah, but not because Vince is the one. Because that would be that. She's still digging."

Tara inspected her fingernails. "So, Cozy found Molly's Girls before we did."

"We need to find a connection between Harry Winslow and the owner of Molly's Girls. We should go see the owner tonight." I hesitated, looking at my notepad. "One Raymond Corondelet."

"I hate strip clubs. I always feel like I need to shower when I leave."

"I usually have to change my drawers."

"I so feel for your wife."

"Hey, you had your chance to object at the wedding."

Captain Dobson entered the floor with a man and a woman wearing business attire. Each of them glanced at us before heading into her office. Through the glass, we could see the seriousness of their discussion. Dobson had trouble controlling her cool.

"Feds?" I asked.

Tara shrugged as Superintendent of Police Gregory Thornberry burst onto the floor, dispensing with his normal greetings. He too, gave Tara and me a once over before opening Dobson's door and joining the debate.

"Think Harry kept true on his threat?" Tara said.

I pulled at my ear. "It's not far-fetched that this is some kind of high profile, D.C. Madam-type shit. I have this bad feeling Chance was right. We might have kicked a hornet's nest."

"Full of political wasps." Tara's wide eyes volleyed to me.

"Looking to… sting… us worker bees."

Tara frowned.

"What? Don't get pissed at me if you can't keep the metaphor going."

"Lord, do I feel sorry for your wife."

The muted conversation lasted ten minutes before the man and woman expedited out of the room. Dobson and the Super remained, speaking in a more casual manner considering their body language. Five minutes later, Thornberry left, however this time he acknowledged us with a nod of his head.

Dobson waved us into her office, shutting her door behind us.

"That looked intense, Cap." I sat, throwing my arm behind the chair.

"Feds?" Tara inquired.

Dobson eased into her chair. "Yes, Feds. It would seem that your questioning of Harry Winslow is interfering with an ongoing federal investigation."

"You gotta be kidding me."

"Thornberry ordered me to cease and desist in the questioning of any employees from Winning One about the Robicheaux murder. Basically, anyone associated with the company."

I faced Tara. "We must be close."

"Cap, we're on the cusp of exposing a trafficking ring." Tara looked ready to blast off into space.

Dobson picked up a tablet just to throw it back down. "Maybe they are, too. They said once they're through with their case, they'll share all their info."

"That's bullshit." I thought of Cozy out there alone. She was a scrapper, but she had to feel scared, out of her element.

"So, what do you really want us to do, Cap?"

She didn't answer. Then Dobson's phone rang, breaking the silence. "Captain Dobson here. Yes. Yes. Where? Isn't that…?" She wrote something down and looked at both of us. "They're on their way."

"What's up?" Tara asked.

"A body was found in an abandoned house in the East. The same house as Cozy Robicheaux's abduction."

"The same house?" I looked at Tara. "Titus?"

"Could be."

"That drug dealing punk?" Dobson asked.

"Sure." I pinched my chin in thought. "He was going to visit Haley and found Cozy instead?"

"But how did Cozy get the body to the East?" Tara asked.

"Maybe Porter took him still looking to get his hooks in Cozy. He knew the house was abandoned. One last act before they killed him."

Tara's eye shot to me. "Murder, now?"

"Maybe. They make it look like a suicide because Cozy recognized him. Whether Cozy killed Titus or not, Titus' body would draw too much attention to their operation. My money's on Porter transporting the body."

"I'll have his car towed in," Dobson said, pointing at me. "So, this means that you would be investigating Titus' murder, which would make Cozy Robicheaux or Edgar Porter the prime suspects, right?"

"Right." I agreed.

"And Cozy Robichaux didn't kill her sister, right?"

"Nowhere near a suspect." I confirmed.

"So Cozy has nothing to do with the Feds, correct?"

"That is correct, Cap." I stood along with Tara, not needing to look at the address she wrote down.

Dobson motioned for us to go. "I'll have a trooper see if Cozy returned to Manchac and pick her up if she did."

TWENTY-EIGHT

With Vince and Sal's death, Cozy had a hard time falling asleep, despite the Jack Daniels filtering through her liver. She had sat in the lotus position on the Day's Inn bed at three in the morning, enveloped in darkness. Murder surpassed anything stimulants could do. In an attempt to calm down, she imagined her happier childhood moments—the teasing, the chasing, the laughing, she had shared with her sister. And her favorite memory, the camping trip when she and Haley both slid into the same sleeping bag one chilly night. She had never felt so warm and safe and loved, and being wrapped in that memory allowed her to finally drift off.

The pampered accommodations at the Day's Inn on Canal Street impressed her, despite only semi-sleeping for three hours, dreaming she had become the Grim Reaper. She had figured Vince not to be Haley's killer, and yet he died anyway. He seemed the type to just hit women, not rent them out. If anyone at that club had anything to do with Haley's death, it would be Ray or possibly Tabby, if only indirectly.

Maybe she had brought Vince to Sal's place with the more sinister motive of creating a confrontation. Did she expect Sal to be calm about bringing that brute into his home? Vince deserved to be punished with ass-rape in prison for his sins, but not shot to death. And Sal died as a result of poor decisions and chemistry. She would have to reconcile those feelings at some point, but not now.

Cozy collected herself, needing to keep busy before meeting Tabby for a drink later in the day. She consulted a map of the Quarter taken from the lobby of the hotel, studying it to get intimately familiar with the city grid. When things get hairy, she was going to need an escape route. She thought about how well Ash had known the Quarter the few times he took her to Dr. Claire. Did he have that good a memory? Was he that good a navigator? No, not unless…

That bastard.

She pulled out the burner phone and dialed a number she knew by memory.

"Hello," her boyfriend's familiar voice answered.

She clenched her jaw, not bothering to disguise herself. "Meet me on the front steps of Harrah's at 3pm - today."

"Cozy?" Ash said, off-pitch.

"Front steps of Harrah's at 3pm" She hung up, fighting the urge to whip the cell at the wall. When she glanced to her right, her reflection in the mirror showed a sitting duck. She still looked too much like her old self.

THE WARM BREEZE tickled the tops of the Palm Trees that had been planted along the side of Harrah's Casino. The low-key exterior masked itself beautifully on the edge of the Central Business District, not sticking out as much as one would think. Cozy approached from the foot of Canal Street, keeping an eye out for Lucas, who always seemed to like to appear at the worst times.

She rounded the corner to the front of the casino to see Ash sitting on the second step, leaning against the railing as if he had lost his savings at the blackjack table. He looked different, less handsome then before she had left home. His hair was styled shorter than before and his sunglasses made him seem arrogant. His charm no longer had influence.

He finally noticed her storming toward him. "Why the hell didn't you tell me you knew where Haley was this whole time?"

He stood, but held onto the railing. "Cozy, what did you do to your hair? Is that you behind all that makeup?"

"Don't change the subject. How did you find out?"

He fidgeted and couldn't meet her eyes. "She didn't want me to tell you."

Cozy hopped up onto the third step and slapped his face. "She's my sister."

When she reared back for another, Ash caught her wrist. "She made me promise not to tell you. I loved her. You don't think I felt a world of guilt keeping this from my best friend?"

"Best friend? I thought you loved me. You were having sex with me while you were coming here to have sex with her? In what world does that make you the good guy?"

"I'm a shit, all right? A dick. But, we weren't having sex. Haley didn't want to be with me anymore. I *do* love you. But, Haley has my heart. She always had. I didn't want to let either of you down. You *are* my best friend."

"I'd sure hate to be your enemy." She broke from his grasp and almost shoved him over the rail. The people walking by had stopped to watch. "What exactly was she into? Give me something."

"She danced at Molly's Girls. That's all I know. She told me how that landlord was always watching her, too. I think *he* might've killed her."

"Maybe you couldn't handle her stripping for other men. You got blind with jealousy and lost control, since she 'has your heart' and all."

He stepped to her. "Jesus, Cozy. You're accusing me? You're crazy."

"You have no idea what's going on inside my head."

"I guess I don't. But are you sure this isn't just a convenient way to get rid of me?"

Cozy palmed her head with both hands. "Get rid of you? Convenient? Don't pull that shit with me. What you did is a bigger betrayal than the douche-bag trio raping me and don't you dare say that's a gray area because they're your friends." She wiped her dripping nose. "I didn't ask for it. It's not a gray area."

"Hales made me promise. I kept my promise. Either way, I guess someone would get betrayed."

"You know things about her life that're eating away at me to know."

"Hales wanted to get out of that apartment and into a house. I thought if I kept helping her, she'd get back with me. She wanted me to bring you here."

It took a good ten seconds for her breathing to relax while staring a hole through him. Then she spat, "I'm done here."

She pivoted to leave, but he grabbed her arm. "I knew there would come a day when I couldn't do any more for you. When you didn't need me around. Here it is."

"You still haven't apologized."

He kept his mouth closed as his eyes broke contact. She pushed him down the steps as pedestrians started pointing their cameras. However, the scene didn't escalate any further as Cozy rushed away down Canal Street, hearing her name shouted several times.

TWENTY-NINE

Noon hour approached as we came out of the house where the kidnapper had taken Cozy just months ago. Every piece of rotting furniture looked clear in the daylight. CSU had just put Titus in a body bag, telling us he had died from a stab wound to the heart several days ago. His killer had perfect aim. The place was still otherwise undisturbed from when it was cleaned by the hazmat crew.

I leaned against the car's fender with Tara at my side, thinking aloud, "Remember Cozy's puffy red cheek? What if Titus went looking for Haley and found Cozy? Cozy wanted to ask him questions, and Titus had other plans. Things got out of hand and he didn't realize she carried a switchblade. And if Titus had a gun, then Cozy now has a gun."

"This makes her someone to look at for the Vincent Dean murder."

"I don't know. Vince was found in the spot he was shot and Sal's heart attack makes sense. It was his gun. She would have had to stage the scene perfectly. I don't see Jerry disproving the obvious theory. At the very most, she was present at the time."

We stared at each other as the sun intensified, each going through our process of deduction when my cell rang. "Yeah, Cap."

"The troopers said Cozy's not at her home in Manchac. Hadn't returned since she left with you, according to the mother. Plus, traces of blood were found in Porter's trunk. Most likely Titus."

"So, he at least disposed of the body. Thanks, Cap. I noticed you called me instead of Gray." I glanced at my partner.

"She said you're doing fine."

"She's such a liar. We'll be in shortly." I hung up.

"Too bad we can't grill Corondelet about Harry Winslow," Tara said.

"We can grill Corondelet about Dean, Haley and Titus. That's not off limits, right? We'll do that later tonight at the club when we can talk to the whole staff. Plus, we can make him more uncomfortable at his work. For now, let's go back to Manchac and put a little more pressure on Aponi Robicheaux."

"Let's do it." Tara patted my shoulder before getting in the car. "You think old Harry Winslow, Esquire could be a patron of Molly's Girls? Could that be the Haley-Winslow-caviar connection?"

"I'd say that's a definite possibility."

"So, Harry or another employee of Winning One or someone at Molly's killed Haley after a party?"

I started the engine. "A good theory. Winslow has a political party with Molly Girl strippers walking around." I adjusted the air conditioning. "Either way, I'm willing to bet Raymond Corondelet is in bed with Winslow."

Tara laughed. "All this from a Jane Doe in the river. So, we go to Manchac?"

"Yee-haw."

THE DRIVE to Manchac just before rush hour took a bit longer than the first time. It allowed me to think of how much I've become involved in the Robicheaux's lives and how I've extracted myself from my own family's lives. Too many cops fall into that hole and it won't be me.

The house appeared sturdier on the second visit, like it had withstood many hurricanes. No movement registered through the window, so I knocked loudly on the screen door.

"Hello? Aponi?"

Tara's attention focused on the road and nearby Cypress Trees for surprises. I couldn't blame her. When the locals get wind that the law was after one of their own, they could get ornery.

I rapped my knuckles on the wood again, this time hearing something stir inside. A moment later, Ashton from the picture answered. The side of his face was red with a small cut as if he had been punched. "Hello?"

"I'm Detective Peyroux."

"Ashton."

"Is Ms. Robicheaux here?"

I noticed he was barefoot when he moved aside to let us in. His clothes hung from his frame like hand-me-downs. "You're the one who took Cozy to New Orleans."

I nodded.

"And now she's missing," he accused.

"Have you talked to her recently?"

"Hell, no." He charged forward toward the kitchen like the man of the house, speaking over his shoulder. "I actually just got back from looking for her in the Quarter. Of course, I didn't find her."

"There's a difference between being missing and not wanting to be found."

Aponi came from the hallway as if she had just awoken, but not surprised to see us. "Detective Peyroux, perhaps you can explain why the state troopers were looking for Cozy. They certainly wouldn't say."

"No one knows where she is. You're not concerned?"

"She called me. Told me she was taking care of Haley's paperwork, so I assumed the police would know where she is."

"Haley's body hasn't been released yet, Aponi." Tara told her.

Aponi gave Ashton a glance. "She's staying in the Quarter to punish me."

Tara stressed her voice. "She's in trouble… serious trouble."

"Let's have some tea." She turned before anyone could argue.

Ashton, Tara and I sat at the kitchen table. Aponi seemed to need to keep her hands busy, a coping mechanism I'd guess.

She took a pitcher out of the refrigerator. "I've never been able to control her. She always sought out danger, that one."

"I'm going back to try to find her again tomorrow," Ash confirmed.

"How many times did you visit Haley at her apartment?" I asked.

Ashton's eyes grew. "None. What do you mean?"

"We interviewed the landlord after discovering Haley's body. He placed you there," I sounded convincing, knowing that Porter never actually said Ashton's name.

He blew air out his lips. "He's wrong. He might've described someone that looked like me. If I knew where she was, I would have brought her home. Or at least let Cozy and Ms. Aponi know she was safe."

"Sure. I can buy that. What about you, Tara?"

"Sure." She shrugged.

Aponi placed two glasses of tea down on top of scuffed plastic Dixie Beer coasters. "You said Cozy was in trouble. What kind of trouble?"

Tara answered. "She might be involved in the murder of a local drug dealer."

"You must be mistaken," Aponi shot back. "But, I'm sure he deserved it."

Ashton chuckled, his pimples glowing.

"What's so funny?" I asked.

"You ever see her dismantle an alligator? Or shoot the eye out of a nutria from fifty yards? You don't mess with Cozy where Haley's concerned."

"She even saved Haley from her father," I added.

The blood left Aponi's face as she stood and wiped down a spotless counter. "Ashton's opinion is a bit biased. What proof do you have of this murder?"

"We can't go into the specifics, but we're just looking to question her for now."

"Well, I know this will all be cleared up as soon as we find her."

I inspected my glass of tea as I slowly spun it in a circle. "Aponi, I know what happened with their father and the stress that abuse must have created."

"Girls tend to exaggerate… not remember things properly."

"Nevertheless, what Cozy believes is what's important at the moment, true or not. Does Cozy have any psychological disorders? Schizophrenia? Bi-polar? Rage issues?"

Again, the two of them glanced at each other. Aponi said, "No, but Dr. Clair, her therapist, thought she needed more therapy past what the court mandated."

"What's Dr. Clair's full name?" Tara asked, taking out a notepad.

"Dr. Clair Shipman. She's got an office in Kenner," Ashton offered. "I took her a few times."

Aponi's eyes smiled at him. "Ashton's been so good to both my daughters."

"Both? How so?" I knew, but I asked anyway.

Ashton spoke softly. "I was Hale's boyfriend for a while."

I took a long drink from the delicious glass of tea, thinking Ashton could have information we need. "Would you say you loved both of them?"

Ashton shifted on his feet. "Love? I think I loved Haley. I might've been falling in love with Cozy. I think I'm too young to know for sure."

Aponi grabbed my tea to refill it. She spoke toward the ceiling, "You think she killed this drug dealer because he killed Haley?"

"It's possible. My guess is, she was attacked and it was self-defense. The most she'd get is tampering with a crime scene."

Ashton said, "Would it be that big a deal if she keeps killing scumbags until she finds the guy?"

"You think it's no big deal to kill someone."

"If they're scum." His lip curled like Elvis Presley.

"You want her to possibly kill an innocent man?" I asked and looked to Aponi.

Aponi moved to the seat next to me, leaning in close to my face. "Detective, my husband is dead. My oldest daughter ran away and was killed. If my youngest daughter leaves me, I'm going to be all alone."

Her wrinkles grew to show her age, yet her eyes were that of a twenty-year-old.

"It seems you have Ashton."

She paused. "Not that it's any of your business, but Ashton's Daddy, Paul Bergeron, is sweet on me and also comes over often. Our families are close."

"How often does Ashton come by when you're home alone?"

"What are you trying to say?" Ashton's voice rose. "I don't care if you are a cop, I'll bust your nose."

Aponi and I shared a look where the meaning was understood. Her shoulders slumped and her head dipped, before establishing her posture again. "Nothing is going on, Detective. What kind of lady would that make me?"

"Lonely… desperate."

Aponi slapped my face, but I had been building to that. I needed her to open up, to expose herself, and my seeming like a total dick was a small price to pay. My eyes returned to hers, which never wavered, piercing like a tribal warrior.

Ashton stood rigidly. "I don't have to listen to this shit." He left the kitchen through the back door, slamming the screen against the wood frame.

She scolded me. "That boy's been like a son to me, a man around the house for me, fixin' things and whatnot. That's what we do for each other out here. I wouldn't expect someone from that toilet of a city to understand." She pointed to the window behind the ragged curtains as if she could see New Orleans from here.

"I apologize for Detective Peyroux," Tara said. "He's used to dealing with thugs and witnesses who keep their mouths shut. It's frustrating."

I blinked in agreement. "Sorry if I was harsh. Maybe you should go talk to him. We'll let ourselves out."

"I don't want you back here. Send someone else if there's news."

She met Ashton out on the pier who burst into an indecipherable rant. I picked up my napkin and placed it around Ashton's glass, a nice gift for Dr. Jerry to process.

THIRTY

They planned to meet at a Daiquiri shop on Bourbon Street because Cozy wanted to try the famous frozen creation. Tabby people-watched at a small table with a large white cup and straw, not noticing her newest squire glide in. Cozy purchased a Jungle Juice in a small Styrofoam cup without an I.D. from the apathetic bartender. She pretended to search for a table before getting close enough to face her boss. She took off her glasses and Tabitha did a double-take.

"Keri? What in the world did you do to yourself?"

"Whatever do you mean?"

"It's so short and auburn. Look at those highlights. Makes you look fierce."

She sat down. "You like?"

"It's stunning, like an after picture. Plus, with that hair, it'll be easier to wear those wigs."

"That kind of leads us to why we're here."

"Shoot." Tabby wrapped her cherry-red lips around her straw.

"I can assume you haven't heard."

"Heard what?"

"I saw a news report this morning. That bouncer you warned me about – Vince? He was murdered early this morning."

"What?" Tabitha's mouth hung open. "Ray didn't call me."

"Maybe he hasn't heard, either. I don't know the details, but he was shot in some old guy's house in the Quarter."

She dug in her clutch for her phone. "I have to call Ray."

"Wait a second. Me and Vince were together last night."

"Keri, you didn't…?"

"Sex? No, God, no. But, he was alive when I left him."

"After I warned you?"

"He followed me to the Moon Walk. I had no idea. We ended up talking a while. That was it."

"Were you involved in this shooting?"

"I left him on Decatur Street with an empty bottle of Jack. But the cops are sure to come sniffing around Molly's. I can't be there for that."

"If you didn't kill him, you'll be fine."

"In what world? People saw us together. The police will put together that I'm dancer where he worked. Tabby, I can't talk to any cops."

She closed her eyes. "So, what kind of trouble are you in?"

"No warrant for my arrest, if that's what you're wondering."

"We have no paperwork on you, so that's good. You're not the first dancer to be skittish of the cops."

"So, I can maybe skip tonight?"

"No. Ray wants to talk to you. I'll call you when it's safe. You have a cell?"

"I do, but no one else has my number."

"You have a phone and no one has the number? You are truly alone, aren't you?"

Cozy reached out and put her hand over Tabby's. "Just keeping a low profile."

"Give me the number."

WHETHER OR NOT MY acquisition of the glass with Aston's prints would hold up in a court of law remained to be seen. I entered it into evidence just before Dr. Jerry left for the day. He promised to get the prints in the morning as he paved through his workload, but my breath I would not hold. After dinner with my family where I made sure to stay engaged with meaningful conversation, I left again to have my interview with Raymond Corondelet.

Molly's Girls had the typical cast of patrons, including a mix of obvious tourists. Like most other places we investigated with an alcohol license, Tara and I located the bartender first. They tended to have a wealth of information, not to mention their own take on things. The longhaired, blond German prototype stopped in front of us and stared me down, smelling our badges.

"Two Cokes, please."

He silently obliged and I left a five on the bar, which probably didn't cover it.

"I assume everyone here heard about Vince?" I asked.

"Yep. That old cop shoot him?"

"We're still working the investigation." Tara said.

I added, "And I understand Haley Robicheaux also worked here?"

"I don't ever learn their real names. You talking about the girl found in the river?"

We both nodded.

"That was Lacy Mastergator."

Tara looked at me. "Mastergator?"

I spoke as if she was a child. "Like masturbator... someone who masturbates. I'll use it in a sentence..."

"I get it. Masta-gater. That's a new one."

The bartender chuckled. "The audience loved it. She'd come out in redneck costumes with a stuffed alligator."

"What's a redneck costume?" I asked.

He pushed the five back towards me. "Overalls, Daisy Dukes, or shirts tied up in a knot under her tits. That kind of stuff."

"What do you think happened to her?"

He settled onto his elbows as he leaned on the bar. "C'mon detectives; stripper, alcohol, drugs, money, sex... any number of things could have got her killed. I don't get close with any of them, so I wouldn't know what she was into."

"Fair enough. Is Raymond Corondelet here?"

"Yep, in the back."

We followed the bartender's finger to a little hallway in the rear corner, dodging a dancer whose body was barely hanging on to its youth. The bouncer allowed us safe passage into a corridor where I found an open door. The man inside stood as he waved us in.

"Detectives, I'm Raymond Corondelet, but please call me Ray. We were expecting your visit. Have a seat."

Other officers had told me that Molly's had a nice working relationship with the NOPD. Any place with a liquor license had to in this city. My cop buddies gave no warning of any underhanded dealings because a cop would do most anything not to be exposed. I noticed that one of Ray's many pictures on the wall was of him and my friend Mayor Chance Picaud, smiling at some dinner function.

"Mr. Corondelet... Ray, I'm Detective Peyroux and this is Detective Gray. Do you mind if we ask you and your employees a few questions about Mr. Dean?"

"Of course not. Quite a few of my customers are policemen. You should come by to enjoy some of the perks we offer the boys and ladies in blue."

"We'll see."

Tara stood. "How about I go talk to the staff while you chat with Mr. Corondelet? We'll cut our time in half so we can get out of here."

"Sounds good, the quicker the better," I said.

Ray watched her leave his office before speaking to me. "Vince's murder has shaken us all up. I actually just got off the phone with his mother. I'm going to take care of the cremation costs."

"That's kind of you."

"We liked Vince a lot. So, my staff and I are totally at your disposal."

"Can you give me your overall impression of Mr. Dean?"

"Sure, but from what I understand, you know who killed him. That old man, right?"

"There are just some unanswered questions. We need to understand what happened that night."

"Vince was a great bouncer, good with the customers and with the dancers. I heard he had some personal issues outside of work, but he never brought them here."

"Like what?"

"This is second-hand, mind you, and please don't repeat this to his poor, grieving mother, you know how Italian moms are, but I heard he was abusive to his girlfriends. Possessive, too. That's what's so strange about his murder; he wasn't a burglar or gay. Not that I know of."

"Everyone has secrets, Ray. Speaking of his girlfriends, do you remember his dating a Haley Robicheaux?"

He shifted slightly. "I feel I need to be honest."

"Please."

"Haley Robicheaux came to work here on contract a couple of years ago."

I didn't react. "Explain contract."

He sighed. I couldn't tell if this was rehearsed or not. "Contract is kind of like an extended trial basis."

"Off the books."

"Yes. She was the type of girl that brought in men, and alcohol is where I make my money. What she made on stage is what she kept. I didn't pay her a dime. She gave me a cut for use of my establishment and we kept it at that."

"Don't worry. I'm not vice or the IRS. We're here to help each other."

He nodded. "Vince was dating her for a while, but they broke up a year ago."

"Her death wasn't a good enough reason to contact the NOPD?"

"I'm ashamed I didn't, but I didn't want to lose other girls through fear, or lose customers for that matter, with uniformed police sniffing around. It was selfish, and the poor girl deserved better. She – Haley – had her own thing going on the side. From what I understand, she was basically prostituting herself, and I was cutting back her hours here. I was ready to let her go."

"And then your problem was solved for you."

He smiled and nodded before snapping his index finger at me. "I understand how that technique would draw information from reluctant witnesses, so I won't hold that comment against you personally. It means nothing to me to fire someone, so why would I resort to murder? Plus, if my girls started thinking they'd be murdered, I'd be ruined."

"And now Vince is murdered."

"Yes." His lids dropped.

"Do you know of anyone here who would want both of them dead?"

"Like a girl that was seeing Vince and was jealous of their past relationship?"

"Perfectly said."

"No one I know of was dating Vince. Tabitha tells all the girls not to date the bouncers."

"Tabitha?"

He pointed to one of the pictures on the wall. "Tabitha Wheelhouse, my manager. What about this retired policeman I saw on the news? You don't think he shot him?"

"There may have been a third party in the house."

"Well, that complicates things for you."

"So, you know nothing of Vince's personal life."

"Nothing." He shook his head.

"Anything else you can think of about Haley?"

"I'll admit, when she first came to Molly's, she was one of my favorites, but this past year, I bowed out of her affairs. Some of the other girls might be able to point out certain customers that especially liked her, but other than that, I can't help you."

I held up a picture of Cozy. "Have you ever seen Vince with this girl?"

He studied the picture. "Keri Sullivan. She just started working here on a probationary period, but she doesn't have any ties to Vince that I know of. She's not from New Orleans."

"We have a witness that places them together hours before his murder," I lied. "Is Keri coming into work tonight?"

"She should be here now, actually."

"Can you call her?"

"She doesn't have a phone. I don't even know where she's staying, but Tabitha might have that information. I figure she's in a motel somewhere. As soon as she's set up in an apartment, I'll have her fill out the proper paperwork."

"Naturally. I guess that's about all for now, but I do want to ask Miss Wheelhouse about Keri before I leave." I retrieved the photo of Cozy, then motioned to the wall. "Tell me, how do you and the mayor know each other?"

He smiled, glad I noticed. "That was taken at LaPlace on Bourbon at its grand opening. Mayor Picaud didn't realize I was the owner of Molly's Girls or he might not have taken that picture with me, but I promised it was for my private use. Nice man. We talked for a while."

I stood, handing him my card. "If Keri doesn't show by the time we finish questioning your staff, can you give me a call when she does? Otherwise, I'll try back tomorrow."

"Of course. Good luck, detective."

I almost expected to feel a hundred folded up against my fingers after Ray reached out and shook my hand. Before I exited his office, I turned. "By the way, what's Keri's stage name?"

"Spitfire. A real find, that one."

THIRTY-ONE

Her vantage point from the crowded balcony lining Bourbon Street kept Cozy well hidden from view. The burner cell rang for the first time. She examined it like a bomb that had just started a countdown, but then she relaxed. Only one person had the number, unless it was someone trying to reach Sal.

"Hello," Cozy answered, putting her finger into her other ear.

"All clear, Sugar. Ray wants you here right away."

"I'm just around the corner. Be there in a sec. And Tabby, thanks."

Cozy kept her wits about her, waiting for a cop to blip on her radar like an enemy warplane. She entered Molly's expecting an ambush if Ray had betrayed her, however she rushed to the changing room uninterrupted. Coincidently, she brought a police bikini for the first show. Before she could undress, Ray poked his head in.

"Keri, you're not working tonight. Put your clothes back on and come in my office."

Cozy felt her blood pressure drop, glancing at the other girls. "Sure, be right there."

She entered the office for only the second time, but with more confidence.

"Am I doing something else tonight?"

"Close the door."

She did as instructed, having a flashback of the greasy detective that had questioned her in an interrogation room after shooting her father.

"You look like you should be on the cover of Vogue. Any particular reason?"

"I needed a change."

"The cops questioned us about Vince and the murdered girl that worked here." He waited for Cozy to respond, but she didn't. He continued. "I noticed you were conveniently absent. Tabitha said you were going to be late."

"Yeah, had an errand."

"You want to tell me why the cops showed me a picture of you."

She twitched a bit, but then collected herself. "Vince followed me to the Moon Walk last night and we talked a while. I suppose there could have been a witness or a security camera."

He spoke in a conversational tone. "And the picture he showed me? How'd that come to be in his possession?"

"My drug addict mother gave them pictures when I ran away. With all my petty bullshit, they don't like me very much."

Ray stood and rounded the desk, stepping behind Cozy. His hands rubbed her shoulders. This time, the grip threatened her collarbones. "Can you imagine how I feel about cops questioning me in my own office?"

"They aren't after you or me, right? They're investigating Vince."

His manicured nails sunk deeper. "They asked me about one of my dancers who also turned up dead. And they asked about you."

"I can't be blamed for Vince following me." She resisted pulling out the switchblade to cut off each finger embedding in her flesh.

"Is there anything else you're not telling me, Keri? Anything at all?"

"Who's clean in this business, Ray? I used to shoplift. I stole things. I made bad decisions. Ray, you're hurting me."

"Sorry." Ray let go and nodded with a flat expression. "I had to tell them I recognized you, because one of the staff was sure to say they saw you dancing."

"I understand. I'll leave."

"Relax. I have an alternate plan but only if you're on board." Ray returned to his chair.

"You know I am." Her shoulders and neck burned from the release of pressure.

"I'm going to call this detective and tell him you showed; I confronted you and then you quit. We'll make it a point to have the staff see you walk out pissed. As far as I'm concerned, you just vanished."

"Why not just say I never showed?"

"Too suspicious for you to go missing after I get questioned about you. Especially with Vince and the other girl."

"So, I'm done here?"

"Not quite. I like how you took care of our VIP the other day."

"Putting your mouth on a dick isn't exactly rocket science."

"Don't devalue your talents. If you dodge jail time, I can use you for private parties and it's very lucrative. There's a party being held at a plantation house on River Road the night after tomorrow. Some very powerful men will be there. I supply the entertainment."

She brightened. "A Civil War, real life plantation? Really?"

"Yes. You and four of the girls will be classed up with elegant evening dresses."

She questioned, "Just four of us?"

"There will be other girls from around the state."

"Cool. So, what's my cut?"

He smiled like a proud father. "All goes well? Could be three grand. I'm afraid I have to ask a personal question."

"Can't imagine what you'd consider personal."

"You can't attend a party during your time of the month… unless we have a guest who requests it, of course."

"Ew. No problems, there."

"Good."

"So, if I wasn't on board, you'd play the cop card and blackmail me?"

"That's not my style. It's this, or I wish you well. You impressed the organizer of this party. He wants you."

"So, how do I end up all gussied up?"

"Your outfits will be supplied to you at the mansion. But, tomorrow evening when Tabitha's done with the books, she'll take you shopping at Canal Place for a nice dress to arrive in. You two can have dinner anywhere in the city – on me. Now leave like you're upset, and be sure to bitch that you're quitting to the bartender."

"Okay."

"Oh, and Keri, be careful with your body. No new bruises or cuts. Clean yourself thoroughly. You have a chance to make a lot of money."

"Consider me a China Doll." She beamed at being invited to a party that had Haley's killer as a guest. Would this be the party where they take her for good and sell her to the highest bidder? Or would she net two or three grand and walk away? She understood how easily these women could fall into this hole.

THIRTY-TWO

Instead of hitting the firing range this morning; I headed straight into the station. Raymond Corondelet sat on one of the outside benches wearing tight designer jeans and a form-fitted T-shirt. Sunglasses hid his eyes, but he seemed alert. He stood and waited for me to reach him.

"Ray, this must be an early morning for you."

He shook my hand. "I don't sleep much. I suppose that's the case with most business owners."

"You want to talk inside? Or grab a coffee?"

"That won't be necessary. Right here is fine."

"What brings you by?"

"Keri Sullivan came in and quit last night." He took of his sunglasses and sat back down.

"Wait – she showed up and you didn't call me?"

"There wasn't enough time." Ray looked up at me, exasperated.

"What does that mean?"

"Honestly? I'm a bit of a hot head. It's gotten me into trouble before. The more I thought about Keri being involved with the police and Vince's murder, the more I stewed. She came in about ten. I confronted her about being with Vince… about the police questioning me, and she ran out of my office before I could stop her." He paused. "She was gone. It wouldn't have done any good to call you so late."

"Why confront her at all?"

"My temper, I told you. I'm used to making the decisions. I run things. I wanted my own answers and that was a mistake. I apologize. What else can I say?"

Liar. I reached out and gripped his hand in a tight single shake. "I appreciate your coming down to tell me, Ray. She might keep in contact with someone on your staff. Tell them to let you know if Cozy contacts them, and then you call me – *at any hour.*"

"Naturally."

THE CASE HAD GOTTEN sticky and far from linear. I sat at my desk surrounded by my notes and the pictures of the Robicheaux sisters. It was possible Cozy, a.k.a. Keri Sullivan, had seen us parading around Molly's last night and made herself scarce, but I had a hunch that Ray might be protecting his new investment. I don't buy the '*wasn't thinking*' bullshit. Ray wanted us off his trail.

Dr. Jerry hadn't called me yet on Ashton's fingerprints like he had promised and the DNA results hadn't come in from the lab, which was always less than expedient. The NOPD was forced to use the slowest crime labs in the country and, due to that, had the worst conviction rate. I'd be lucky if that glass didn't end up in one of the lab worker's kitchen cabinet.

My desk phone rang. Again, it was the uniform at reception downstairs.

"What's up, Ted?"

"Seems you're a popular guy. There's a Miss Mozart down here to see you."

"Mozart?"

"Sure, why not?" he asked, deadpan.

"I'll be right down."

One of the dancers from Molly's fidgeted as I popped into the reception area. The tattoo of a snake wrapping around her neck gave her away. She waved with a weak smile, wearing smart reading glasses, jeans and a Neville Brothers T-shirt. Her hair was pulled back with a scrunchie.

"I'm sorry. What's your name again?" I asked.

"Sophie. I was hoping we could talk somewhere private."

"Let's go next door and get a coffee."

We crossed over to a beignet place and found an open table hidden from the street by a tree in a planter. She had been reluctant to tell Tara anything at the club, but clearly something was on her mind. I ordered two coffees at the counter while she ripped a napkin into tiny strips. At the club, make up applied like cake frosting had covered many imperfections on an otherwise plain face, however sitting here; she could very well be a college student.

I placed the coffees down and sat, waiting for her to speak.

"I know Ray just left."

"You followed him here?"

"Sort of. I knew he was coming. I was just with him." She ripped another strip from the napkin.

I sipped my coffee, making this conversation as easy as possible for her. "You two involved?"

"Better shifts, more protection."

"He told me Keri showed last night."

"She did. I saw her leaving pissed off. I want to clarify some things."

"I imagine you couldn't speak freely at the club?"

"I won't testify to anything. I'll deny this conversation." Her eyes were on me, despite facing forward.

"Sure. We're just talking over coffee."

"I thought I could keep this to myself, but it's about to happen again." Another perfectly torn strip.

"What?"

"Is this off the record?" Her deep brown eyes continuously scanned the street.

"This isn't an official statement. We have many informants that give us information and don't get involved."

She took a break from her napkin for a careful sip of her coffee. "I know what Haley Robicheaux was doing the night she was murdered."

"Go on."

"I don't know how she was murdered or who did it, but I know why she was in the river." She waited a beat, but I kept my mouth shut. "Ray supplies women to these uber-secret parties. The guests arrive like everything is on the up-and-up, but there's some crazy shit that goes on."

"You know who throws these parties?"

"No. But there's this guy that comes in the club once and a while. It seems the parties coincide with his visit, put together in just days. I guess to prevent word of mouth. This one party with Haley was at a warehouse on the river. There have been other parties where the girls don't come back, but this is the first one that turned up dead."

"If I show you a picture, could you identify him?"

"Sure, but I won't do it in a line up."

I pulled out my cell and went online, pulling up an image of Harry Winslow. "Is this the guy?"

"No, that's not him."

I hid my disappointment, wishing I had pictures of all his employees. "Okay. What other girls were working the party that night?"

"Don't know. The girls are told not to talk about it. I don't want another friend to end up dead. It could be any one of us."

"How many parties have there been?" I handed her my napkin to continue her nervous habit.

"I know of three. From what I hear, any deep south politician worth their weight in corruption has been to one."

I patted her hand. "There's no way anyone will track this information back to you. I don't think you'll be in harm's way for telling me."

Her eyes dropped. "You'd think."

"Would Ray hurt you?"

She didn't answer.

I asked, "Do you think Ray killed Haley?"

"I think he could have, but I don't think he did."

"Why?"

Her eyes darted around. "Two reasons. One, Haley was a money-maker."

"So, her hours weren't being cut back?"

"Hell, no. She was one of our most popular girls." She smiled for the first time. Her overbite was cute.

"And Ray let her keep all the money she made?"

She surprised herself with a full laugh, putting her hand over her mouth. "Oh, no. Haley danced under the 'no questions asked' option, which meant Ray probably took half her take."

"I see. And the second reason?"

"If Ray killed her, you wouldn't have a body." She balled up the strips of napkin and looked into her lap. "I stopped getting close to the girls because they just come with too much baggage and then when you like one, they just stop coming to work."

"What's Ray say about these girls that don't come back?"

"He preaches the unpredictability of troubled girls in this industry. How can you argue?"

"Why do you stay?"

"Money. That, and I'm not the brightest bulb. After this, my options will be the fast food industry."

"Go back to school with your money."

"I appreciate the effort. As stupid as it sounds, I dream of a fairy-tale ending where a lonely man with money – ugly, fat, I don't care – a man that adores me for I how I make him feel will tell me he loves me and wants to take me away to be his wife."

"Like that movie."

"Sounds pathetic with feminism and all, but I would treat him like a king. I would like that."

Our conversation ran dry of information, but I wanted to keep her close. "You think you can find out where the next party is being held and when, without putting yourself in danger?"

Her fingers needed a new napkin to tear apart. "I'll try to bring it up casually, but I won't ask directly. If someone says something, I'll let you know."

"That's all I can ask."

MANY ELEMENTS from the case were beginning to gel, but I feared everything rested on the next party Miss Mozart had confided to me. I told Tara of my recent visit with Ray and the dancer, as she was working a different case. Just after returning to my desk from a delicious lunch, I received a restricted call on my cell.

I answered while paying more attention to my laptop. "Peyroux."

"You can't trace this. I'm on a burner."

The hairs on my neck stood on end like a ghost brushed past. "Cozy?"

"I got one question and you need to answer me honestly. My life depends on it."

"Ask me."

"I know you questioned Ray and Tabby at Molly's. Did you tell them my real name?"

"No. As far as they're concerned, you're Keri Sullivan." I quickly typed the name Keri Sullivan into the database, realizing there were five ways to spell that name.

"Good. It's possible they know who I am, but I can't be sure."

My fingers ran through my hair. "Cozy, you can't play that game. Tell me where you are. You are in way over your head."

"Just outside Shreveport. I don't want to die. I'm going to Canada and never coming back."

"Really? You made it to the north side of Louisiana after just quitting Molly's Girls late last night? Without your car." I finally rocked back in my chair to let the conversation happen.

"I stole one. Drove through the night."

"You're lying, Cozy. Did you kill Titus?"

"Titus was rapist and a drug dealer."

I waited a beat. "I know what you're going through."

"Their payment to the legal system is very different from their payment to me."

"Let me help you, Cozy. You trust me to do that, right?"

"I do, Lucas. But, I have one more question."

"What is it?" I rubbed my eyes.

"Why did you pull away from me when I hugged you?"

This time I hesitated. "… because I really wanted to hug back. It scared me."

"We ever meet again, Lucas; I won't let you pull away."

"Let's meet now, Cozy." My elbows fell forward onto my desk.

"Goodbye, Lucas."

The phone went dead and my body coiled, ready to spring into action, yet there was nothing to be done.

THIRTY-THREE

Evening had fallen as dinner at Antoine's continued on longer than a meal should. Cozy and Tabby left arm-in-arm after the rain had subsided, strolling on the wet slate of Jackson Square, adding movement to the dark patches of shadows. Several pockets of kids stood around as if planning something sinister, but this was just their Friday night. Dates held hands in no rush for the night to end. Cozy envied them.

"Thanks for letting me stay on your couch," Cozy said.

Tabby leaned into her as they walked. "No problem. You ever hold a black light to those motel sheets?"

"I imagine it would look like the Emerald Room."

"True. We should have added another hundred-dollar bottle of wine to take with us."

Cozy moaned, saliva rushing into her mouth at the mere memory. "The food and wine were so good and so expensive."

"Get used to the nicer things."

Cozy put her arm around Tabby's waist and kissed her cheek, which sent them reeling a few feet to the left. "I like you, Tabby-cat."

"Ditto."

Once inside Tabby's surprisingly large two-bedroom apartment on

Royal Street, she uncorked another bottle of wine as Cozy toured the local art on display. Posters of past Mardi Gras hung next to each other. Brightly colored African art sat perched on shelves. Tabby hadn't felt the need to fill every space with furniture or knick-knacks. There was room to breathe.

They relaxed on the plush, cream sofa with unobtrusive, soft music filling in the silent moments. They chatted about the inspirations for art and music, keeping their glasses topped off. When the conversation wore thin, Cozy snuggled to her side and sang to the music while leaning back on Tabby's arm.

Tabby inhaled the scent of her hair. "You're just a babe."

"It's all relative." Cozy reached over for her last sip of wine on the nightstand. "We killed two bottles."

"You want a third?"

Cozy put her glass down and faced this worldly lady, staring with drunken eyes into a striking deep well of brown.

"You're not even twenty yet." Tabby said, examining every contour of Cozy's face.

"And yet, I've lived a lifetime."

Tabby extended her glass to the end table without looking. Their lips touched gently at first, each pulling back as if asking permission. And then they joined together again and Cozy couldn't help but curl her toes.

THE SHEET HAD BEEN PUSHED DOWN to their waistlines. Tabby propped her head up with two pillows as Cozy rolled over and threw her thigh over Tabby's hot legs. She moaned with sleepy eyes and gently kissed Tabby's nipple before resting her cheek on it.

Tabby stroked her arm. "You were amazing and I'm not saying that 'cause I'm drunk. I actually didn't think I'd finish, but you made it happen."

"Same here." Cozy exhaled.

"I'm sleeping with a criminal."

"What?"

"Wanted by the cops… you."

"I wanted to ask you, what kind of questions did that cop ask?"

Cozy felt her tense up. "Just general questions about Vince and Haley and you, but Ray told me you explained about your momma."

"Is Ray in trouble?"

"No. He's covered."

"What did you tell the cop about me?"

"About you? Nothing. That we had no contact info."

Cozy stretched up and kissed her tenderly. "What did you say about that Haley girl?"

Tabby's expression turned curious. "That Haley was about to be fired from the club just before she died." Tabitha kissed her hair, running her hand down to the small of her back.

"Convenient."

"That sounded accusatory."

"I imagine myself in that girl's place. I just want to know what happened."

Tabitha shrugged, her lids closing. "What else can I say?"

"Could Ray be protecting the guy who killed that girl?"

Tabitha stiffened. "You're asking some very dangerous questions. What's going on, Keri?"

Cozy shrugged and then inched down to squeeze one of Tabitha's breasts like a water balloon, taking the nipple in her mouth. Tabitha sighed. "Stop."

"Alright."

"Are you nervous about tomorrow night? Is that what all these questions are about?"

"I know my way around a dick and the little button." She bit her bottom lip with a smile.

"That's only part of it." Her speech was sloppy. "These men want their fantasies. You might have to fawn over them or dominate them, or hell, they might want you to shit on them. They might expect you to know what they want and get pissed when you don't. They may think they are in charge, but you have to control them."

"How do you do that?"

"Confidence, sugar. Each girl develops their own method. If you're unsure about how things are going, you might find yourself uninvited to these events."

"You nervous for me?"

"Sure. You don't come off as experienced and that's why they want you. Everyone will want you. Hell, I wanted you."

"You got me."

"You know I'm not a lesbian, right?" Tabby's eyes were closed. "At least not full-time."

"Neither am I, but with you, it just seemed right."

"It did."

Cozy separated from Tabby's body and propped herself against the headboard. "Should I be worried about these freaks?"

Her eyes opened for just a moment to see that Cozy shifted to a higher position, looking down on her. "I don't think so. It's like I'm a doctor telling you the risks of an appendectomy. Ninety-nine percent go fine."

Cozy watched her chest swell with each breath in the candlelight. "Would Haley be the one percent?"

"Haley wasn't killed at the party, Sugar. It had to have happened right after. Bad things could always happen. I want you to be careful."

"You miss Haley. You get really sad when you talk about her."

"We really liked each other."

"Like, how we're liking each other?" Cozy had to force her mouth shut.

"Sometimes gender doesn't matter."

"Sometimes we all need a friend."

"You're having second thoughts, aren't you?"

"I didn't come all the way out here from Manchac for nothing." Cozy clenched her jaw and squeezed her eyes shut.

Tabby paused for five drunk seconds, and then it registered. "Manchac? You said you were from Empire. Haley was from Manchac."

"Empire… That's right. Someone told me Haley was from Manchac. I'm drunk." Cozy hoped the darkness hid her skin warming up.

Tabby scooted to a sitting position. "Now, I remember. That alligator pendant was Haley's, wasn't it?"

Cozy let out a breath. This bell couldn't be un-rung. After an eternity of silence, she confessed. "Haley is my sister – *was* my sister."

"What the fuck is this?" She threw the blanket off and stood at the edge of the bed.

"My name is really Cozy… Cozy Robicheaux."

Tabitha attempted to keep balance and poise while putting on a robe. Her face became hard and aggressive. "What exactly are you doing, *Cozy*?"

"Maybe I should start from the beginning."

Tabby pulled a gun from her dresser and held it on her with wide eyes and steady hands. "Damn well you better."

"I guess the story starts when I got shot in the throat." Cozy pulled the covers up to her chest. She explained the entire story where she lay, as if there wasn't a weapon pointed at her. Tears had slowly gathered and fell from time to time until she finished. Cozy sheepishly looked at Tabby. "… And that brings us here." Cozy smiled and the last tear dropped.

The gun bobbed in its descent. Tabby eventually put it back in the drawer. "I'll make a pot of coffee."

Fifteen minutes later, Tabby held Cozy's hands at the kitchen table. "That's incredible. The fact that you're ready to throw your life away makes me sad."

"If I can't avenge my sister, I might as well kill myself anyway."

"So, wait." She looked at the bed. "Was all this a way of eliminating me as a suspect?"

"I didn't have to sleep with you to do that. I knew in my heart you didn't do it. Deep down, I think I wanted to experience what my sister did with you. Like, maybe it would bring me closer to her."

"Did it?"

"I don't know. I was doing the same thing with her boyfriend back home; but that was more to hurt her for abandoning me. This isn't the same."

"Why?"

"The memory of Haley still exists in you and I like you for that. So, I guess the question now is, what are you going to do about this?"

"Nothing, sugar. Absolutely nothing."

"You're not going to tell Ray?"

"I tell Ray and he might have you killed… seriously. He's unpredictable. He has a long fuse, but once you reach the end of it, he just explodes."

"Great. I'll have to be careful when I question him."

"Question Ray? You *do* have a death wish." Tabby gently pecked Cozy on the lips. "I know Ray didn't kill Haley. He doesn't murder you, he just throws you away. Whether he knows who did is another story."

"All I want to do is get him to tell me who was with Haley the night she died. That's all."

"If you think you can get him to say, be my guest. But be very careful. When he figures out what you're hinting for and he shuts you down, don't push it."

"Right. Act like it's not important. Will he be at the club tomorrow?"

"Not 'til late, so you won't have any time with him. Here, I'll give you his home address and you can see him early tomorrow." She reached for a pen. "But, you better think up an amazing excuse for showing up at his house."

"You won't betray me?"

"My loyalty to Ray is hanging on by a paycheck." Tabby gave Cozy a lingering kiss on her cheek. "If I betray you, then I betray Haley."

Cozy smiled. She could see why Haley loved Tabby.

THIRTY-FOUR

Cozy woke with Tabby spooning her, their bare bodies creating an intoxicating scent. Her hangover wasn't even a consideration. The moment couldn't get more perfect. Was this love? Or would Dr. Clair say this was some kind of Electra complex with a mother figure instead of father? Both her parents had been lacking, but Cozy had to live with her momma's warped sense of reality. No, Tabby was too young to be a mother figure and she didn't want any other sister. Tabby was just perfect.

Cozy had eaten a bowl of instant grits with Tabby before returning to the hotel. Tabby had told her to come back for six that evening in the new dress to get her makeup done. With the entire day ahead, Cozy showered with the hotel-supplied toiletries, double-checked the gun she got off Titus, and headed out the door with a weighted purse.

She rode the shiny, old-school streetcar down St. Charles, hypnotized by the shadows of the Oaks whizzing by before getting off at Napoleon Avenue. She strolled towards the river like a resident with her large handbag snug to her side. The charming houses were impressive, but she found that without the bayou, she was like a fish out of water.

Blocks later, she approached the address Tabby had supplied and saw two men in Ray's driveway. Each cradled one end of a large sack, obviously weighted, throwing it into the back of a cleaning van. *A body?* They didn't look like a cleaning service. Confident they were gone; she stood paralyzed in front of a magnificently manicured home. She admired the garden, the rose bushes and freshly painted exterior shaded by a large Magnolia tree, its huge white blossoms resembled decorative lampshades. She couldn't believe such slime lived inside.

Ray answered the door alone as Tabby had promised, not liking his conquests to know where he lived. He was wearing only a towel and a head of wet hair.

"Keri. Who told you where I lived?"

"Internet. Everything's on the Internet."

"Tabitha told you."

"Don't blame Tabby."

"Tabby, is it?" He chuckled like he knew of their intimacy.

"I'm freaking out about this party, Ray. I need you to put me at ease or I won't do it."

"Come in. Forgive my towel, but I'm getting ready for a meeting downtown."

"I won't keep you for long." She took a step in.

"You're the first dancer I've ever had in here; not counting Tabby."

"That's hard to believe." Cozy trailed her boss into his expansive living room. He pointed her to a leather studded couch in front of an actual bear hide with the head still attached. It looked as if he smoked cigars and drank brandy in this room often. When she approached the coffee table, she noticed two empty cups of coffee and a napkin torn into long, narrow strips.

"Company?" She pointed.

"I'm in a bit of a rush. Your question?"

A cleaning service that left a shredded napkin next to their cup? Her mouth dried instantly. "You live here all alone?"

"Yes, but that can't be your question."

"It's not."

"Must be a tough question to ask." He gave up and sat in his towel, patting for Cozy to take a seat.

Cozy stepped up to edge of the sofa, still amazed at the classy décor that contradicted this man's profession. She put her knee on the cushion next to his thigh and sat on her foot. She leaned in, running her finger through the hair on his chest.

"I'm scared of embarrassing myself tonight."

"No you're not. If anything, I'd say you're angling for more money."

"No." Cozy squinted at him.

"You're playing games and I have a meeting."

"Fine." She pushed herself onto the end cushion and dug into her purse. "I got something for you."

"Can't wait."

"Here, put these on." She threw a pair of handcuffs on his lap.

"Keri, this isn't the place…"

She pulled out the gun and pointed it at his face. "Put them on."

He sighed as if he was inconvenienced, reached under a throw pillow and pulled out his own gun. "I had such high hopes for you."

"Why the fuck you have a gun under your sofa pillows?"

"I have guns hidden all over for moments just like this."

Ray picked up the cuffs and tossed them back at Cozy, startling her into firing unexpectedly. A loud ping filled the room as Ray's gun popped out of his hand with a spark. After a frozen moment in time, Cozy let out a loud, short laugh. "Like Clint Fuckin' Eastwood."

"Unbelievable." Ray shook his hand as Cozy affirmed her grip. "How the hell?"

"Just lucky." Cozy kicked the cuffs to Ray's feet. "Now put those on or I aim for your head."

Cozy rounded to the backside of the sofa and intently watched as Ray's stinging hand fumbled with the cuffs, making sure they snapped closed. Moments later, the stunned prisoner held both cuffed hands in the air and then let them fall back into his lap.

"Good. Now, I want you to sit that contraption of a chair. What is that for? S&M?"

He stood and followed her command. Cozy reached out to pull the towel off his waist. He hesitated before snuggling his butt onto the solid metal chair. "This contraption is an antique barber's chair from the French Revolution, meant for royalty."

"Perfect." She kicked his gun across the room and then eyed the back of his head. With one slow practice aim, she brought the butt of her gun down as hard as she could on the spot where his neck met his skull. Luckily, he didn't slump forward enough to fall out.

RAY REMAINED naked in the brushed nickel, gold-plated throne of a chair, still handcuffed, duct-taped to the backrest, along with his legs. Cozy watched him wake with a struggle. This was a hairy man, and she shuddered at the thought of his removing the tape.

Ray's eyes strained to focus. "You duck taped me?"

"I call it duck-tape, too. Someone tried to tell me it was *duct* tape, which makes sense. Both are right. I found out it was called duck-tape during the Second World War. Used to keep ammo dry. You know, *water off a duck's back*. Then, it started being used for ducts. Interesting, right?" Cozy's kept calm, waiting patiently for Ray to get a grip on his situation.

"Either you're a psycho or you're pissed off at me. One of those, I can fix."

"Can you bring my sister back to life?"

"No. I can't."

"So, are we done playing that game?"

"Honey, ever since you showed up to Haley's apartment, I've led you every step of the way."

"You had Porter try to kidnap me?"

"No. He learned about you from going through Haley's apartment and did that on his own. He's a pervert. Once he told me you recognized him, I eliminated the problem."

"Why not just kill me instead?"

"I like money and I didn't like Porter. Porter told me you killed Titus, so I told him to clean it up. I knew you would eventually come to the club if Porter planted a business card. Why do things the hard way?"

"Tell me who killed my sister."

He stopped fidgeting as if he had regained control. "I didn't kill

Haley and neither did Porter. Not to speak ill of the dead, but she was a huge meal ticket. I would never do that."

"But you would also think she was a dime a dozen."

"No. Haley. You. You're not a dime a dozen. Quite the opposite. You'll make me lots of money at this party. Would have, anyway."

"I believe you. I think one of the guests killed her and dumped her body and you know who did that."

"Haley left alive."

"Like you'd rat out the killer."

"I can get witnesses that saw her leave. Get my cell phone."

"No one is going to admit they attended, much less say they saw her leave."

Cozy patted down a strip of tape onto his chest. He peered down with a gaping mouth. "What are you doing?"

"You're a hairy fucker, aren't you?" She quickly ripped it off, leaving a decimated forest on rash-red, irritated skin.

His face twisted with a sceam. "Bitch! I'm going to kill you."

"Oh, so you *do* kill people. Who did Haley hook up with?" She applied another strip of tape across his nipple.

"Let's go to the police together. I'll tell them everything I know about the girls at the party. Hell, bring the cops here."

She pulled the tape off with serious effort. Blood came to the surface of skin as if permeating a cloth. Ray cried out like he had been branded. "You're dead. You bitch. You're fucking dead."

Another short length torn off the roll created a tacky, ripping sound. "You think I'm stupid."

Ray's purple face glistened as he spoke swiftly in short breaths. "Senator Folsom requested Haley, but he didn't kill her. When everyone left, Haley was alive. I swear, she was alive."

"Then, Folsom's my next target."

"Dead end. He won't know what you're talking about." His eyes slowly met hers.

"You have video?"

"Yeah," he laughed through the pain. "I got loads of video of that."

"Watch your tone. I suppose you might believe that to be the truth. I'll find out tonight."

"You're going to leave me tied up?"

"If I don't kill you, yes. You're still a scumbag. And I can't have you coming after me."

"You kill the senator, you'll be put away for life."

"Once justice is served, I don't plan on hanging around."

"Oh, you're fucked up *and* crazy." The fight returned to his face. "Do I have anything to bargain with?"

Cozy wedged his legs open, wrapping the tape around his testicles, giving them a light tap. "I looked around the place. It's beautiful. I found the Fort Knox safe behind that picture in your bedroom. How original. I imagine that's where you keep your illegal accounting, client list, money and stuff like that. You give me the combo – you live. You refuse, you die with no hair on your balls, perhaps no skin, either."

"You're in over your head, little girl."

"Maybe." Cozy put her face in his. His sweat mixed with the fresh smell of soap. His labored breathing wafted mouthwash. She whispered. "I killed my father. I killed Titus. I want to kill you, Ray, but I'm giving you a choice. A chance for redemption."

Ray jerked his head at Cozy's face and bit into the air, just inches away. His body rocked as his teeth clacked together in an effort to take a chunk from her. She backed away silent and wide-eyed, bending over to pinch the corner of the tape on his balls. She gave it a short tug. "Ever been man-scaped?"

"Wait, wait, wait." He grunted like a punch-drunk fighter.

"If this doesn't work, then I got a nice little torture technique I read about. The Vietnamese used it on prisoners of war and let's just say you'll never pee the same way again. All I need is a hammer."

"Jesus Christ."

"The combination, please."

THIRTY-FIVE

The next item on the morning's agenda was figuring out Cozy Robicheaux's state of mind from her therapist. Dr. Clair Shipman's home doubled as her office right off Williams Boulevard. She answered her door wearing a dark blue blouse, black pumps and a gray skirt, clearly not lounging on the sofa. From the front step, the inside looked to be filled with expensive furnishings.

"You must be the detectives." She looked to be in her forties, with short hair and a sleek face. Her nose and chin were pointed; an intelligent kind of sexy, if that made sense.

"Lucas Peyroux and Tara Gray," I said as we entered her chilly home. "Thank you for seeing us."

"Let's sit in the parlor. Can I get you something to drink? Coffee? Scotch?" She waited with laser focus.

Tara and I declined and were instructed to sit on a firm white couch that had no arms. At our knees was a coffee table with looping metal legs underneath a glass top. I felt as if the plastic wrap had just come off her furniture. Dr. Clair eased into a large, white and teal striped chair that could fit two people.

Dr. Clair started. "You must understand that I can't divulge anything from our private sessions. I told your Captain this."

"We understand." I leaned forward with my forearms on my knees. "But, we need to get some idea of the person we're searching for. How she thinks. What she's capable of."

She waved her hand at us. "Cozy Robicheaux? She could be my life's work, that girl."

"What can you tell us?" Tara asked.

Her face grew serious. "Let's see. What do we all know? Her alcoholic father abused her sister for years before Cozy killed him. The emotional guilt of watching it happen while not being touched can be extremely damaging."

"How so?" Tara asked.

"Beyond the obvious, as strange as it sounds, her father beating her sister and not *her* could be viewed as a type of neglect."

"You're shitting me." Tara said.

"In Cozy's eyes, her sister mattered enough to get abused. Good or bad, it's still attention her sister was receiving from a parent. Attention that wasn't worth the effort on her."

"I get what you're saying," I said, remembering the hug we shared. "It made Cozy feel small, like she didn't exist."

"Instead of shrinking, she did the opposite and acted out. Her mother is in denial. Her sister abandoned them, most likely having serious issues herself. The community she lives in thinks she's promiscuous, to be polite." She paused as if assuming we would come to her conclusions.

"Has she ever been suicidal?" I asked.

"Hypothetically, someone can commit suicide by pointing a gun at a cop, right?"

"Sure. Is that why Cozy's like an adrenaline junkie?"

She remained stoic. "I'm just saying people don't need to use the direct route of suicide."

"You may not have heard, but she just found out her sister Haley is dead."

"What?" She put her hand over her mouth. "How?"

"Murdered and tossed in the Mississippi."

"I saw that story on the news. That's why she missed our session."

"We can't locate her. We think she's trying to find out who killed Haley and has gotten in with some bad people."

"That's troublesome."

"Is Cozy capable of killing someone she believes killed her sister?" I asked.

"In my professional opinion… in the right situation… *someone* in Cozy's state of mind could kill and with no remorse."

"Are we talking multiple personalities?" Tara asked.

"No, nothing like that." She waited a beat. "Oh, dear, this changes everything." She paused again before continuing. "Her reality has been warped by her parents and her environment, and she has learned to justify anything she does. She had to make up her own rules her entire life."

"What do you mean by that?"

"As a child, she had to decide what behavior her parents favored best to either receive praise or to keep peace. In random textbook examples; she might have had to decide what outfit wouldn't warrant verbal abuse or at what hour she needed to come inside from playing, or the best times to use the bathroom so her father wouldn't be disturbed."

"She could view anything that gets a positive result as good behavior?" Tara questioned.

I leaned back on the sofa. "So, if she – a hypothetic person – thinks someone is a bad person, she wouldn't have any qualms about killing them?"

"Not exactly. In my opinion, someone like Cozy wouldn't kill her boyfriend for cheating on her, but she could rationalize killing him if she found out he molested a little girl." Dr. Clair crossed one leg over the other as if enjoying this.

"So, she could rationalize killing someone who's guilty by her moral standards?"

Dr. Clair gave a slight nod.

"Is she delusional?" I asked. "See things that aren't happening?"

"I can't say if delusions are occurring, but if they do, then she could start hearing what she wants to hear and seeing what she wants to see. No one can predict that."

"Did she mention a favorite place in the Quarter?" I had my notebook at the ready.

"No, I couldn't say she did."

"What about Ashton? How is that relationship?"

"I'm afraid I can't comment much on that. But, he strikes me as needy."

"What about her mother?" Tara asked.

"My personal opinion is that she's of no real help in Cozy's healing. She doesn't put much faith in psychiatry, but she seems glad Cozy has someone to talk to." Dr. Clair appeared disappointed. "I've given you my assessment, but I can't give you any personal information she's divulged in session. I skirted the edge as it is. I would be obligated to inform the authorities if she posed a danger to anyone, which she hasn't."

"So, we're dealing with a time bomb," Tara said.

Dr. Clair kept silent, staring at the bleached hardwood.

THE DAY LOST momentum with paperwork concerning Dr. Clair, but then Dr. Jerry called. Tara had left for the day and since I had no other cases, it had to be about Haley Robicheaux.

"Jerry, you have news on my prints?" My pen rested in my hand.

"How do you do that?" He paused a second. "The prints on the glass match the cell phone."

"Definite?"

"Seven points. Close enough?"

"Touchdown as far as I'm concerned. Thanks, man." I put down my cell and glanced at my computer. Good things come to those who wait: the lab results had just come in. The DNA from the hairbrush matched the body, so this was indeed Haley Robicheaux. And the DNA from Edgar Porter matched the samples taken from when I shot him. Did any of this help? No, not really.

Ashton Bergeron had lied, having proof of contact with Haley in New Orleans and not telling anyone. He would be picked him up for questioning in the morning. I updated Tara, not very optimistic about the progress. Unfortunately, I would be going home this evening without anyone in custody, but at least Heather would be happy to hear the updates with the case. I pushed away from my desk and left for the day.

The drought in my bedroom had been going on for too long and I didn't care if we needed to rent a hotel room. I had no one to blame but myself, and I had to make it right. My anticipation focused on Heather during my entire drive home - her hair, her lips, and the warmth of her body. I ignored the speed limit until slamming the brakes in my driveway, glancing at the glow of the lamp in the front window. I entered the house and immediately located my wife in the kitchen, wearing my over-sized, long sleeve dress shirt and nothing else. Two glasses of wine were on the table.

"Not pushing you. Just thought you were doing better since you and Cozy talked."

"I am. Alicia?" I asked, looking at the wine.

Heather unbuttoned the shirt from the top. "At Jane's, sleeping over. House is ours."

Bypassing the red wine, I drew to within inches of my wife's body and she didn't move as my arms pulled her close. Our kisses were short, intense bursts of pent up desire that led to pulling off our clothes where we stood. Our aggression forced us against the stove where I lifted her onto the counter, dividing her knees as she fell against cooking utensils hanging from hooks, but she wasn't about to complain.

THIRTY-SIX

"When are you going to leave your wife?" Receptionist Amy Schultz sprung from the hotel bed wearing just her underwear and a loose T-shirt.

Harry Winslow almost walked through her as he took off his jacket. "I'm not. Quit asking that fucking question."

He had a different answer this time. He didn't say 'soon' with a kiss on her cheek and a new bracelet. Harry shut the bathroom door and the shower went on, leaving Amy to ponder the disrespect.

He had later apologized after a few drinks, blaming the stress of his job, but the sting of his betrayal made this night's sex akin to a one-night stand; the body was the same, however she didn't know Harry anymore. For the first time, she saw Harry as the out of shape, middle-aged adulterer he was. The shame bore through during sex, where she lost all animation.

Afterwards, Amy laid motionless in the hotel bed, breathing deep through parted lips, eyes closed, but wide-awake thinking about her apartment, the bills and her future. Harry Winslow's seven-minute missionary position, although fierce on his end, had no effect on her insomnia. She thought he had fallen asleep until the bed shook like a tiny earthquake as he slid from the covers. The amplified sound of his jacket swishing on the chair and the unfolding of a piece of paper made his movements easy to follow. He slithered into the bathroom where she could barely make out his echoing whispers.

"…I know you said don't call you…"

"…can't be traced…Peyroux…got nothing…"

"…Apex…She'll be there…"

"…don't threaten me…"

The talking stopped and a minute later she heard pissing, and then the toilet flushed with a roar. A pill bottle shook, and the faucet came on for a moment before hearing the click of the child-proof cap. He returned to the jacket resting on the chair and then climbed into bed with his back to her, summing up their entire relationship.

She waited an entire hour for his pills to take effect. She crept from under the blanket and made her way to the jacket while Harry's stomach rose and fell with a grating snore. She pulled the piece of paper from his pocket, set the flash on her camera phone, and took a picture. Satisfied with its clarity, she slipped the paper back into its home.

After expertly dressing in the dark, she wrote 'I quit' on a piece of paper with lipstick and laid it on her pillow and then whispered *fuck you* in his ear. And with one final glance, she shot Harry the bird and left the hotel room. She relished the thought of personally delivering this picture to that attractive detective.

THIRTY-SEVEN

For the first time in weeks, I didn't wake before my alarm went off and Heather had been good for another go, although without the morning-breath kissing. We even showered together, but she was disappointed to learn, although not in a sour way, that I needed to work for a few hours on a Sunday.

However, Dobson was fine with my collecting overtime, so I traveled to Manchac solo because Tara didn't want to miss church. I didn't believe that Ashton Bergeron killed Haley, but he lied and I needed him to illuminate some things about their relationship, with each Haley and Cozy.

Ashton's house appeared no different than the other residents; new planks had been nailed next to old ones with peeling yellow paint and dirt paths with random embedded bricks leading around back. Large Cypress trees towered over the front porch, providing deep shade. The overgrown brush nearly covered the entire walkway to the front door. His domicile, like most of the others, was also situated over the water.

Two NOPD uniforms staked out the back pier in case of an escape. I didn't expect Ashton to run or put up a fight, but stranger things have happened, and I'd rather have my ass covered. I banged on the screen door, which rattled against the jamb. Soon after, a man in frayed gym shorts and no shirt answered. His torso was sweatered with sparse gray hair in contrast to his thick, brown moustache.

"My son ain't here."

"I'm Detective Peyroux. You're Ashton's father?"

"Paul Bergeron, yes, sir." Only half of his mouth moved when he spoke. "You're welcome to come in and look."

"I will if you don't mind, just so I can tell my boss I did." I stepped inside. "We believe he has information about Haley Robicheaux's murder and the whereabouts of Cozy. We know you want to protect your son, but we need to find him."

He slapped my shoulder as if we were old friends. "You mind if I get a beer?"

"Feel free." I did a quick search of the closets in each room.

"You want some tea?" He yelled, just as I entered the kitchen.

Paul opened a brand new silver side-by-side refrigerator and pulled out a full pitcher of tea with lemon medallions floating in it. The glasses he pulled from the refurbished cabinets were spotless. The outside of the house seemed like a disguise for the luxury within.

"You got some nice appliances," I said.

"Not what you expected?" Paul smirked.

"Honestly? I didn't think much care went into these camps."

"The bayou moisture and humidity can ravage these homes over time. Most folks out here don't live on much. My seafood place is doing real well and I splurged a bit. We're a prideful people, sir."

"Point taken. I also believe you didn't invite me in to talk about crawfish season."

"You saved Cozy's life. That's all I need to know. I can sense you're a stand-up guy. I can also tell you my son is a hundred percent cocky with fifty percent of a brain. So, let me guess; my son's got himself involved in something."

"Directly or indirectly, yes he has. Right now, we need to question him."

"Ashton doesn't tell me what's going on in his life. But, there is something I'd like to show you."

"Okay."

He held his palms up. "Wait here. Help yourself to some chips."

Paul disappeared into the hallway. I sipped my sweet tea, taking a few chips from an open bag of Zapp's on the table. When Paul came back into the kitchen, he had something in his hand.

"Now and then I go through his stuff like a good dad should. A few months ago, I found this in his pocket."

He placed several bar napkins from Molly's Girls in my hand with scribbling on them. I kept my mouth shut as I tried to read the crude lettering, which just had some numbers added together and a couple of French Quarter street names, but in two sets of handwriting

"Ashton probably spent the night at one of those loser friends of his. This morning, I'd bet my ass he's at the Wharf having pancakes."

"Wharf? Right off I-55 coming in here?"

"Yep."

The Wharf's breakfast rush had dwindled to just a few tables. Ashton and two bulked-up men with tattoo sleeves were sitting in the corner booth, yakking it up. Their table looked to have been cleared, but not cleaned. Each man still nursed a full cup of coffee.

"Hey guys, I heard the food here is terrific." I let my badge hang over the edge of the table at belt height.

Ashton lost his glee. "Good morning, Detective Peyroux."

"You done eating?" I scooted next to the mangy one, sitting directly across from Ashton. "What's your names?"

Ashton spoke. "That's Joe. That's Tray."

"Tray and Joe? Two of the date rapists?"

The two men glanced at each other. "What?"

"I heard all about you boys from Cozy. I'm thinking about looking into that before the statute runs out. I'm guessing you took digital pictures and video, and guess what boys? As long as there's Internet, they never go away."

"Wait, wait, wait," Tray stammered. "There is no video or pictures on the net. And there was no rape."

"What about the witnesses?"

"Everyone at that party will tell you she wanted to go in that room. Hell, every one of us in that room will tell you she wanted it. Tell him, Ashton."

"Dude." Ashton put his hand over his eyes.

I stared at him. "Did she want the rape, Ashton?"

Tray shifted in his seat. "Stop saying rape. It wasn't rape. You weren't there. I'll admit, she was in no condition to agree, but she didn't fight it either. As shitty as it sounds, it was just a misunderstanding."

"Oh, sorry judge, it was a *misunderstanding*. Tray, Joe, you guys can leave."

They each scooted out the opposite side of the booth and walked away without any farewell. I pointed at the waitress to get some coffee. "You want to explain?"

He didn't look at me, but real tears formed. "Yes, I was in that room and yes, I participated, but you can't tell Cozy. It would destroy her. She was just lying there, smiling and moaning and running her fingers across my arm. But, I was as drunk as anyone there. I know it was wrong, but..."

"You got some balls to start dating her."

His head tilted at me. "I was nauseous with guilt. After that night, I started hanging out with the Robicheaux sisters because I felt so bad. I wanted to do things for her and her family. It was just by accident that Hales and I started dating. Cozy loved that her big sister was seeing me."

"You did it out of guilt."

"Deep, deep guilt. I was sixteen when I made the hugest mistake of my life." His lip never sneered and his eyes were earnest.

I let him sit with that statement before pointing where his plate had been. "What'd you eat?"

It took a second for him to answer. "Pecan pancakes."

"They cook the pecans in the batter or are they just topped off?"

"Cooked in." He relaxed. "This ain't no amateur joint."

The waitress came with a cup of coffee and topped off Ashton's. She left for another table and I continued. "Listen, date rape aside, I'm going to ask you a few questions and your answers will determine whether I drag your ass back to New Orleans in cuffs."

"Okay." His pimples flared.

"Were you aware we had found Haley's cell phone when her body was recovered?"

"No, sir. I had no idea."

I sipped my coffee, letting the words settle. "There were prints on the inside cover, but only one was usable. Guess whose print it was."

"I would guess Hale's."

"Remember what I said about your answers and cuffs. You dad showed me the Molly's Girls napkins."

"Fuck." He slumped against the backrest.

"Start from the beginning."

"Alright, alright, but let me tell you right now I didn't kill her."

"Noted."

He exhaled before choosing his words. "I started taking little weekend trips to the Quarter to look for Haley."

"How'd you know to look in the Quarter?"

"The Quarter's the best place to live if you don't have a car. If she was in that area, I figured I'd run into her at some point, right? Well, sure enough I found her stripping at Molly's Girls."

"And you kept it to yourself?"

"She begged me. We had long talks about her future and what to do with her money and where she would live."

"Is that what was written down on those bar napkins?"

"Can't believe my dad showed you those." He rolled his eyes. "We were figuring out how to get her life legit. You know, paying taxes and all that shit. She actually wanted a 401k. Then, she was going to have me go rescue Cozy."

"Tell me about the cell. She just got it, so you obviously saw her right before the murder."

"No." He waved his finger spastically. "I helped Haley pick out that older model phone. She pulled the back cover off, but I put it back on for her. She had just got her driver's license, too. She had her birth certificate and Social Security card, but was really excited about having the license."

"She was old enough to be out on her own. Why all the secrecy?"

He hesitated with an answer. "She needed to be away from Cozy for a while. Not forever, just 'till her life got straight. Things happened to her, things that no one should go through."

"Don't do that. Don't offer me teasers. You have a murder charge hanging over your head. I'm giving you a chance to convince me otherwise."

"When Haley moved to New Orleans, she was pregnant and got an abortion."

"Your baby, Romeo?"

"No, I wish it was." He tapped his spoon on the table, unable to look at me.

"Then who? One of these Bubbas out here?"

"No. Think about whose sick baby she wouldn't want to have."

"Her father."

He nodded and his eyes filled, not able to part his lips.

"He used to rape her?"

"Just the once, she claimed. She said it never happened before. And, I believed her, sir. The first night I found Haley in the Quarter, we got drunk and she told me everything. Poor thing was crying so hard she could barely speak. The bastard thought he could beat Haley into a coma and that's when Cozy shot him."

"Does Cozy know about the rape or abortion?"

"Cozy never knew any of that. Haley protected her."

"So, you wanted to stay with Haley in New Orleans despite the incest, despite the abortion."

"We're all fucked up in one way or another, right?" He wiped his face dry. "I wanted to make it work, but Haley didn't."

"No?"

"She dated some guy a while. Then, she started seeing this woman from the place she worked. She was in love according to her."

"A dancer?"

"A manager."

"Tabitha Wheelhouse?"

"Yeah, Tabby. With Haley's life, can you blame her for going lesbo?"

"What's your relationship with Cozy's mother?"

"I figure if I hang around, do stuff for her, she might give my Dad a chance. He deserves to have someone. There's nothing going on with us, detective."

I sipped my coffee, thinking Ashton had bought a reprieve for the moment. He actually seemed like a nice kid in a tough environment. "I'm not going to take you in, but don't leave town alright? Not even to New Orleans. If I find out you crossed the parish line, I'm locking you up."

He nodded, and drained the rest of his coffee.

As I left The Wharf, my cell phone rang. It was Tara telling me to meet her back at the station.

"MAN, have I got some updates for you," I announced out loud while bounding into our work area. My partner relaxed at her desk in her nice, blue church dress and she wasn't alone. The young lady from Winning One waved from my desk with a demure smile, looking more like a beauty queen contestant than receptionist. She had on khaki shorts, slip-on sneakers, and a Cowboy Mouth band T-shirt.

"You remember Miss Amy Shultz?" Tara asked. "The desk called me when she showed."

Amy spoke, "I called the number on your card, but it went to voicemail."

"I didn't get the call. What's going on here?" I rounded my desk and held my hand out for her to shake.

She pulled out a piece of paper and pressed it into my palm. "I have something you might be interested in."

Tara gave me the stink eye. "She insisted on waiting for you."

I opened the paper, which looked to be a scan of someone's writing. It had the capital letters 'MA' and a phone number. "What's this from?"

Amy held up her phone. "That was Harry's. I took the picture and printed it out for you."

"Whose number is this?" I asked while handing the paper to Tara.

"I don't know, but it has something to do with your investigation."

"Technically, we don't have an investigation anymore." Tara sat on her desk as I found a chair. "You're going to have to explain from the beginning."

"I quit last night. Harry and I have been having an affair for about a year. It took me this long to realize he was never going to leave his wife. Last night a light bulb went off in this stubborn head of mine. After he thought I fell asleep, he pulled out that paper and called some guy, but I could only make out a few words here and there."

"How do you know it was a guy?" I asked.

She blinked. "Oh, I don't know. I just assumed."

"How do you know it has to do with us?" Tara asked.

"That I do know because he said Peyroux."

"You know the name of the person he called?"

"No, but I'm guessing the M.A. are his initials."

"How much of the conversation did you make out?" Tara asked.

"He was being threatened. He said your name – Peyroux and he also said Apex."

"Apex?" I asked.

"Definitely Apex. Could that be a European name? The 'A' in M.A.?"

"I'll get a trace on the number," Tara said.

"Whatever we do, we can't let the Feds know."

Amy became concerned. "The FBI? Is Harry being investigated by the FBI?"

"We can't comment on that. Does Harry know you took this picture?" I asked.

"Not a clue."

"So, are you ready to be truthful about that party?"

Her eyes widened. "That was the truth, Lucas. I didn't know of any party."

"That's alright. He didn't want you to know." I pinched the bridge of my nose.

"What is he into?"

I ignored her question and tilted my head, motioning for Tara to follow me out of earshot of Amy. I whispered, "We stopped questioning Harry. I'm guessing M.A. stands for Winslow's boss – whoever that is."

"Obviously, not Raymond Corondelet."

"Are we at the point of ignoring orders?" I bit my bottom lip while waiting for answer that never came.

ALICIA ATTACKED THE SOCCER BALL, aggressive about what she wanted, just like her father. Pure joy crossed her daughter's face every time her foot made contact and Heather suppressed the resentment for Lucas working so much lately, especially when it didn't seem he needed to.

The game ended. After all the post-game shenanigans and victory speeches, Alicia sprinted back to the sidelines. The other parents packed up and left like specially trained Navy Seals on their way to Pizza Hut to celebrate, clogging up the side street. Alicia and Jane were the last ones left on the field chatting it up. When they finished, Jane ran in the opposite direction and Alicia strolled towards her.

"Alicia, let's go. Hurry up." Heather put her hand on her daughter's shoulder. All of the other parents were in their cars, lined up to get out of the neighborhood.

"Chill out, Mom. Look at the street. We're not going anywhere."

Heather stopped about fifty yards from the car to pull out her key. She turned to look at Alicia, whose ponytail whipped in the hot breeze. Her face was dirty and the jersey's underarms were wet. "I know. I just want to get in the air condition."

Not a second later, the car exploded into a fireball. Heather instinctively covered her daughter's head. Alicia shrieked, staring at the wreckage in a state of shock. Bystanders gathered and got out of their cars. Cell phones took video. Time stood still, until screams broke the silence.

"Holy crap! Why did our car blow up?" Alicia asked in a squeaky voice.

"I don't know, honey. I don't know. But, I'm going to call your father."

Heather and Alicia took slow, cautious steps toward the car. Sirens in the distance grew louder by the second.

I OPENED the unlocked door and entered Harry Winslow's house without knocking or ringing the bell. I listened for the scratching claws or bark of an attack dog, ready to shoot it. The house was sprawling, decorated in marble and mirrors, but my momentum took me right into the industrial sized kitchen where his wife hovered over a spread of hot dogs, potatoes, and burgers.

She startled, grabbing a knife. "Who are you? I'll use this."

"I need your husband. Where is he?"

"You want Harry? You don't knock? You barge right into our home?" She pushed the knife forward.

"I don't have time to explain. Where is he?"

"You don't tell me who you are, I'm calling the police." She reached for her cell phone.

I held up my badge. "Mrs. Winslow, I *am* the police. Is he out there? Outside?"

His two kids had just escaped through an open sliding glass door and I covered that ground in seconds. When I reached the patio, Harry was already heading towards me with a long fork wearing an apron. My right hand found his throat, pushing him backwards as my left hand kept his weapon at bay. I pushed until he fell into his patio chair with my weight over his.

"Hi, Harry. How are you? Doing good, I hope." I banged the barbeque fork out of his hand and eased up on his throat. "You weren't going to stab me with that, were you?"

"You're that detective…" He choked. "What are you doing?"

"Leave my daddy alone, mister." The older kid said as his sword swatted my thigh.

"I'm a policeman, little man. I'm not going to hurt your dad. He just scared me with that big fork." Guilt set in as his older brother pulled the kid inside.

"I'm calling 9-1-1," his wife yelled. "The real police." She stood there with the phone in her hand, waiting for her husband's okay.

"You gonna be calm, Harry? If I get off you, can we talk in a civil manner?"

Harry nodded. "It's fine, honey. This is a misunderstanding. Put the phone down and keep the kids inside."

I backed off and pulled a chair next to him. When the sliding door had shut, I said, "One of your imaginary party guests tried to kill my wife."

"What?"

"The Feds are either protecting one of their own or someone high up. You squashed my investigation of your company, so why was there an explosive device placed under my wife's car?"

"Someone put a bomb in your wife's car?" His hand rubbed his stomach as if sick.

"Yes, and it detonated. Luckily there were no casualties."

"I have no idea about that."

"Really? What about Apex? Tell me what you know."

Harry pulled a pill bottle from his shorts, popping one in his mouth. "They do that to your wife's car, what do you think will happen to me?"

"At this point, I don't give a shit about you. Maybe your wife would like to know the kinds of benefits your pretty blonde employees really get."

He lowered his voice to a growl. "That ended."

"Who is M.A?"

"You know about Apex? You don't know shit."

"I need to know who's in charge. Your best chance is to tell me."

"Over half the people we cater to have the kind of connections that the mob would envy. Once wind got out that there was an investigation, they got very nervous. Made lots of calls, many of them to me. I'm the one that orders the Almas Caviar that was found in that girl's stomach. I'm the reason my clients are nervous. I'm lucky to still be alive and you really think I have the power to call it off?"

"I don't think you have any power at all. I need to know who does."

"If I were you, I'd concentrate on protecting your wife and daughter. That bomb was a warning, or they'd be dead."

I almost struck him across the face. Harry Winslow, Esquire, was a mid-level link on the food chain, nowhere near calling the shots, unless he was a great actor. There always seemed to be a bigger fish. I stared at him and God help me, Chance came to mind.

THIRTY-EIGHT

Tabby leaned in close to apply the smoky shadow around Cozy's eyes. That, with the new hairstyle, made her virtually unrecognizable from the homeless girl who had appeared right off the street. Cozy wore a green, strapless evening gown, much like she had seen in bridal magazines, but was curious about the outfit they expected her to wear at the party. Another glass of wine would help calm her nerves.

Tabby poured two glasses. "So, Ray was cooperative?"

"Not at all. Very closed-lipped."

"You must have tried to work that bayou charm."

"My charms had no effect on that man. After he changed the subject a couple of times, I decided to let it go. But, I'm not through by a long shot. I'll find out who Haley was with at the party tonight from one of the other girls."

"If you ask any questions, Ray will hear about it."

Cozy finally made eye contact. "I'd rather not talk about Ray."

"Sure, but it's just that he hasn't called me yet and he isn't answering. With your going over there, he should have rang me up as soon as you walked out the door."

"Who knows with that guy? How do I look?"

"You are absolutely stunning." Tabby inspected her creation. "You could pass for fifteen or twenty-five, depending on what they're looking for."

"So, you know who I'm getting tonight?"

"Senator Folsom, I think."

"Folsom?" *This wasn't a coincidence.*

Tabby continued, "Usually, the participants pick the girls out, but you were chosen by the VIP you serviced the other night specifically for the Senator." Tabby entwined her fingers with Cozy's, who stood with a bland expression. They faced each other in a moment of silence. Tabby placed her hands on Cozy's waist. "Like I've said; you can't fish for information with the Senator. Questions are not allowed."

"I know."

"If you have it in your head that he killed your sister, you might do something you'll regret."

Cozy turned away. "Either way, is Folsom all that innocent?"

"Don't go down that road."

"What?"

Tabby caressed her forearm. "It's not up to you to decide who's guilty or their degree of guilt. You've already killed two people in your lifetime."

"I'll be good." Cozy didn't lift her arms, but forced a smile as Tabby pulled her close.

"What are your plans afterwards?" Tabby asked. "When you're done with this mission of yours?"

"Depends on if I get caught. You?"

"Rethink my life. Maybe get out of the game."

"Ray won't be too happy with that, I imagine."

"He'd be hurt, but he knows my heart isn't with Molly's anymore. Maybe I should call him again."

Cozy touched her wrist. "Oh, he did say he had a meeting in Baton Rouge."

"Baton Rouge on a Sunday?"

"Something about a casino."

"He's probably hob-nobbing with the politicians up there. The mayor and City Council isn't enough anymore. He so wants to get close to the governor. I think he may run for office one day. I think this city would love that he owned a strip club." Tabby rose onto her toes to kiss Cozy on the forehead.

TABBY CHAUFFEURED Cozy and three other girls down the oak-lined entrance of a magnificent three-story plantation home situated behind acres of vibrant green grass. She had never seen anything so majestic and, considering its history, so tragic. Tabby informed her passengers that this place was used for weddings, private dinner parties and political fundraisers for many black politicians – ironic, given the number of slaves that had been abused on this very land.

Tonight, the entire staff had been given the day off.

They veered around the side of the house to the servant's entrance. If things went as planned, Cozy could possibly try to reunite with Tabby one last time. Vegas odds would say that she would never see Tabby again. As the other girls piled out, Cozy leaned in for a quick, discreet kiss on Tabby's lips.

A man in a dark suit and glasses held the door open without a greeting, giving everyone a clear entrance. Cozy scooted in with the other girls and was escorted to a luxurious room with pristine antique furniture, where a spread of sliced fruit, crab cakes, finger sandwiches and lemonade sat in plain view. Each of the curious ladies found a chair and waited in silence. Cozy figured they were all being watched on some multi-screen video feed in another part of the mansion.

Two more women entered the room dressed to impress. They exchanged a glance, but didn't fraternize much like kids at their first school dance. She wondered if there were more escorts in the other rooms and, underneath it all, how sick that this was just an excuse to have a sex party.

"First time?" A tall, slender blonde asked. She didn't wait for an answer as she downed a full glass of lemonade. Her eyes twinkled blue against pale skin.

Cozy smiled, patting the chair for her to sit. "Yeah, does it show?"

"You're wide-eyed. This is my third party. An Arkansas

congressman has taken a liking to me. Well, he likes what I do for him."

"Do I want to know?"

"It might help relax you to know what you're getting into. Hold on a second." The blond got up on long boney legs and refilled her glass. She returned taking a large swallow.

"Thirsty? That's going to make you have to pee really bad."

"Exactly."

"Exactly, what? Won't your having to pee make it uncomfortable for you?"

"Oh, sweetie, you are so cute. He *wants* me to piss on him. Sure, any one of these chicks can squat over him and let loose, but apparently I have the strongest stream he's ever seen."

"That's gross."

"My talent for peeing makes me a shit-load of money. You have to be prepared for anything. Just remember, you're not here to get off – they are. What they like has nothing to do with you. You just have to play along."

"Thanks. That's good advice."

The blonde finished the lemonade and let out a charming belch before filling it up again.

THIRTY-NINE

After leaving Harry Winslow in a nervous stupor, I stopped at my in-laws where my wife and daughter were still holed up due to the press camped out on our front lawn. So far, the Public Affairs Officer gave a press conference stating that the car bomb was under investigation, but that wouldn't satisfy them. Let those vultures sit in front of my empty house. Captain Dobson had assigned a squad car to my in-law's house just in case.

Heather and Alicia were sitting at the kitchen table with her parents Carl and Ruth. A thick, circular rug lay under their feet and a stained-glass fixture hung above. There was barely any room between them and the walls.

"Why is your main priority to investigate this man?" Heather chastised. "We almost died."

"Because it's not going to end. If we don't find Cozy, they'll kill her."

Carl and Ruth stayed quiet, probably having given Heather their opinion earlier. Carl's hand rested on his wife's wrist. They held their tongue, but they had never been shy about sharing their opinion of me, or my job.

Heather stayed calm for Alicia's sake. "Do you love your job more than us?"

I grabbed a nearby bar stool as I was the only one standing. "How can you ask me that? That bomb was a scare tactic."

"Well, we're scared." Heather pounded the table.

"This isn't about my job or my love for my family. This is about humans being treated as animals in a network so powerful that the FBI looks the other way. They are taking other parent's daughters. Like Alicia."

"Don't you dare mention her name in the same breath as those people." She grabbed Alicia's hands. "Jesus, Lucas."

"As far as they know, I'm not investigating their operation anymore. There won't be a reason to retaliate." After a bout of silence, I spoke again. "I'm going into the station. I'll keep you updated." I leaned in and gave my wife and daughter a kiss, but I felt it wasn't welcomed.

As I CAME into the station, Tara had just finished tapping on her keyboard and then ran to the printer. "How's the family?"

"Hanging in there."

"I can't imagine. Don't worry, we'll find those bastards."

"What you got there?" I pointed at the laser in her hand.

"I think I got something on Apex."

"Tell me." I sat down, considering a meeting with Chance.

"There's an Apex Industries that's an importer-exporter of clothes, alcohol, and other shit. They run the Claiborne Container Terminal on the river."

"Trouble is, I have to put my family into protective custody just to ask any questions." I looked over the laser.

"I'm with you, either way."

"I know. Giving up goes against every fiber of my being."

"So, what do we think of Apex?" Tara flicked the laser while in his hands.

"That freight dock would be a perfect front for trafficking. Do they bring in the women for Harry's parties or does Harry supply women for export? Does Raymond sell one or two of his strippers to make some extra cash? Haley could have been one that fought back. That video she made had other bodies with her."

"Corporate offices for Apex Industries are guess where?"

"Spring-Love Square? Probably above Winslow's offices. The problem here is that we'd have to catch them in transport. Once we ask the first question, they'll shut it all down and then plant another bomb."

"This is your call, Lucas."

"Heather and Alicia are with her parents and two cops are sitting outside. They lost the element of surprise. It's late. Let's go home and look into Apex tomorrow and see how this plays out."

Tara grabbed her purse and a man's voice boomed from the doorway. "I wouldn't do that, Lucas."

"Chance."

My friend approached in jeans and a powder blue collared shirt. "I came as soon as I heard about the car bomb. The news stations are going on and on about mob hits and terrorist strikes. How's Heather and Alicia?"

"They're good. What do you mean, you wouldn't go to Apex?"

Tara came to my side. "What business is it of yours, Mr. Mayor?"

"These are very powerful people with everything to lose."

"Chance, I love you more than my real brother, but your friggin' picture is hanging up in Raymond Corondelet's office. You are the last person to be telling me how to handle this investigation."

"You think I had something to do with this?"

"The bombing of my wife's car? No, but you're in a position to know things that you would never tell me. The corruption runs so rampant, how can you be the mayor and not know the players?"

"What I know is the type of people they are. They're ruthless and power-hungry and will destroy anyone in their path. All small-time, local politicians start out wanting to do good things, but as we rise, we all reach a level where we either play ball or stop rising up the ladder. Check your soul at the door kind of shit. I'm still clean. I haven't been asked to play ball yet."

"Will you, if that gets you governor?"

He turned away from me. "I honestly can't answer that question right now. Harry Winslow is my campaign manager and he's lining up contributors. If they're dirty, put them away for life, but I have nothing to do with their business practices."

"Winslow is dirty. He practically told me how dirty he is. You have to get out now, Chance. If you're not a part of it."

"Then, let's you and me go talk to Harry again. Put the Apex thing on hold for now."

Tara spoke, "I can find out who the employees are. Maybe we can isolate one and limit the damage."

I nodded. "That's worth considering."

"As it is, you're disobeying Captain Dobson's direct orders and interfering with a Federal investigation."

"It's a fake investigation, Chance."

"Fake or not, the Bureau is involved."

"So, fire me."

"Come on. Let's go to Harry's and the three of us will hash this out."

WE TOOK separate cars to Harry's home. I pulled behind Chance's Towncar in the circular, bricked drive. Chance got out of the car while on his cell phone in unison with his driver. He hung up as we started for the door.

"Wait here," he told his driver, who immediately fumbled for a smoke.

The humid air filled my lungs, making them heavy. Chance unbuttoned the top of his collar as if that would get him to relax. He rang the bell.

His wife answered in shorts and a heavy plaid shirt. "Chance? *And you.*"

"Sorry about that, Mrs. Winslow." I bowed my head.

"I can forgive your intrusion. If my car blew up, I'd want Harry to be as passionate about finding the answers. Not that I know what information Harry would have."

"He knows people."

"Well, Harry has to be the most popular man in New Orleans today."

"Why do you say that?" Chance took a step, but hesitated.

"Oh, where are my manners. Come on in. I just put the boys to bed." They entered the kitchen. "First Detective Peyroux here busts into the house and has some kind of serious conversation with Harry and then two FBI agents show up on my door step."

"The Feds?" I asked.

"Yes. At least they said they were. Two large, rough looking men."

"They show identification?"

"No. Harry said to let them in. They went into his study for fifteen minutes and then left. Harry hasn't come out since. Do you know what's going on?" Her expression switched to concern.

"Hasn't been out since?" I parroted.

Chance touched her arm. "Why don't you wait here."

Instead, she headed towards the study, but I stopped her abruptly. "Seriously. I should go in alone."

"You're scaring me."

"Just wait here with me." Chance calmed her down.

I stopped at the door and knocked on the dense wood. "Harry?"

No answer.

"I'm coming in, Harry."

I entered to see Harry slumped over his desk as if he fell asleep while working. Chance appeared at the door. I rushed to Harry's side, noticing an empty pharmacy bottle by his hand with a few pills scattered about. Harry was cold. He didn't have a pulse.

"Oh, God." Came from the doorway.

Mrs. Winslow, with her hands over her mouth, faltered backwards.

"Call 9-1-1." Chance yelled.

She ran down the hall and Chance wiped his forehead. I searched the desk, finding a note under his other hand. It simply said *I'm so sorry*.

Chance's shock was real. "Do you think he really killed himself? Or those FBI agents...?"

"You know what I think." I searched the room for some magical evidence as Chance wiped his hands on his thighs in panic. The shelves were all in order, his desk clean. The drawers in his desk had legal pads, invoices and bills. A display of Mardi Gras memorabilia caught my eye. He must have caught a coconut from the Zulu parade for the past thirty years.

I glanced in his garbage can. It was completely clean except for one tiny, balled up piece of paper. I reached in and uncurled it. It was a business card on thick stock.

"What have you got there?" Chance asked.

"A business card from LaPlace on Bourbon. Mark Alexander, proprietor." The initials M.A. were seared on my brain.

"Harry hires LaPlace to cater his parties – used to. He knew Mark Alexander pretty well." Chance finally looked to be getting his senses back.

I put the card in my pocket. We left the home office and trotted into the living room where Mrs. Winslow paced while on the phone. She put the cell against her shoulder with tears falling down her cheeks. "Police are coming."

"I have to leave," I said.

"We both have to leave," Chance added.

"My husband just committed suicide! Where are you going?" Here wild eyes darted between us. Her arms spread as if to stop us.

I held my hand up. "I'm so sorry. Tell the police that I'll make a statement later. I can't explain, but I have to go. I'm sorry."

Chance followed, shutting the front door. He yelled to me in the driveway. "Where are you going?"

"Back to the station. I just can't be here. I'm not supposed to be investigating him, remember?"

"You're going to talk to Mark Alexander." He stopped at his car. The driver had the engine running already.

"Were are *you* going?" I asked to deflect his accusation while opening my car door.

Chance sighed, looking back at the house. "Alexander does his books on Sunday nights. He's probably at the restaurant right now." Chance pursed his lips as if he had seen my future.

MARK ALEXANDER'S greased hairline retreated towards the back of his head, but his European goods looks more than compensated. However, close up, I could tell he had the remnants of large abnormality that covered most of his forehead. He stood when he saw us enter.

"Your hostess brought us through the kitchen." I inspected Alexander's office with Tara at my side after climbing a flight of stairs. "Quite amazing."

"The kitchen is the heart of the restaurant. It must beat properly." His accent was New Orleans, but didn't flow naturally, like he had learned it. Alexander continued to stand, waiting for Tara and I to take our places opposite his desk.

Tara eased into a chair made of twisted white pipes with a flat square to sit on, more suited to be a work of art. I maneuvered into the chair's cousin, the same pipes twisted into a letter 'A'. They were sturdier than they looked.

"Interesting chairs," I commented.

"I bought them from an art student at UNO. Form and function."

"You support a lot of the arts and charities around New Orleans."

Alexander shrugged. "Least I can do for the city that has given me so much."

"Thanks for taking our questions." Tara said.

Mark Alexander tilted a gracious nod with smiling eyes. "My scar," he said after noticing my eyes shifting.

"I'm sorry."

"Don't be. An unfortunate accident with a deep fryer in my youth."

"Ouch. Lucky you weren't blinded."

"True dat."

"Do you know this man, Harry Winslow?" I put a picture on his desk taken at a fundraiser we found on the Internet.

He glossed over the picture. "Obviously, I do. He insists I call him Harry, but we're business associates, not friends. I've been to a couple of his functions, as I like to dabble in politics. Sometimes it helps my business. I catered some of those functions."

"What about this girl? Do you recognize her?" I placed Haley's picture in front of him.

He peered at it. "If our paths crossed, I don't remember. But, I meet many people that I forget."

"She was a guest at one of Harry's parties. She was found in the Mississippi River."

"Yes. That's sad. The manager of her apartment complex was just murdered, too. And your wife and daughter were almost killed by a car bomb. Terrible coincidences, eh?"

"I see you're up on current events." Tara spoke for me.

"I just watch the news. Half of it is crime related." His elbows rested on his desk, making a pyramid up to where his hands met his chin.

I threw my left foot onto my right knee, adding to the chair's symmetry. "We're trying to avoid getting a warrant for Mr. Winslow's client list. We really want to ask about one guest from a party that no one will admit to."

He folded his arms. "As far as I know, none of Mr. Winslow's parties fall in the realm of secret. And I have not been to one of his events for months."

"Harry Winslow was found dead this evening. *That* hasn't been on the news yet."

His small eyes finally opened. "That's horrible. How did he pass?"

"Hasn't been determined yet. You're Russian, right?"

He sat straight, appraising me. "Yes. How do you know?"

"Not by your accent. You got New Orleans down. It's your name - Alexander. Plus, we can't find a record of you before the past decade. It's like you didn't exist and then you come to New Orleans and buy LaPlace on Bourbon. How does that happen?"

"If you are through asking me about Mr. Winslow, then please leave. I am very busy."

"Have you heard of Apex Industries?"

He stared at me – hard – like I insulted him.

I continued, "Apex controls the Container Terminal. They import Top Notch vodka." I said, more than asked.

"Yes, one of our many spirits. Your point?" He shifted in his chair.

"LaPlace on Bourbon… is this your hobby?"

"I find hobby to be a dismissive word and you've obviously never owned a restaurant."

"I've eaten here recently with Mayor Picaud."

"Ah, Mayor Picaud. A class act, soon to be governor. I trust that you enjoyed yourselves?"

"I'm more of a poboy man myself, but yes, I must say the entire experience was excellent. Would you say that you and the mayor are friends, or just business associates?"

"What business is that of yours?" His eyes dropped. "I understand that you and Mayor Picaud are close. He spoke highly of you when he requested the table the other night."

"I want to know the nature of your relationship."

"I see. Perhaps I can put my social life in perspective for you and your lovely, lovely partner. I don't have any friends that are business associates and I don't have any business associates that are friends. The two don't mix."

"I cleared my throat. "One more thing, Mr. Alexander. Are you the head of a human trafficking ring operating out of your docks? Do you sell women?"

In my peripheral, Tara reared back with saucer eyes, but said nothing.

Alexander gave us no reaction at first, but then laughed. "That's ridiculous."

"So, you don't go to Molly's Girls to pick out the new crop? Cater Winslow's parties to find the gems to sell overseas? I'll bet beautiful American girls go for huge bucks."

His eyes grew darker. "I work hard and I often work late. You want to know why, detective?" He paused. "Because I have no family. No family to go home to. You are a lucky man to have a loving wife and daughter."

"You Russians love to veil threats, don't you."

He waved me off. "Leave my restaurant before I file a complaint."

I pulled out my weapon to inspect it. "I know warnings are popular these days. Well, here's a warning. I'm holding you responsible for *anything* that happens from here on out. Eye for an eye. I love that saying."

Tara grabbed my arm. "Lucas, let's go."

"Listen to the lady detective, before you secure greater regrets in your life."

I stood and leaned over the desk, putting my face within inches of his. I didn't say a word. I didn't blink. I didn't move. A few moments later, Tara pulled me back and we exited.

A CALL to Heather gave me temporary relief, but my day wasn't done. The afternoon sun had long dipped out of sight, allowing nocturnal establishments to lure tourists to the streets. Molly's Girls vibrated with life and the customers were gaining, most saving the stripper experience until they were good and lit. Tara and I maneuvered through the tables to the back hallway where I recognized the bouncer from last time.

"Detectives, how are you?" He folded his arms as if on instinct.

"Ray here?" I asked.

"Mr. Corondelet didn't come in today. Miss Tabitha's here."

"Can you get her for us?"

The bouncer didn't move, but spoke into his collar. "Miss Tabitha, you have guests."

A moment later, the stunning dancer-turned-manager strolled out wearing an elegant red evening gown. "I assume you're not here for the show."

"You look like the queen of the debutante ball."

"A canceled engagement, I'm afraid."

"You expecting Mr. Corondelet anytime soon?"

"That's why I'm here now. He should be here, but I believe he's running late from a meeting in Baton Rouge, probably gambling. He's not picking up his phone."

"We need to talk about Keri Sullivan… or Cozy Robicheaux if you didn't know her real name."

Her tough exterior immediately evaporated. "You guys want a Coke? Follow me to the bar."

The music was just loud enough to cover our conversation. Tabby ordered us three Cokes and then offered a secluded table nearby. We sat close, like familiar college friends, with Tabitha in the middle.

Tabitha started without prompting. "I know she's not Keri Sullivan. Last night, Cozy confessed to me that Haley Robicheaux was her sister and how she's been searching for the people responsible. She's in trouble, isn't she?"

"She's wanted for the murder of a local drug dealer and is a person of interest in the shooting of Vincent Dean. I'm afraid there may be more in her wake."

"She killed someone?"

"When was the last time you've seen her?"

"Last night we had dinner at Antoine's. It was late and we were drunk, so I let her sleep on my couch."

"She obviously doesn't believe you're the killer," I said. "With your being alive."

"I suppose."

"Where is she now?"

Tabitha glanced back and forth at us, settling on Tara's gentle eyes. "I don't want to go to jail."

Tara spoke with concern. "Why would you go to jail?"

"For being an accessory or accomplice… whatever it's called for knowing beforehand."

"You would only be arrested for obstruction of justice if you lie to us now," I explained.

She exhaled while looking up at the muted glow of the strobes. "I know where Cozy is."

"Where?"

"I'm afraid of what she might do if cornered. You can't hurt her."

"That's the last thing we want. We'll give her every chance."

"I know the NOPD. You'll roll in with sirens blaring and scare the shit out of her. Then what?"

"It's just me and Detective Gray. We'll go in alone."

"I have a number to her burner cell. Would you be satisfied if I could just get her here?"

"She'll run. Tell us where she is." I said.

"She won't run. She's at one of Ray's parties." Tabby already had the number dialed. "Pick up, Cozy. Pick up." She waited, the hope drained from her face. "They probably took her phone. She's not answering."

"We'll go pick her up, alone and safely."

"It's an hour away. You're going to call it in, and then who knows what the Keystone Cops out there will do."

"We won't call it in." I touched her hand. "Tabitha, I give you my word Tara and I will drive out there to get Cozy ourselves."

Her lips pulled up into a tiny smile. "You two have a special relationship, don't you?"

"Despite myself, yes. Where is she?"

Tabitha hesitated, sucking in her cheek. "She's at The LeCoure Mansion on River Road."

"Don't call her again, but if she calls you from a different location…" I squeezed her fingers. "…tell her to meet you back here and then give us a call. Like you, I don't want to see her hurt."

FOR TWO HOURS Cozy mingled with some of the country's most powerful political figures in a grand ballroom. High ceilings held crystal chandeliers and tall round tables without chairs were strategically placed apart on an immaculate red carpet. Men in bow ties passed around little bites of food and glasses of bubbly. She observed many old and unattractive men talking with young, beautiful women. Nothing odd about that.

A bell sounded and the men acted as if it was last call. All the women filed into a satellite room and waited. Eventually, a sturdy man in a glittery Mardi Gras mask escorted her by the hand up a winding staircase, past portraits of Confederate soldiers. They stopped at a room where the man held out a key for Cozy to view. He turned and unlocked the oversized door.

"The safe word is coconut." He stepped aside.

"Coconut," she repeated.

The man didn't enter the room, but he shut the door once she entered. The four-poster bed had a mattress that seemed unusually high, but more luxurious than any she'd ever felt. The furniture matched the era of the house, as far as she knew, including uncomfortable looking paisley chairs with busy patterns and a dazzling chandelier. Elegant paintings with gold leaf frames adorned the walls and in the center of the room lay a large green area rug on shiny brown hardwood and not a speck of dust.

Her outfit had been laid out, specific to her size, as Ray must have planned on her showing. Cozy stripped down naked in complete silence, putting on a red, leather, skin-tight dress with thigh-high boots. She strutted back and forth, getting used to the character she was to play. *He wants to be dominated*, she thought with a smile. She could pull that off.

"On your knees, dog." She swatted the horsewhip onto the mattress. "Lick my boots." She laughed, pretending to kick him in the ass, and then growled in the mirror with a devilish sneer. "You… are… pathetic."

A knock on the door startled her. It opened a crack and an older man with graying hair peered inside. "Mistress Keri?"

Time to begin. "Get your sorry ass in here. Now."

"Yes, Mistress." He shuffled in, wearing a sharp pinstripe suit and power tie.

"You think I'm impressed? Strip out of those rags before you make me really angry."

After he tossed his shirt and pants aside, Cozy secured a dog collar and leash on top the dresser, wrapping it around his wrinkled neck. They played the game, back and forth for twenty minutes and Cozy held her own. She had to force herself not to gut this disturbed individual by remembering he had been with Haley. He probably spent most of his day treating people like shit; always in control and this was his way to let go. She lured him onto the bed as she knotted up lengths of nylon rope that had been supplied. Once gagged with his hands tied to each post, she got down to business.

"Coconut! Coconut!"

The senator's arms and legs were pulled tight, his erection long gone. Cozy closed the mouth-zipper shut on his leather mask. "Say it all you want, it won't make you safe."

She waved her switchblade and his eyes grew wider than the narrow slits that allowed sight. He frantically mumbled something as his frail body flopped like a fish. When his energy finally subsided, she took his thumb and placed the tip of the switchblade under the manicured nail, scraping at its underbelly. "I need some information."

Incoherent sounds vibrated under the mask as his fingers stiffened, not yet curling under. His eyes pleaded with her.

"You want to say something? Okay, but if I unzip your mask, you have to stay quiet. One shout for help and this blade goes in your throat." She pushed the tip against his jugular. "Got it?"

He nodded and she pulled the zipper open. He fumbled through his sentence. "What do you want?"

"Tell me about Mistress Haley."

"Haley? The dancer that turned up dead?"

"So, you know her. This is a promising start."

"I did not kill her. We had sex. That was all." His aging skin hung off his face.

"Of course you're going to deny killing her, Senator. I'm about to pop off your fingernails one by one."

"All I have is my word. I'm a senator, damn it. Why would I risk my career by killing someone?"

"It's because you're a senator that you *can* kill someone. People like Ray Corondelet will always clean up your messes. Oh, well." She zipped the mouth closed and stuck the tip of the blade halfway up his thumbnail before he could wiggle it away.

The mask muted the old man's agonizing screams. His bloody hand jolted from her grasp and she exhaled, making a show of her patience. When his moaning subsided, she unzipped the mask while blood dripped on the corner of the mattress.

He whispered, "If I say anything, they'll kill me or disgrace me and my career."

"Then the question is: when do you want to die? Because if you're still not talking by the time I'm done, I'm killing you anyway. You tell me what I want to know, you'll live through the night."

"This isn't happening. I'm a very powerful man." But his failing voice betrayed that statement.

Cozy zipped the mouth shut again and secured his arm under her armpit. When she couldn't get him to unclench his smeared red fist, she jabbed the knife between his knuckles like she was shucking an oyster. When his hand opened, she ran the knife under the exposed thumbnail again. With a full body jolt, he gazed at the nail that resembled the open hood of a car.

After a series of growling muffled cries, she unzipped the mask for him to speak, this time as a weak, scared old man. "Okay, I'll tell you everything. Okay? Please."

"Just remember that I already know a lot. If you lie, you lose another nail. Go."

"Haley was going to be sold."

"Sold?"

"It's the truth. Some of the girls that come to these parties get sold. I don't know to who."

"Like slaves?"

"Sex slaves. Most girls return home so as not to draw suspicion, but the special ones are offered to the highest bidder. The party's like an audition. Like an auction."

"I believe you. The thing I want to know is who was selling her and who was buying her."

"I don't know. Foreigners come to this. I'm not involved in that."

Cozy took his pinky finger and brought the knife to rest under his nail.

He shrunk like a slug with salt. "The girls are kept in a warehouse on the Apex Industries property until they decide to move them."

"Where's that?"

"It's the Claiborne Container Terminal on the river… right off Napoleon."

"Who's in charge there?"

"I don't know anyone from Apex. I just know the girls are brought there because the place is immune from inspections. It's protected."

"I'm pleased with your cooperation. Go on."

Saliva collected on the mouth slit of the mask. He stammered, "When they get enough girls, they put them in a cargo container to be shipped. Sometimes mass quantities of girls are imported, but they don't come to these parties. I hear some of the less desirable ones are donors for black market body parts. Ray controls that. I don't buy or sell; I just participate."

"You sick freaks. Why was Haley killed if she was going to be sold?"

"I don't know. Maybe she fought back or pissed someone off. Maybe she knew what was happening and slashed her own face." His body bounced as he sobbed. "I swear she was alive when I left her."

Cozy backed away, and sat, pulling off her stilettos with eyes on Folsom. His body sagged like Jesus on the cross. She put her regular dress back on, and then searched Folsom's coat pockets until finding his cell phone. "I'll bet you're very photogenic. Does your wife and kids know how photogenic you are?"

His voice calmed, speaking like a father. "There is no place on earth for you to hide. These men will find you and kill you, you know. Or sell you like the others."

Cozy looked outside the window to the tree with its outstretched limbs. "You let me worry about that. I'll be long gone before they feel the need to bust down the door."

"You don't need to send those pictures. My wife already knows."

"Who said anything about your wife? Don't worry, Senator. If your information pans out, I'll destroy the pictures and video. But, if you're lying, well, the American public would like to know the habits of their elected officials. I'm turning your GPS off, too."

The light flashed on. Ray's pupils reacted to an explosion as intense as the Hiroshima bomb. Despite feeling like tiny laser beams had seared his brain, he needed to see who had entered his home. Fearful that Cozy had returned, he stayed still – not that he had a choice.

"Aren't you a sight?" The tape was ripped off his lips.

"About time you got here. Get something to cut me loose… and get me some water. God, I'm fucking thirsty."

"Let me guess… Cozy Robicheaux, vigilante."

Ray's eyes had finally adjusted to the light. "When I get my hands on her, I'm going to skin her, and then kill her."

"No, you won't. She's worth too much. So, what'd you give up? Did you tell her anything?"

"Nothing of real importance." His head rotated in a stretch.

"You're lying."

"I told her nothing," he insisted.

"So, she left you here alive and left with nothing."

Ray squinted. "Yeah… she's got nothing."

"Then, you're a lucky bastard. I just got a call; she worked the same magic on Folsom, but he spilled his guts. He's got to make up some reason why he lost a thumbnail and needs stitches on three of his fingers."

"It only took three fingers for him to cave? Couldn't happen to a nicer guy."

"More bad news. She's in the wind."

"She escaped the party? How incompetent can your guys be?"

His associate looked closer between Ray's legs. "She got away from *you*. But unlike you, Folsom didn't get waxed or have his nut sack torn off. Ah, it's not that bad, but it looks like she took a lawnmower to you."

"Cut me out of this tape, damn it." He tried to rock his body. "Do you at least have your people looking for her?"

"The senator told Cozy about the operation. We're moving the girls tonight."

"That spineless bastard." He struggled against the tape again. "We need to find her before she goes to the wrong cops or finds a news station for Christ's sake."

"Relax, she hasn't shown her face yet. Believe me, I'd know."

"Why does it seem like you're enjoying my pain? How many times do I have to say it? Get me out of this fucking duck tape." Ray shook violently, but failed to move the dense, metal chair.

"Not until I talk sense into you. You can't kill her, Ray. She can't even have a bruise."

"I'll find another one just as hot for the buyer. Jesus, they're crawling all over the Quarter."

"You aren't thinking straight."

"Fine." He made a point to show that his breathing relaxed. "I'll track her down tonight and deliver her to Apex. Just cut me loose, please."

"And where do you plan on looking, Ray?" His partner waited. "Whether she goes back to Manchac or appears on Peyroux's doorstep, we'll reel her in at a later date. After that, we should probably cool it for a while."

"Huh?"

"The gasket's leaking. We need to stop and seal the leaks."

"Are you that naïve to think we're going to stop?"

"You're not the one who makes the final decision."

Ray's eyes became soft. "We plow on. These parties, these girls, the money… we're a good team with a network of powerful people that look out for us. Don't freak out on me now."

"True, but this is the closest an investigation has ever come. Even the Feds can't get them to stop. A friggin' car bomb can't get him to stop."

"The Feds are a means to an end. We operate under a huge umbrella. We're fine. Cut me loose."

"You're okay?"

"Yes. You talked me down. The important thing is to get the shipment out. Then regroup."

"Don't expect me to be gentle."

"Does it look like I've just had a bubble bath? Get it the fuck off."

"Let me get a knife." Dress shoes tapped across hardwood,

returning from the kitchen with a pair of scissors instead. "I figured this might work better, considering your night."

Once the tape had been cut away from his wrists, ankles and chest, his visitor left. Ray stood in front of the bathroom mirror, his body vibrating in a rage. His skin appeared to have melted in some spots and his remaining body hair was mangy, with lacerations and bruises on his face. He couldn't go to the hospital. Best to take pain pills, clean up, and bandage the bad areas. After he retrieved the stolen client list Cozy found in the safe, he had to make sure that bitch suffered an excruciating death.

WALKING on the side of the unlit road in the middle of nowhere reminded Cozy of the myth about the teenaged girl walking home from prom in a bloody dress, who is picked up by a stranger in a passing car. When the driver finally pulled up to the girl's address, she had disappeared from his front seat. He then learns from the people living at the house that their daughter had been killed the year before hitchhiking from the prom. She felt chills shudder up and down her spine.

It took an hour of trudging along the side of the road towards Uptown before finding an open cab to take her to the hotel room. She changed into jeans and a T-shirt, grabbed her purse carrying the gun, and kissed the alligator pendant before headed toward the club. One last stop before this whole thing came to a head.

The finality of her mission loomed. With a Saints cap and fake Walgreens glasses, she hiked into the heart of the Quarter, weaving in and out of faceless pedestrians on Bourbon, as it was blocked off to traffic at night. The crowd-heavy street allowed for perfect cover until entering Molly's Girls like any other dancer. She pulled her cap and glasses off and stopped at the bar. "Can I get a cup of water, Chris? I'm here to see Tabitha. She's in the back?"

He slid the water to her. "Yeah, she's back there."

Cozy walked into Tabby's office and closed the door, falling against it with her back. "Thank God you're here. Jesus, what a trip."

Tabby was on her cell, but held up a finger to Cozy. "Just calm down. Breathe Ray… breathe. Yeah… that's right… okay." She hung up and threw the phone down. "That was Ray. He's lost it. He's got his gun and he's out looking for you because you tortured him. Cozy, you lied to me."

"I gave you deniability. Where is he now?"

"He wouldn't say, but he was just on the phone calming down Senator Folsom, who you also tortured. Cozy, I don't think you're going to make it out of this alive." Her hands wiped down each side of her face, waiting for a response.

"If not, so be it. But, they're going to get a hell of a fight." She gripped her purse.

"Well, I expect Ray to show up here at some point." Tabby stared at her.

"I better not be here when he does."

"Want to tell me about Folsom?"

"Likes to be dominated. Yet doesn't like real pain."

"Is that all?" Tabby perked up straight, waiting in silence. Cozy scooted forward, holding back the tears. She reached out her hands and Tabby hesitated in reciprocation, but caved. "Talk to me."

"You ever wonder why some of your dancers don't come back from these parties?"

Tabby pulled her hands back and turned away. "Ray says they quit."

"He sells them, Tabby. They get sold and shipped to Russia, Brussels, fucking Prague. Some stay right here in the United States. Can you believe that? In our own country. That senator told me everything, and believe me, Dick Cheney couldn't have got more out of him. Haley was going to be sold before they murdered her. Doesn't that piss you off?"

"Sold? No, Ray would never sell his girls. Would he? Oh, God."

"It's true."

"True or not, these are very dangerous people. They will kill you if they don't already have a bounty on your head."

"I don't have a lot of time, then."

"I had to tell the cops about the party, but I also had to call them to shut it down. The police are probably at the mansion right now, but these guys prepare for these situations with a clean -up crew. They won't find anything, so my guess is those detectives are coming right back here."

"I'm going to the Apex dock to get the evidence I need to shut this down. The party was tonight, so I'm guessing the girls will be moved tonight. Your career is done here, Tabby. I love you."

"I can't go with you, Cozy. This is your mission, however tragic the ending."

"Tragic for who?" Cozy hopped to her feet. "We can be together after all of this, if you just give in to it."

"It's not meant to be, honey." Tabby stood and rounded the desk.

Cozy accepted her advance, putting her face in Tabby's neck, squeezing tight. After a moment of listening to Billy Idol's Mony Mony through the thin walls, Tabby cupped Cozy's cheeks and kissed her tenderly.

"If you end this tonight, if you get the vengeance you want for your sister and make it back to me, then yes, I'll run away with you. But, you have to get out of here. Now."

"Walk me out?"

"Sure."

With their fingers entwined, Tabby led her into the hallway, but before entering the main room, she stopped short and clenched Cozy's hand. "Ray's here."

At the entrance, Ray's eyes scanned the crowd until falling on Cozy. He reached behind his back and came back with a gun and barreled toward her, needing to dodge other patrons and dancers who hadn't noticed anything wrong yet.

"Oh, shit. What do I do?"

"Damn, he was on his way here the whole time."

"He's probably upset with me," Cozy said with a nervous laugh. "I'll leave out the back."

"He'll chase you down. The bathroom has a window," Tabby offered. "He'll think he has you trapped while you escape. Hurry, before he makes it back here."

Cozy was well on her way toward the bathroom when a shot

echoed and splinters of wood exploded in front of her. Screams from the main room overpowered the music as her shoulder slammed against the bathroom door, opening it just enough to squeeze through, not realizing Tabby had been behind her the whole way. Cozy fell onto her butt near the sink as Tabby barricaded the door with her entire body.

"Lock it." Cozy whispered.

"There are no locks. Go! The window." Tabby propped her back flush against the door until her butt hit the tiled floor, using her hands and feet for leverage. Bullets penetrated the door above Tabby's head.

Cozy climbed onto the toilet of the middle stall and opened the tiny window wide, revealing a well-lit courtyard shared by the adjoining building. "What's back there?"

"There's an alley that will lead you to Royal. Go."

"What about you?"

"I'll be fine. Get out of here." Her body jolted forward as something akin to a battering ram thumped against the door.

Cozy gave her one last smile as the door almost jumped off its hinges. Ray got his foot in the bathroom and used his leverage to push Tabby across the floor. When Cozy saw the gun, she wasted no time sticking her arms and head out of the window, pulling her body out and landing hands-first in a garden. More shots followed and she prayed his aim was at her and not Tabby. She cringed when she realized she forgot the purse with the gun in the office.

Her feet uprooted hunks of a flowerbed while escaping, scurrying through the dark alley to the wrought iron gate and onto Royal Street where she steadied her pace to match the crowd. If anything happened to Tabby, Ray's torture would be nothing like the first time.

FORTY

The LeCoure Mansion had been abandoned. No cars were in the lot or around back where staff usually parked. George Singer, the overweight, bearded plantation manager, met us on the front steps as we arrived, looking around perplexed. After a short introduction, he opened the huge double doors wide.

He flipped on a switch that lit up every chandelier in sight. "I thought they'd be here all night. This place is clean as a whistle. Maybe they canceled it?"

"Who should be here?" Tara asked.

He pulled a piece of paper from a large manila envelope. "Ryan Diamond. He rented the place for a retirement party. Paid with cash."

I moseyed near the adjoining rooms. "No credit card on file for a damage deposit?"

"All cash. Came in a fancy briefcase and all."

"That didn't signal any red flags?"

"Unusual, yes, but what method of payment is illegal?"

I turned away from him. "So, no paper trail."

"Only this form and copy of the receipt I gave him, which I can assume by the looks on your faces probably has false information. He showed me a driver's license with his picture on it. Gave me his business card." George handed it to me.

"You didn't verify this business address?"

"These weren't college kids on Spring Break. We host these kinds of parties all the time. Usually we offer our staff to serve drinks and hors d'oeuvres, but they paid extra to clear the house tonight. Normally, we'd never do that, but he…"

"He let you have a taste," Tara finished.

George's puffy cheeks flushed under his impeccably groomed beard. "Thirty thousand for the night. Four grand in my pocket. Said he was happy to pay extra for the privacy. Too much to turn down, detective."

"Would you recognize him?"

"Sure. Older man, maybe upper sixties or a good-looking seventy. He was a little over six feet, short gray hair, very expensive suit. And thin lips. I remember lips because I look at them while people talk. I'm slowly going deaf." He pointed at his ears.

"Sorry to hear that… to know that," I said.

"He was driven here in a limo. It was supposed to be a retirement party with professional types."

"Any video cameras around the property?" Tara asked.

"Sorry. The guy requested they be shut off. Said some big-shot celebrity was coming to perform and didn't want to be recorded."

"Seriously?" I asked as my teenage daughter would.

"You should hear what some of these celebrities want. One time John Goodman had a party here and…"

"Mind if we look around on our own?"

"Knock yourselves out. I'd like to see if anything was stolen myself."

As expected, our search of the mansion resulted with a goose egg. We watched from my car as George's tail lights floated down the Oak lined entrance and disappeared onto River Road. Tara fidgeted in the passenger seat as I stared into the ghostly darkness, disappointed having just missed the party.

"Cozy could be in the Mississippi by now," I said.

"Don't think like that. It seems they knew we were coming. They cleared that place out pretty fast."

"Think Tabitha's call warned them? Like that was an abort number? She was dressed as if she'd be attending some kind of gala."

"That makes the most sense," Tara agreed.

"Tabitha and Captain Dobson were the only ones who knew where we were going."

Tara popped a stick of gum in her mouth. "Wheelhouse didn't have to tell us where Cozy was in the first place."

"Knowing she could warn them in time."

"Or Captain Dobson… or anyone Dobson might've told. That's just great. Is it too far-fetched to think those feds are working both sides of the fence?"

"I never thought of that." We stared at each other under the glow of the dashboard. I spoke after a moment of silence. "C'mon, let's get back to Molly's and question Ms. Wheelhouse."

Just before putting my car in drive, Tara's cell rang. "Gray." She listened for a moment. "What? No. What? We're on our way."

"Where to?"

"Your in-law's house."

My eyes grew wide. "Why?"

"There's been a fire. Your in-laws' house burned down."

WE ARRIVED TO A SMOKING, charred shell of a house. Two fire trucks were parked in front, but their hoses had been put away and cops had the block cornered off. I advanced as far as the firefighters would let me with Tara at my side.

"I'm Detective Peyroux. Where's my wife? My daughter?"

The fire captain answered, "Calm down, detective. So far, we haven't found anyone inside the house. It appears to have been empty."

"I looked around the crowd for Heather. "Empty – you're sure?"

"We checked thoroughly."

I looked at the cops that had congregated while dialing Heather's cell again. "I need to find out where my family is." My eyes went from the driveway to the street and I didn't see Heather's car. Her cell phone continued to ring.

Tara waited in anticipation. "Maybe they went out to dinner or a movie. The good news is no one is in there."

"Or they were *taken*." I took a deep breath of burnt wood. "She's still not answering."

The responding officer put his hand on my shoulder. "Let the fire chief do his job here and we'll let you know if we find anything at all."

I nodded. "Where's the security detail that was watching the house?"

"Don't know of any detail."

My cell rang and I looked at the display. "It's Chance," I said to Tara.

"Answer it."

I slid my finger across the screen. "Chance."

"Where are you?" He sounded frantic.

"Believe it or not, I'm standing in front of my in-laws' house that was burned to a crisp and everyone is missing, including the cops assigned to guard it."

"I just heard about the fire. They're with me. Everyone... Alicia, Heather, and her parents."

"Why are they all with you?"

"I got nervous with Harry and you going to Alexander. I didn't know something was going to happen specifically, but like I told you, I know the type of people you're investigating."

"Scumbags."

"Just breathe easy. Everyone's safe."

"Jesus, Chance. As soon as my heart defibrillates, I'll be right over."

OUR EMBRACE LASTED AN ETERNITY, Heather and Alicia cried in my arms as my in-laws sat upset, albeit impressed with the Mayor's palatial house. Chance's assistant offered everyone tea as we sat around the dinner table. He had brought pizza at Chance's request and stayed to help. The same detail that had been positioned outside of my in-laws' was staked out in front the entrance and on the street.

"I don't know what to do anymore," I said to the room.

My daughter spoke up, "Why are they trying to kill us, Daddy?"

I took Alicia's hand. "Because I'm trying to send some very bad people to jail."

"Then stop. Let someone else do it." Tears ran down from her searching eyes.

"Listen to your daughter," Heather's father demanded. "You're going to get us all killed."

My shoulders collapsed. "Then, we should stop."

"My people in Shreveport are fine. I'll support any decision you make, Lucas." Tara lifted her glass of tea at me.

Chance walked in front of us, used to having control. "Lucas, you know my opinion. But, my home is open to Heather, Alicia, your parents and with all the protection it has to offer. I can have round the clock staff and security."

"That's great, Chance, but they have to leave the house sometime." My eyes found Heather, however our connection was disturbed when my cell rang. I answered. "Peyroux."

"Lucas, is Tara with you?"

"Yeah, did something happen with Corondelet?"

"Jesus, I hate when you do that." My captain spoke more seriously, "Yes, I need you and Tara over at Molly's Girls."

"What's going on?"

"I got a call from the station. Shots fired. Witnesses say Corondelet shot up the place. Uniforms are there trying to sort it out, but apparently Cozy Robicheaux was there, but bolted and Corondelet's on the lam."

"We're on our way."

"Lucas, wait."

"Yeah?"

"This may be my last official order to you. I'm resigning."

"Wait – why?"

"Just know it's been a pleasure working with you. And don't blame yourself. I was on board the whole time."

"They got to you."

"We'll talk soon." She ended the call and I found Heather's curious face. "Shots fired at Molly's Girls. Corondelet's gone ballistic. He was trying to kill Cozy."

Her face softened and she nodded, standing behind Alicia with her arms around our daughter. Heather's face nestled near her ear. "Baby, there's a young girl out there, just a little bit older than you and she's in trouble. Your Daddy has to find her before these men hurt her."

"Will you find her tonight?" Alicia asked.

"There's a good chance."

Alicia and I nestled into a hug, something I had been missing for a very long time. Her grip on me tightened as she spoke, "Go find her, Dad. We can stay here one more day."

TWO SQUAD CARS and an ambulance had taken position in front of Molly's Girls. The entire block was quarantined, however people were able to watch from their hotel balconies, some drunk and dangling beads for the boys in blue.

I approached the first cop just outside the door. "What happened?"

"According to witnesses, the owner, Raymond Corondelet, came into the main room firing his gun. Everyone scattered and ran out. One witness says he walked towards the back offices before shooting. One of the bouncers said he might have been shooting at an ex-dancer named Keri."

"Any casualties?" Tara asked.

"No casualties, however two people were injured while fleeing and the manager, Tabitha Wheelhouse, has a concussion. Officer Harvin is trying to get her in the ambulance." His thumb jutted over his shoulder.

"Frank Harvin's here? Wonderful. Thanks officer." We walked towards the ambulance, seeing Tabitha being escorted by the arm by

Harvin in plain clothes as a paramedic waited. Tabitha appeared agitated, trying to pull from Harvin's grip.

We heard her voice rise. "Let me go." She yanked her arm away and when Harvin reached again, her elbow shot up into his mouth, splitting his lip. Tara and I sprinted the rest of the way.

"Whoa, there." I separated Tabitha from Harvin, who was bent over, wiping blood from his chin. "Harvin, why do people feel the need to kick your ass?"

"Fuck you, Peyroux. She assaulted me. Arrest the bitch."

"For what?" Tabitha screamed. "I refused medical treatment and you were forcing me into the ambulance."

"She's right, Frank." Tara added. "You have no cause to subdue a witness like this."

"She has a concussion and I was holding her steady. I'm filing a complaint. That was assault. I'm not letting this go." Harvin turned to engage the paramedic who had retrieved supplies to treat his lip. They walked to the back of the ambulance.

"That was an *accident*."

Tara touched my arm. "I'll check inside. You interview Tabitha again."

"Alright. Meet you back out here."

I opened up the door of a squad car and let Tabitha sit with her feet hanging down on the street. The paramedic's partner ran up with an ice pack for her cheek. She smiled at me. "Not a typical night at Molly's Girls."

"Looks like you had quite a scare." I stayed outside the car, but faced her.

"Ray kind of flipped out."

"You want to tell me what happened?"

"He came in shooting, looking for Cozy. We were in my office just before he got here."

"What happened to Cozy?"

"I told her to turn herself in and I think she was going to. Ray came in with guns blazing. I scooted Cozy out the bathroom window. Don't know where she is now." She lifted the ice pack to show a bandage over a laceration and a swollen face.

"No idea where Ray would go look for her?"

"Not a clue."

"Any idea where Cozy would be?"

"She might be back at her hotel room at the Days Inn. Maybe she's at a police station."

"You need to get checked out at the hospital, but it's just a suggestion." I back up a step with my hands up in surrender.

"I'm alright."

"The place you sent us to was cleaned out. No party. Sort of like they were tipped off."

"I didn't do it. She didn't answer my call. That was it."

Tara's voice called out from behind. "Lucas, got a minute?"

I gave Tabitha a lingering pause, then turned to put some distance between us. "What's up?"

"Looks like Ray came in and shot at Cozy, who escaped through the bathroom window."

"That's Tabitha's story."

"There are bullet holes leading to and into the bathroom. Someone left out the window."

"I still believe she's protecting her. Ms. Wheelhouse's demeanor wasn't that of someone who was attacked. Her body language was too relaxed.

"What say we let Tabitha go for now?"

I nodded. "Sure, whether it's Cozy or Ray, she's going to lead us to one of them."

Tabitha climbed out of the squad when she saw my approach. She asked, "How much longer?"

"I'll send the responding officer over to take your statement and then you'll be free to leave. Sorry about officer Harvin. He tends to be a little overenthusiastic."

"I'm fine. And you'll find Cozy? You need to find her before Ray does."

"Their pictures are being distributed. We won't stop until we find her." I yawned on purpose. "We'll dispatch several officers to stake out their home addresses and then we'll start fresh in the morning. God, this has been a long day."

"I just want this all to be over with." Tabitha sat back down in the back seat.

"You'll be out of here within minutes. We'll contact you tomorrow if we hear anything."

"Thank you, detective."

FORTY-ONE

The backseat of the cab reminded Cozy of the strip club, despite being spotless. Perhaps knowing what sticky, disgusting substances had to be cleaned off her seat on a daily basis kept her from touching anything.

The black cab driver spoke with an accent she guessed to be African. "This is a strange request to be taken to the Container Terminal at this hour."

"Is it?"

"You meeting someone? That is not a place for a pretty, young woman such as yourself." His eyes saw her in the rearview mirror.

"I'm good."

"Men are not to be trusted in the dead of night. You do not want to hear how many girls from my village were taken by force – by men making their own rules."

"Sorry, but I'll be fine."

But, would she be? The cab pulled to a stop. Cozy stepped onto the dark, isolated parking lot of Apex Industries. She could wait for the right opportunity, she supposed. If Senator Folsom admitted to the party hosts that he blabbed, then they should be getting the girls out of here tonight.

No cars were in the lot, but they could be parked in the warehouse for all she knew.

Tabby didn't want her to kill innocents, but who in the flesh trade really was? The problem was that she didn't know the top dog. If nothing happened tonight, then she would live another day to find that out. However, if things got going, she would have to play it to the end. There were girls being sold through this dock and this was probably where Haley had been killed.

She squeezed between the gap of the padlocked chain link fence. The property floodlights exposed the cranes, forklifts and general walking routes marked with yellow lines, which were protected by guard rails and short, thick poles sticking out of the cement. Everything left in the elements was unsecured, but having a guard making rounds wouldn't be unheard of. No sign of movement yet.

The nearest structure was a warehouse stretching two stories with APEX written in giant bold letters across one wall. She saw no windows save one by an entrance door that sat to the right of four huge openings made for semi-trucks and forklifts. She surveyed the area one last time before approaching the normal-sized door, feeling more exposed than she ever did on stage. The solid knob turned left and right, but wouldn't move a millimeter due to the deadbolt.

There was a lot of land to cover. The reserved parking spots up front told her that this building was the main hub of activity for the business, so she doubted if the girls were kept inside. Instead, she hugged the outside wall of the warehouse until reaching the far end where barrels and pallets were stacked, but still no place for entry. The corner floodlight illuminated where the foundation ended and a gravel road began, leading far off into the darkness. Squinting, she could make out a distant light pole over a smaller, fenced in structure a couple hundred yards away. *That isolated location made more sense.*

Cozy ran with little pebbles collecting in her shoes, until coming to a gate at the end of the road. She easily scaled the eight-foot fence and was more comfortable to be hidden in the shadows. The rusting warehouse was about the size of a supermarket with one large set of chained double doors, a single entry door and no windows. She turned the knob and the door opened with a cracking noise, causing a spike in adrenaline. If anyone was inside, they'd heard her.

"Hello?" Her voice choked.

Without an answer, she felt against the wall for a light switch, finding a fuse box with a large lever on the side. Turn on the lights? What the hell was she thinking? She progressed forward in the darkness. The aroma of cleaning products filled the air, reminding her of the cleanup with Titus.

Within moments of visual adjustment, she could see from the illumination through the skylight that the warehouse was empty. Firstly, why would there be a locked fence for a completely empty warehouse and secondly, why wouldn't this empty warehouse be covered with dust and cobwebs?

Instead of crossing through the middle, Cozy stayed to the perimeter, coming across an area near the rear with assorted items neatly organized including stacked buckets, several empty garbage cans and a coiled-up water hose leaking into the nearby drain.

She almost stepped onto a stained mattress. There were maybe twenty of them sporadically stacked. Next to them were corresponding iron half-loops set in concrete that was a different pour from the rest of the foundation. They were big enough to hold shackles and the fresh grooves in the loops indicate they had been used often. Haley could have been here. Folsom had told her about loading the women into a cargo container. Perhaps that's where they had been moved. Her shoulders hurt from the constant tension. Ray had nothing on the rage she felt.

Once outside in the dark humidity, she kept to the shadows on her way to the cargo containers stacked on several acres next to the Mississippi River. There was no way to find the right container from the hundreds stacked on the land before her. Letters of the alphabet signified the rows. Further into the depths of these containers, she found the naming convention progressed into three-digit numbers and then something in her memory clicked. She pulled out a folded piece of paper that had been sitting loose in Ray's safe. It had a list with the same numbering system with one row highlighted in yellow. She squinted to make it out, continuing on until finding the specified row on the paper: column D, row 240, container CGR10345.

The corrugated blue metal box sat alone, not on top of or under any other container. Still, it was disguised among the others of different colors. A titanic pad lock prevented her from entry. Muffled voices pulled her ear to the container, however she found they weren't coming from within the box. *Guards?*

Men approached from some yards away, two at minimum, talking casually. Cozy ran tiptoe to the opposite side of the container and waited as the men drew near. They stopped, speaking in a language she guessed to be Russian. The men laughed, one of them tapping on the metal wall. Dressed in plain clothes carrying machine guns, these were unlike any security guards Cozy had ever seen.

She didn't feel herself tilting backwards until it was too late. Her back thumped against a container, and she tried to catch herself in an effort not to make noise. She failed. The voices on the other side of the container grew loud in alarm. Cozy could feel them rounding the corner, so she flung herself into the adjoining row, hoping to get lost in the maze of redundancy.

The men had split up; she could hear distinct pursuit to her left and right. With her switchblade in hand, she tracked one of the men's clumsy movements parallel to her until he came into view. His annoyed expression and casual demeanor meant he wasn't hopeful of finding anything, probably thinking it an animal that had made the noise. He dropped his automatic weapon to his side and that show of carelessness would be his downfall.

Cozy sprang onto his back, driving her blade into his throat and twisting it with torque. A gurgled moan fizzled to a wheeze before he fell onto his side. Blood shot from his neck like a fountain. *These guys better be human traffickers. They have to be.*

She collected his gun. It felt light in her hands, more than she expected. She slipped between containers once again to wait for his partner. Eternal moments later, shuffling feet ran past to the dead body. She could hear his frantic calls into the radio, which would be good to get the boss on the scene. Just when the man finished speaking, he spun around, expecting an attack. What he received was a hail of bullets in his chest causing his arms to jerk out like a new dance move. He didn't fly backwards, only fell to the ground.

Cozy picked up the radio from his feet and clicked the button. "Who is this? Give me a name, coward." No answer. "Get down here, fucker." She released the button waiting for a response that never came.

However, another voice spoke from behind. "You took out two of my men."

"Ray." A blunt kick to her stomach sent her reeling, losing her weapon before turning onto her back. He hovered with the devil in his eyes.

His head popped back with a quick chuckle. "I never liked that guy."

Her muscles froze while the butt of the rifle came at her in slow motion. She never felt the wallop on her face, just a flash of light before she could even raise her hand. Her body operated on its own accord, rolling onto her side to reach for the gun, but Ray kicked it out of her reach. When she tried to stand, he put his heel in her stomach. Why was there no pain?

He bent over her face. "Hard for me to believe a little nothing such as yourself caused all this havoc. We're having to move the girls out tonight because of you."

"Cops are coming," she moaned.

"Shut up. At first, I planned on paying you back, but then I realized, you've walked into a much grander form of retribution." He glanced at the cargo container. "Due to the time and place, I won't have that chance to hear you begging me to take your life. But, it greatly pleases me that you will suffer a fate more horrible than death, the slow torture of your soul."

She spit at his feet. The last thing Cozy remembered was his fist flying at her head and she still didn't feel a thing.

HER EYES OPENED TO BLACKNESS, only slivers of dull illumination allowed for any perspective. *Ah, there was the pain.* At first, she thought sweat had rolled down her nose, but she touched her forehead and felt the mushy gash. The smell of urine and defecation hung stagnant in the air. Cozy's head ached as she pushed herself into a sitting positing, immediately feeling the skin of another person.

"Who's that?"

No one spoke, but she could hear breathing and movement, like being in a pit of snakes. Cozy held her hand out, feeling for what might be a leg. "Who are you? Are you okay?"

This person was lying down, either asleep or unconscious. Ray had put her in the container. These were the girls to be shipped out. How long had they been waiting in that warehouse? Days? Weeks?

"Is anybody there?"

"Ssh. No talk," an accented whisper said, "They hear you, they take food and water away… beat us."

"What's your name?"

Silence.

The racket of heavy equipment and motors grew near. Something smashed against the container where a few of the girls offered an abbreviated moan. The buzz of machinery through the metal meant they were being moved. Cozy stood and banged on the walls, screaming to be let out. None of the others joined in, having already been broken, drugged or just resigned to their fate.

"The police are on their way," she screamed again, pressing her forehead against the wall.

When the container started floating, she knew it had been lifted. Vertigo forced her back into a sitting position, and she closed her eyes to focus on not passing out. Her entire face felt swollen.

If she left this port, there would be no saving her from a life of horror, being sold to the highest bidder, spending her remaining youth doped up in a distant land, turning tricks until she was used up and thrown away. Or maybe she'd be the personal whore of an oil tycoon, a sheik, passing her around to his rich friends at parties.

Oh, shit.

FORTY-TWO

In many of the one-lane streets of New Orleans, the frequent red lights and congested traffic often meant the car in front of you would stay the same until they turned onto a side street, and that made tailing someone fairly easy. We positioned ourselves two cars behind Miss Wheelhouse as she pulled from a garage in the Quarter until she turned her lights off in the parking lot of Apex Industries. Even if we had lost her, we quickly deduced that this was her destination.

I slowed to a stop at a safe distance. "Well, this is interesting."

"Is she meeting Cozy or does she just think she came here?"

"Why would they want to meet here?" I asked. "This has to be Cozy's next stop on her revenge tour, although she couldn't expect anyone to be here at this hour, so I'm vexed. This is so vexing. This vexes me."

"Gladiator quotes now?"

"I'm impressed you got it."

"Whatever. We have to assume she learned something about the dock while at the phantom party."

"I think we should stop Wheelhouse before she goes in. Confronting Ray or Cozy could be taking your life in your hands."

"That's true. Let's go."

I coasted to the side of Tabitha's car just as she got out. She stopped to rest against the door with her arms folded. "I should have known."

"Can you blame us?" I approached her side with Tara staying three feet back.

Tabitha waved her hand at the Apex building. "I wasn't totally honest with you. Cozy thinks someone who works here is behind Haley's death. This is the only place she knew to come."

"You should have told us."

"I know. Part of me wants to help her get away with it. Jesus, I don't know why I came out here. I'm going to get myself killed."

"You love her," I said.

Tabitha turned her face away and didn't reply.

"What did Cozy tell you exactly?" Tara asked.

"That she was going to break in to his office and try to find something incriminating."

"So she could kill him with a clear conscience," Tara spoke what we were all thinking.

"You have to stay here, Tabitha. We'll go in for her." I opened the car door for her to wait.

"With pleasure." She fell into the luxury vehicle. "I know I keep saying this, but please don't hurt her. She's been through so much."

I closed the door. "I know."

Tara grabbed my arm. "You hear that noise? Some kind of machinery fired up." We scanned the sprawling Apex property. "Something's going down. I'm calling for back up."

"Do it quick." I gestured. "Let's go."

With our weapons drawn, and back up on the way, Tara and I covered each other as we sling-shot through the property until coming upon two men operating the gantry crane. Raymond Corondelet stood on the barge orchestrating the floodlights and the positioning of the container.

"What are they doing?" Tara asked.

"Midnight loading after shooting up his club? I'd say something spooked Ray."

"Wait for our back up?"

"I suppose. I count four men. I don't see Cozy anywhere."

Car engines rumbled behind us. I peered over my shoulder. "Don't look now, we have company and it's not ours."

Back where Tabitha parked, several sets of headlights entered the lot and shut off. A cacophony of men's voices and laughter drew near from where we had just been. "Ray called for reinforcements."

"We're trapped. What now?"

I sighed. "Don't move. Hope they don't notice us."

"Bitch, this is serious." Tara used her hand to stifle a laugh.

A huge man carrying an assault rifle stumbled behind the pallets we were using for cover, dropping the cigarette out of his mouth in surprise. As he swung his weapon around, Tara and I both fired, hitting him in the chest.

"We just announced our arrival," Tara told me wryly.

I grabbed the discarded assault rifle and aimed it at the sound of the voices. As soon as we saw the outline of men with weapons drawn on us, I sprayed a round of bullets, taking down the first wave of attackers. I counted three others that scattered into shadowed corners, possibly wounded. Then sirens far off in the distance began to grow louder.

"We need better cover," I said. "Let's get closer to the barge. Follow me."

FORTY-THREE

The container hovered in mid-air, floating as if by magic. Cozy could feel it moving sideways, swaying enough to give her motion sickness. She clutched at her revolting belly. Occasionally, slivers of floodlight found entry, showing a carpet of female bodies lying about. She had long since given up on talking sense into them, the ones that were awake anyway. She would take her own life before being forced into prostitution or becoming some disgusting man's sex slave.

But then, abruptly, the crate halted. They weren't on a forklift, so it had to be one of those cranes used to load the barges. Maybe something went wrong. Maybe the police had arrived and Ray was caught. Would anyone even know that this container was full of women? Without warning, a tug almost knocked her to the floor. They were moving again. No doubt being placed on a barge in route to a freighter that would take them to Europe.

She felt the descent like a slow elevator until the floor contacted something solid beneath them. *Open those doors*, she begged to her momma's spirits. Just give me one chance at escape.

At first, the silence drained all hope, but then gunfire erupted. Men yelled in a different language, some screamed in English, but with heavy accents. She sensed they were near the container, shooting away from it, protecting it. A metal ping rang inside the box and she could see a hole exposed by the floodlights. Whoever it was, they had shot back.

"Help!" she screamed, her fists banging the walls.

Clanking at the front of the box surprised her; it sounded as if they were trying to open that bastard of a padlock. Cozy sidestepped bodies the best she could until pushing against the opposite side of the noise. She heard sliding as the locking mechanisms shifted. And as if the spirits had answered her prayers, the doors swung open. But it wasn't the freedom she expected.

Ray stood on a three-foot ledge at the door's opening. He grabbed her around the neck as if knowing she would be there, spinning her to face out over the barge deck. It took a moment to settle the sudden dizziness, like being on the edge of a cliff. The container had been placed on top another container, stacked askew like two Lego's that were off by one row.

It didn't matter why Ray had decided to pull her out. It was her one chance at a miracle. However, one step forward and they would both plummet a good ten feet. Ray pressed behind her, but she could see his weapon pointing at Detectives Lucas and Tara not too far below.

Ray growled, "Go ahead and shoot, Peyroux. We all know how well the last time turned out."

FORTY-FOUR

Tara and I stood three feet apart with our guns drawn on Ray. I whispered, "S.W.A.T.'s here, but they aren't going to converge until they assess the situation and form a plan."

"Let's hope this standoff lasts a while." Tara said.

"We never tested my breakthrough at the firing range."

"That was simulated. This is reality. Your head will know the difference. But we can't take the shot anyway," Tara warned.

"I'm ready if we need to." I felt the sweat running down my back. My gun was aimed, but this time the barrel remained steady in my grasp. Cozy's face wore a mask of dried blood, all the way down her neck. *I made the right choice then, and I will again.*

Ray's face scrunched in anger. "Wheelhouse, you want to do the honors, so we can get this situation under control?"

I heard a click behind me and turned to see Tabitha Wheelhouse pointing a nine-millimeter at my back. Her expression was cold and calculating, her words came out like molasses. "Drop those weapons."

Tara and I both raised our guns at the same time. "Crap. Didn't see that coming."

"You speak for both of us," Tara mumbled.

"Most of our guys are dead, Ray. More police just showed up," she yelled.

"One call and they will be told to leave the barge alone, but only if these two aren't around to fuck it up. Kill them."

Tabitha drew closer and yelled past us. "Ray-baby, I've never killed anyone before."

In unison, we placed our guns at our feet and rose with our hands up. "You helped Cozy escape from the club just hours ago. I don't get it."

Tabitha's entire body stood rigid. "Ray wanted to kill her. She's worth more alive."

Tara spoke. "You heard the sirens pull up. The parking lot is full of cops. Even if that barge gets away, they're going to stop you on the river."

Ray screamed, "What are you chatting about? Pull the fucking trigger."

Tabitha kept talking like she wanted to stall. Her eyes were wide. "You have no idea who's involved in this, do you? That barge won't be stopped. And as far as witnesses? There won't be any." Her gun trembled slightly.

"Tabby, quit fucking talking and kill them."

"You swore I'd never have to," she barked at him.

He kicked a foot toward her in anger. "I lied. Do it."

"Just try to get them from there, baby."

That would be a tough task. Ray aimed his weapon at me first, shutting one eye as he lined up his shot. We had to make a dive at our weapons. But with two guns trained for a kill shot, one of us would take a bullet.

As Ray steadied his arm against Cozy's squirming, a dark figure moved behind him, jumping at his knees. It was another girl from inside and she managed to knock all three of them out of the container, onto the floor below.

"Ray!" Tabitha yelled.

While he was distracted, Tara and I lunged for our guns and turned to fire on Tabitha. Her only shot landed between us as if she couldn't choose. Tabitha's chest cavity saturated with blood as she stood in shock. She fired another shot in the air before falling backward. With Tabitha out of commission, we used the ramp to run onto the barge to find Cozy straddling Ray while he lay on his back. She had the barrel of his machine gun in his mouth. The other girl was face-down, not moving.

"Cozy – don't." Tara and I trained our guns on her.

"Why not, Lucas? This is where it all ends for me. I'm going to jail, right? The least I can do is take this scumbag out."

"You're giving him the easy way out. The real punishment will come from life in prison."

She looked to be considering my statement when Ray reached for the barrel. Cozy pulled the trigger, but all we heard was an impotent click. The weapon must have been damaged in the fall. Ray pushed her off, but couldn't get to his feet before I was on top of him, pulling his hands behind his back for Tara to cuff.

She slapped on the cuffs with no regard for comfort. "Damn straight." Tara wiped at her forehead.

We turned our attention back to Cozy and the other girl. Ray must have broken their fall. Cozy appraised Ray with disappointment while the other female just lay on her side moaning, but none the worse for wear.

"Tara." I knelt beside the unknown female and straightened the hair from the girl's face. "Who does this look like?"

"Son of a bitch."

Cozy noticed the surprise on our faces and turned to see the girl who had just saved her life… Haley Robicheaux. Her mouth opened enough to let air escape, but she couldn't inhale to get it back. A spark of recognition flared within Haley's glazed eyes. The corners of her mouth turned up. Both of Cozy's arms extended in awed shock to hug her sister as they sat side by side on the ground. Tears continued as she struggled to speak, but gave up on speech and simply bawling into the side of Haley's neck.

I turned my back to call Heather, but didn't let Tara see me wipe my eyes.

THE RED AND blue lights flashed through the sparse streets, however the siren had been rendered mute. The squad cruised at the speed limit. The young cop driving stayed wide-eyed as the older one yawned. These officers assigned to bring Raymond Corondelet to Orleans Parish Prison took their time, reflecting the attitude of the city.

The younger cop spoke as he drove. "Why do you suppose Dobson's replacement gave us Corondelet instead of putting him in the wagon or waiting for the Feds?"

"The Feds would take all the credit. And it's best to keep this guy separated from his crew."

"Just weird. Not having an escort or anything. I mean, this is a pretty big deal."

"Enjoy it, rook. You're gonna have a story to tell your pals."

"You boys been on the force long?" Ray asked from the back seat. Through the grate, he studied the two morons hand-picked to transport him.

The cops ignored him, keeping their attention on the road as they drove down Jackson Avenue towards Claiborne, a portrait of youth and inexperience tending to serious business. At this hour, no one was on the road in this part of town. Ray glanced between the two, one of which was young and nervous, the other was older, weighty and soft having hit his career ceiling. Squawking came over the radio, but they ignored it.

Ray twisted his head around to look through the back windshield when he noticed the bright glare of headlights on the cop's bumper. "I imagine you don't make much money as a beat cop, right?"

"Just keep quiet, sir," the older one said.

The driver popped his eyes into the rearview mirror. "What the fuck does this guy think he's doing? Doesn't he see the fucking flashers?"

His partner responded, "Must be drunk. Maybe thinks it's an ambulance. I knew this one guy so drunk he got in a squad car thinking it was his."

Ray felt the car decelerate as the driver ignored his partner. The squad drifted to the parking lane and slowed to a near stop, expecting the drunk to pass.

"I should call this in," the young cop suggested as he coasted.

"Let's see what kind of douche bag we're dealing with here." The older one motioned.

Ray watched the car creep by to pass on the driver's side when two girls, one in the front seat and one in the back, both pressed their bare breasts against the glass and then continued on while waving their hands in the rear windshield.

"Nice," the young cop said with a laugh. When he turned to his older partner for confirmation, a bullet entered his frontal lobe and left out the back of his skull.

"So messy," Ray said.

The older cop got out of the car and opened the back door. He reached in and took the cuffs off Corondelet and waited as he slid out.

"Alright, the boss said you'd just get me in the shoulder or leg or something, okay?" He handed over his gun.

Ray raised the gun to the cop's head and fired without explanation or apology.

THE SCENE RESEMBLED CHAOS. So many law enforcement individuals scurrying around doing the job in which they were tasked. Tara and I spent the past five hours answering questions into the early morning hours, combing through documents and warehouse inventory and basically making sure no one would screw anything up. I counted seven squad cars, four ambulances and three fire trucks parked on the property with lights flashing like the world's largest disco. Police and firemen dodged each other as cargo containers were opened and inspected while news helicopters buzzed overhead with spotlights at the request of the NOPD. There would be no cover up.

The twenty women found in the one container were taken to a nearby hospital before immigration determined who was American and who needed to be deported back to their country of origin. I made sure S.W.A.T. knew that Cozy and Haley Robicheaux were to be separated from the group due to special circumstances. After I saw them off in the ambulance, I called Heather again.

"It's five in the morning, babe. Did I wake you?" I asked.

"Actually, after you called, Chance got an update that Corondelet was arrested, so we decided to go home. Hope that's okay."

"You still have the detail?"

"Yes. That's the only reason we left. My parents went to my aunt's house."

"Guess what? Cozy's sister is alive and well. I'll tell you all about it when I see you."

"That's great. I can't wait."

"I'll be there in an hour or two if I can finish up with this madhouse."

"I'm proud of you, honey. I love you."

"Love you, too."

We had followed up with the Robicheaux sisters at the hospital to make sure the staff knew the situation, leaving Cozy handcuffed to a hospital bed next to Haley in the same room, both staying overnight for observation. We didn't know what kind of jail time Cozy would receive – if any – as that would be up to the D.A. and her extenuating circumstances were sympathetic at worst.

Tara and I had promised to support them during what was sure to be a crazy few weeks upcoming. Just thinking about the press coverage and paperwork gave me a headache. I was curious to how Aponi would handle Haley not being dead. She didn't want me to deliver any more news, so I would honor that request and send a trooper.

My cell phone read 6:13 a.m. as I closed in on home, thinking of the joy on Heather's face. Who was I kidding? My wife will be happy for me, but it wouldn't change her mind. She didn't like my job and she would rather I quit, although she'd never say that to my face. As a detective, I knew this to be true.

Just blocks from my house, my cell rang with Tara's name. "Don't you dare tell me Ray escaped."

"Ray escaped."

I waited for her to laugh. "Bullshit, Tara."

"Seriously. The squad was found just off Claiborne Avenue. The two officers were executed."

"How does something like that happen?"

"You said it yourself, these guys always have an escape plan. Any one of those Russians could have been lying in wait. Hell, for all we know, it was a cop on the payroll. Who the fuck knows."

"I'm pulling up to my house now."

"You don't think he'd show up there?"

"Ray doesn't think rationally when in a rage, remember? I think he wants to show up here."

"I'm sending a unit to sit outside."

"Good, because I don't see the detail that's supposed to be here."

"Trouble?"

"I'll call you right back if I see anything."

I pulled up to the curb by the neighboring house, deciding not to park in the driveway just yet. A different light illuminated the living room; not the lamp that was always on. Could the bulb have blown? I'm not buying it. I called Heather's number waiting a few rings before she answered.

"Hi, *Lukie*," she said with emphasis.

I knew right away. She never called me Lukie since it was my last girlfriend's pet name for me.

"Hey, sorry I'm still out and calling so early, but I'm going to be home in about a half hour and I have a craving for scrambled eggs. Just thought to call to see if you want breakfast so I can tell you all about tonight."

She knows I despise eggs.

She said, "You and your eggs. Why don't you come home first and we'll go out to Camillia Grill."

"Excellent idea. See you soon. Love you."

I hung up the cell with adrenaline about to flood out my ears. I slipped out of my car and ran to the back of the house where I stealthily climbed in the bedroom window, doing a handstand before rolling onto my back.

A man's voice vibrated through the hallway, but I couldn't make out his words. I peeked through a crack in the door, making out

Heather and my daughter, who were tied back-to-back on two chairs in the dining room. They appeared scared, but not hurt. Ray paced, waving a gun. He wanted to kill them in front of me.

And I thought Cozy had a one-track mind for vengeance.

I retrieved my spare Baretta from the closet, opening the metal lock and pulling out a gun I hadn't fired in five years. However, it had been cleaned and loaded and ready to go. Back at the door with limited vantage, I could still make out Alicia facing me at an angle and Ray behind her in full pace. He returned into my vision every so often, reminding me of that serial killer swaying back and forth with Cozy in his arms.

My chest leaned against the doorjamb with my right arm extending into the hall, pointing my Baretta at the spot where Ray returned into a target frame of about six inches left to right and two feet above Alicia's head. Heather and my daughter sat motionless, faces wet with gags in their mouths. I needed to get down the hall and into that room without Ray noticing, which seemed impossible at this point.

Ray came back into my line of sight, seeming to know instinctually not to step in front of them where I had a clean shot. I focused with my body propped solid. Cozy's face formed in my mind except blood wasn't flowing from her throat. I imagined her smiling, saying 'don't be a baby.'

Alicia erupted with a renewed struggle, crying out against the gag and managing to push it from her mouth with her tongue. Her scream rang out like a power surge. Ray whipped around to her side and slapped her face before stuffing the gag back in.

He put his face in hers. "I don't need you alive for this, my dear."

Ray stood straight then rounded to her backside, gently petting her hair. He faced me, putting his gun against the back of my daughter's head. He chuckled and pulled the gun up as if tormenting was foreplay. My muscles locked as the scene played out like a dream sequence.

It seemed Ray sensed my presence as he stopped to glare down the hall. His expression of surprise woke me as his gun rose from Alicia's head and fired a shot that embedded in the wall just inches from me.

A rush of blood pumped from my heart and I squeezed, hitting Ray in the shoulder, exactly where I aimed. As he fell backwards, I sprinted to his side, kicking the gun from his hand. After another swift kick to the bullet hole, I put a slug into both of his legs, ensuring he wouldn't go anywhere.

I untied my wife and daughter who hysterically embraced me.

"Why don't you two go wait in the bedroom?" I pointed.

"Why?" Heather asked. "You need to get the police here."

"Actually, a squad's on their way now." I looked at Ray who was holding his wounds in agony, but still conscious. Malice filled my being for the man who just threatened to kill my wife and daughter. I felt myself standing in Cozy's shoes. I calmly said, "He has information about who's behind the whole operation. I want to see if I can get it out of him before the cops come and he shuts up for good. Go on, I don't want you to see this."

With a lingering kiss, she complied with concern in her eyes, taking a dazed Alicia with her. When the bedroom door closed, I turned to Ray, who eyed me like a man who knew his fate.

"Oh, Ray, there is no one on this blessed Earth that would want to be you right now."

"Fuck you and that bitch Cozy."

"There's one difference between her and me. She left you alive."

Ray's accent instantly switched from New Orleans *Y'at* to Russian. "I'm prepared to die, Peyroux. I expected it every day in Russia, working for the mob."

I kneeled by his head, hiding my surprise. "Russian mob? I didn't even ask you anything about that."

He winced. "Just wanted you to know what you can expect in your future."

"Me?"

"You want to know who is behind this? A brutal, ruthless Russian family. My boss will replace me. He will replace everyone you arrested and you'll never know who it is until it's too late. And he won't stop until your entire family is dead." He yelled towards the hall. "Dead, Peyroux!"

"Or maybe you're full of shit."

"Why lie to you now? You might even arrest the man that will kill your wife and daughter, leaving you alive so you can witness the death of anyone else you are close to – or will become close to. Because that is what we do. My boss is not even in this country. How's that for a start to this little interrogation?"

My mouth went dry. "Actually, it's a good start."

FORTY-FIVE

Cold handcuffs hung loose on the hospital bed railing as Cozy slid them back and forth. Haley, still loopy from being drugged, slept in the next bed. No matter what happened, jail or no jail, she would be happy forever, knowing her sister was safe.

A black man with a bright smile and pin-striped suit bypassed the cop at the door and took command of the room, carrying a satchel at his side. His fade was well-trimmed and his glasses made him look more attractive than he might've been. He took a quick glance around, and then zeroed in on the handcuffs.

"Ms. Cozy Robicheaux?"

"That's me."

"I'm District Attorney Lionel Theriot." He stepped up to the bed, holding the satchel with both hands. "Mind if I ask you a few questions?"

"Do I need a lawyer?"

"That's up to you, but before you decide that, maybe you should hear me out."

"I don't have to answer any of your questions."

"From what I hear, you're a very smart lady. I think you can figure out what questions you might want to answer."

"Doesn't matter."

"Actually, Ms. Robicheaux, this could go very quickly and to your benefit if you give me the right answers."

"I'll do my best." She focused on sliding her handcuffs.

"Your fingerprints have been found at Raymond Corondelet's residence. Seems like a lot of stuff went on there… kidnapping, possible torture."

"Who knows what kind of weird sex that guy liked?"

He smiled. "Seems his safe had been opened and some items retrieved from it."

"Like money?"

"One item in particular being a hand-written log of names and dates. Something that wouldn't mean much at first glance."

"How would you know of this mysterious hand-written journal if it's missing?"

He took a second. "We have a source."

"I'll bet. Tell Senator Folsom hi for me."

"Yes." His eyes fell to the satchel, which he had yet to open. "Full immunity for the list."

"What does that mean exactly?"

"The dead drug dealer, Titus Jones? Unsolved. Salvador Santiago shot Vincent Dean - a break-in. Senator Folsom said he fell onto his hand – won't explain further." Mr. Theriot approached and sat on the bed, putting the pouch to the side. "It means that no matter what you did, no matter what you say, no matter who accuses you of anything, you will not be charged."

"Even the feds?"

"Especially the feds. They have even more reason to be embarrassed, but I won't go into that. Rest assured, everyone is on board."

"I guess the only reason you're here is because no one found it yet."

Theriot's dark cheeks flushed. "No, they haven't been able to locate it. Cozy, you don't want to play games here. You know the high profile names on that list and they have everything to lose. But, for you to get the deal, you have to prove to me you have it."

"The list of names are really of animals."

They exchanged a knowing stare. "And the legend?"

"Cut through the shit, Mr. D.A. I would imagine a lot of people would be interested in that… a lot of people. And if I give you the list, those same people will allow this to happen again."

His face grew solemn. "So, you know who's on the list?"

"Yeah, Mr. Panther, I do." She paused to let him gather himself. "They think disguising Senator Folsom with Rhino or Judge Jenner with Skunk is smart, but only if the legend is destroyed."

"And the legend is where?"

"It's with the list."

"And where is the list?"

Cozy stared at him, momentarily spending time on his mouth, nose, chin and finally his eyes. She then turned her attention towards Haley covered up to her chest with a sheet. "I did it all for her, you know."

"Once the story gets out, you two will stand to make a lot of money from interviews and book deals. We will have to impose a gag order pertaining to certain facts, but that doesn't matter. The more mystery to the story, the more people will eat it up."

"Of course." Cozy slid the handcuffs back and forth a few more times.

"What about retaliation after I give you the list?"

"Trust."

Cozy laughed. "I'll trust that no one will kill me, if you trust that I don't have a copy waiting to be released upon my death."

"Touché. You are one smart bayou girl."

"I want confirmation on that immunity deal. And before I agree to give you the list, I want Detective Lucas Peyroux to be the one who retrieves it and delivers it."

EPILOGUE

Three weeks later. Tara, Cozy, Haley and myself sat on a Bourbon Street restaurant balcony. Tara folded up the newspaper and threw it under the table. "Dobson still won't fight for her job."

"Even if she was to get reinstated," I said, "she said she doesn't want to come back and she won't say what they have on her."

"I don't know," Tara huffed, "she was a great cop."

"What's she going to do?" Cozy asked.

"She's moving out of New Orleans, that much I know," Tara said. "She can probably start over in a small town somewhere. She's gained back thirty pounds."

"I can't believe everyone thought Jeannie from the club was me in the river," Haley said, inhaling her French Fries.

I said, "You had the same body type with no tattoos and she had no family."

"I snuck my phone past the guards and handed it to Jeannie after they rounded us up. When they discovered it on her, they – they – you know what they did. Then they killed her."

"I'm confused about why they did it in the first place." Cozy looked at everyone. "Why plant the hairbrush in your place? Why did they have to?" Cozy asked.

Haley looked down. "When Ash started showing up, they realized people would ask questions if I went missing. All those girls have no one looking for them. I had no one to look for me until Ash showed."

I swallowed quickly to add, "We found traces of blood that matches Jeanie's blood type in Vincent Dean's car. And his cell's GPS places him at English Turn at the estimated time of death. Vince also had a five-thousand dollar deposit in his bank account. We think Ray put him up to it."

Haley said, "Vince was kind of like a son to him. I think he may have been looking to get him into the business."

"So much trouble just so they could sell you into slavery?"

Tara was already half-finished her sandwich, leaving crumbs all over the red and white checkerboard tablecloth. "You two were worth it to them. They have a rating system. You have the bottom of the barrel, like prostitutes and drug addicts, the girl-next-door average type, and you two… The crème de la crème. Big price tags on your heads."

Cozy shook her head. "And Tabby was in on it the whole time. That's why Ray was ready for me with the gun at his house. Tabby called him."

"How'd you get out of that?" I asked.

Cozy snickered. "I accidently squeezed the trigger and shot the gun out of his hand like we were in the old west. You should have seen his face." She made the sound effects and pretended a gun flew from her hand.

The table burst into laughter.

I said, "It's a shame you had to hand over Ray's list of clients, but at least it got you immunity." I looked at Tara. "And Ray will never hurt anyone again."

Cozy stared forward. "You still didn't get the head guy. Pretty soon, their operation will be up and runnin' again. Look, I was messed up in the head – *am* messed up in the head. I'm getting better, though. When the D.A. demanded mandatory counseling, deep down inside, I was glad. I want the help."

Haley put her arm around her sister. "You're not fucked up, dawlin'… just a little askew. We'll work it out together here in NOLA. The whole city's crazy."

"By the way." Cozy stood and pulled the alligator pendant from her pocket. "I've been saving this for you."

Haley gasped and pulled her hair from the back of her neck, allowing Cozy to clasp the necklace. When Haley let her hair drop, she stood and the two sisters embraced. "Never thought I'd see this again."

"I still think Mark Alexander had a hand in all this," I said.

"Too late, now." Tara shrugged.

"He came in the club one night. I went into the private room with him." Cozy shuddered. "What if I run into him and accidently kill him?"

"You won't." Tara smiled.

"How'd he get off, anyway?" Haley asked.

"By not leaving a single shred of evidence."

"Alexander's dirty." Tara added. "Damn Russian mobsters."

"Add the best lawyers and friends on the client list and you have exoneration."

"Go ahead." Tara nudged me. "Tell them."

I conjured a smile. "I quit the force."

"What? Why?" Cozy nearly choked.

"When Ray nearly killed my family, I knew it was time. My work came home and threatened my family. I will never let that happen again. Before I killed Ray…"

"… in self-defense," Tara added.

"… he warned me about the Russian mafia coming after Heather, Alicia and you Robicheaux girls. There's too many of them and not enough of me. I couldn't chance it."

"What will you do?"

"Security work and consulting with the NOPD. I can still make a living."

"You're going to be bored." Tara said.

"Heather says I need someone to save. This time, I like to think, I think I'll be saving myself."

Tara raised her drink and everyone followed suit. "To saving ourselves," she said.

"To saving ourselves," we all said as our glasses tapped together.

ACKNOWLEDGMENTS

I'd like to thank Dan Shanahan for his valuable input, Alicia Franklin and Maxine Groves for their beta-reading skills, Andy Fitz for the many consultations over fine beers and thank you New Orleans.

E.J. Findorff was born and raised in New Orleans, but currently lives in Chicago. He graduated from the University of New Orleans and served six years in the Louisiana National Guard. He is a member of the International Thriller Writers Association.

Please visit my site to subscribe for news and events and free offers.
  www.ejfindorff.com

ALSO BY E.J. FINDORFF

UNHINGED

KINGS OF DELUSION

A FRENCH QUARTER VIOLET

THE UNRAVELING

ONE HUNDRED BULLETS

Please visit my site to subscribe for news and events and free offers.

www.ejfindorff.com

Lightning Source UK Ltd.
Milton Keynes UK
UKHW020204071020
371126UK00003B/264